The *Boardinghouse*

Return to Ivy Log

Other books by Sue Chamblin Frederick

The Juan Castillo Spy Series
The Unwilling Spy
Madame Delafloté, Impeccable Spy

The Ivy Log Series
Grandma Takes A Lover

The Boardinghouse

Return to Ivy Log

Sue Chamblin Frederick

Copyright © 2015 by Sue CHAMBLIN Frederick

ISBN: 978-0-9852104-6-5

Word Jewels Publishing

Acknowledgments

To my five brothers and sisters who thought my wild imagination was dangerous – see, you guys, I've channeled that imagination into terrific novels.

To Robert (Rob) L. Bacon of "The Perfect Write" who tirelessly contributes his wisdom of the writing world to both published and unpublished authors. His manuscript evaluation and editing are solid gold! You're still the smartest guy I know, Rob.

To Steve W. Johnson, the best layout person in the world and author of *Not Much Of A Crime, Pier Pressure* and others.

To Steve Guthrie, International Program Director, Mountain Madness, for his mountain climbing and rescue expertise.

To the folks at Jim's Smokin' Que in Blairsville, Georgia. They do barbecue just right!

To the eagle eyes of the proofers: Gary Frederick, Brenda Cochrane, Iris Whittington and Beth Lindquist – you never miss a thing!

A big Thank You to Ted and Alease Kelly at The Inn at Folkston. Their bed and breakfast is snuggled away in Folkston, Georgia, where an abundance of Southern hospitality awaits.

And, to the folks of Ivy Log, Georgia, for letting me take literary liberties in building their fictitious town. Before I began work on *The Boardinghouse*, I traveled to Ivy Log to get a feel for the town . . . but there was no town. Ivy Log is a community of wonderful mountain folk who live at the top of Georgia. So, I gave them a town with a Main Street, The Church of Ivy Log, *The Boardinghouse* and a town square with the tallest blue spruce in Georgia. Thank you, Ivy Log.

VISIT THE AUTHOR AT: **www.suechamblinfrederick.com**

Part 1

Chapter 1

A small town has a distinct rhythm, like the bumblebee's constant hum or the slow unrolling of molasses from a glass jar. So, it was no surprise when the dawdling pace of that summer manifested itself into boredom; a swelling monotony that could only be relieved by fervent gossip, malicious tittle-tattle that pushed the little town into the throes of a passionate fury. But, that was only the beginning.

The ruckus began not long ago around noon in The Boardinghouse Restaurant in Ivy Log, Georgia, where the whispers of disgruntled folk had begun well before daylight. The whispers evolved into rumblings about a lemon pudding cake, a concoction so delicious that folks drove from all over Union County every Tuesday to stake their claim to the little scoop of heaven that was baked in the hot ovens of The Boardinghouse.

In small towns, the work of the devil is exceedingly easy — perhaps because of the latent boredom combined with the shallow thinking of its inhabitants. After all, what else is there to do on lazy days when the winds of discontent blow across the faces of folks who need just one small reason to gossip, to evoke hard feelings, to find fault in the most miniscule aspects of another's life?

Even a zealous sermon at The Church of Ivy Log that extolled the significance of The Ten Commandments did not prevent naughtiness from simmering among the pews or darkening the hearts of devout worshippers. The same sermon that encouraged loving thy neighbor and forgiving trespasses failed to deter the wickedness that sometimes crept into the lives of those who were, for the most part, good people. A good, however, that for some was purely for show.

Oh, if only Paula Jennings hadn't bragged that the renowned cake recipe had originated in her family 50 years earlier. When Pyune Murphy heard that, she asked to see the so-called Jenning's recipe. Paula's face twisted into a smirk, and her turquoise eyeshadow seemed to darken.

"Well, Pyune, honey, you know I don't give out that recipe to anyone . . . especially you."

No one really knows what happened next. They just know that the two women had a catfight at The Boardinghouse - in front of the crowd that was waiting in line for their lemon pudding cake.

Though the recipe loomed at the forefront of the brouhaha, the real issue simmered underneath and festered there, much like the wound from a fishhook on an already tender finger. It was all about *love*.

~~~

The summer lost itself in the leaves that fell at the end of October, spreading a false peace throughout Ivy Log and settling quietly among the daily lives of its citizens.

Far to the north, winter waited impatiently, the old man with the white beard and the large belly chatting fervently with the snow makers of the universe. Together, they decided on a glorious, white winter for Ivy Log. The massive storm began humbly in western Canada and moved east, the whispers of wind and snow becoming a roaring giant that ended up in the Appalachians, with weather considered worse than The Great Appalachian Storm of 1950.

The snow came - 23 inches of it – leaving the small town a perfect template for the winter-wonderland pictures on the December pages of millions of calendars.

Sitting high in the north Georgia mountains, Ivy Log proclaimed itself as the loveliest town in the Appalachians, its citizens boasting a Christmas tree almost as tall as Brasstown Bald, an exaggeration of course.

The spruce, 30-feet tall and decorated with yards of gold garland, had survived the onslaught of the storm, but unrelenting wind and heavy wet snowflakes had caused the limbs to sag like a tired old man.

Children with sleds zipped down Main Street until daylight faded; the promise of more snow during the night becoming the topic of exhilarating conversations at dinner, since it was understood that snow brought Christmas — and Christmas brought presents.

~~~

In the early morning, long before the resident rooster found his voice — and hours away from the arrival of the December sun — Pyune Murphy turned on the cavernous ovens at The Boardinghouse, the soft pop of the gas the only noise in the cold kitchen. While coffee brewed, she waited at the window and watched one of the restaurant's many cats amble down the top of the woodpile, then gingerly pick its way across the frozen ground to the tin pan it hoped would hold scraps of food later in the morning. Pyune tapped on the window and the blue eyes of the longhaired tabby found hers, a begging meow pantomiming through its long whiskers, a wisp of snow lingering in them.

Along the front of the restaurant, Main Street lay deserted and wrapped in snowflakes seemingly spitted from an irritable sky. At the corner of Mulberry and Elm, the upstairs bedroom — in Adela Queen Harper's rambling white house — was empty. She lay nine miles away, at Nottely Lake, in the arms of Frank Carberry, his breathing slow and constant as she reached over and smoothed his cheek.

Conversely, in her two-story brick house on Dellwood Avenue, Paula Louise Jennings slept alone in the master bedroom, magnolia wallpaper wrapping around the walls as if the room were in perpetual bloom. It was here that Wiley Hanson had made love to her the previous evening.

At this very moment, however, high in the Appalachians, Wiley Hanson pushed his chainsaw into a felled oak a quarter of a mile from the top of Brasstown Bald. He cut up several limbs and piled fireplace-length logs into the back of his pickup truck and headed to town, thoughts of Pyune's hot biscuits on his mind.

~~~

The wind switched direction, now coming from the north-west and bringing fast-scudding clouds high above Ivy Log, as if they were in a hurry to meet up with mountain ranges farther east. Pyune looked up from her bowl of cake batter and held the spoon in the air, a flutter coming to her chest. The changing weather reminded her of anticipating Christmas morning when she was a little girl — and not knowing what to expect.

Adela stirred in Frank's arms and opened her eyes. She sat up and watched the faint light of the breaking dawn peek through the pitchfork branches of winter trees. She left the bed and walked down the hall to the window that faced the lake and saw a wedge of Canada geese atop the tree line. When she looked at the morning sky, the hair on the back of her neck prickled.

On Dellwood Avenue, Paula pulled the covers over her head and talked in her sleep. She even yelled out once. Something about the devil. She sat up straight in bed when her pillow fell to the floor with a thump. "Is anybody there?" she hollered. There was no reply.

Wiley slowed his truck on the narrow mountain road above Ivy Log and looked down at the small, sleepy town, the warm light from The Boardinghouse windows promising the best coffee this side of Chattanooga.

~~~ ~~~

Chapter 2

At sunrise, the preacher left the busy highways of Atlanta and turned onto the road leading northeast to Ivy Log, his worn bible in the seat beside him. His cat, Delilah, slept in the back window of his late-model Buick, unconcerned about where her master was going or whether the pulpit would be welcoming.

~~~ ~~~

Chapter 3

Wiley banged a snow-encrusted, gloved fist on the back door of The Boardinghouse and stamped his feet while he waited in the cold dark of the early morning. He heard one of the woodpile cats meow behind him as Pyune opened the door.

"Lordy! If I don't get a hot cup of coffee real quick, I do believe I am a dead man. Frozen like one of them carcasses they find in the Hens-A-Laying."

"I will assume you meant Himalayas and not Hens-A-Laying," Pyune said.

Not commenting, he stepped into the warm kitchen and shuddered, the snow from his boots tracking the worn oak planks. He removed his gloves and studied the cups hanging from a row of hooks under a spice shelf, looking for a mug stained brown with coffee — one for serious coffee drinking.

Wiley said, "High today gonna be twenty-three. If you ask me, that's cold." He chose a thick mug, its faded image of Roy Rogers and Trigger making him smile.

"Yes, it's cold. Colder than it was yesterday." Pyune poured his coffee and pulled out a kitchen chair. "Did you bring me some firewood?"

"Course, I did. Got to unload it, but I thought I'd get a cup of coffee first. Got any biscuits made yet?"

"They're in the oven," she said, now sitting across from him. "Do all your firewood customers feed you biscuits? Or am I the only one?"

"Well, here's the way I see it, Pyune. Your biscuits are made with real butter, and my granny used to make them with real butter. It's what makes them so good. I won't eat other folks' biscuits because I do believe they use fake butter."

He laughed and then scowled. "I'm of the opinion that God did not intend for things to be fake. And that includes people too." Pyune gave him one of her hard looks.

Wiley took a deep breath and eyed her deviously, "What?"

"I didn't expect a lecture on biscuits." she said.

"Well, that's what you got. Now, hand me over one or two a them biscuits." He slurped his coffee and settled back.

"Not ready yet. Drink your coffee and keep your britches on."

He looked away and chuckled to himself.

Wiley Hanson was an enigma, as evidenced by the incongruities in his life as well as his personality. He was a mountain man, as he liked to call himself, but unknown to most folks, he'd earned a doctorate in environmental engineering from Georgia Tech. Yet despite his lofty intellectual credentials, he remained a simple man. Regardless, his mountain twang and atrocious grammar combined with a hint of higher education to create a remarkable mixture of corn pone and academia.

He cultivated this guise hoping his college-infused intellect wouldn't alienate him from his true roots: the mountains and mountain life. To expose his intelligence would deny him the pureness of who he really was.

Though his Ph.D. cemented his love of wisdom, he had looked in the mirror one day as he trimmed his beard and saw the clearness of his eyes and felt the truth of his existence. When he leaned closer and studied the mix of gray, white and black in the wiry hair on his face, he wondered if there were a secret message, hieroglyphics maybe, resting there; a puzzle, a sign, a hidden meaning that had been placed there by those who came before him; a message that would give him assurances that it was all right to have left the mountains and gone to the city to become educated; that it hadn't changed him.

He had left the manicured campuses and the stately brick buildings and returned to the mountains as Wiley, a man whose genes carried the blood of his ancestors. He'd never let his heritage go, although he would admit that more than once he'd been tempted to do so — and always by a woman.

"There is something else I'd like to know." Pyune's skin shimmered in the kitchen light, her eyes black marbles of laughter. "What about this new preacher that's coming here?"

"What about him?" Wiley asked, finishing his coffee and Pyune pouring him another.

"I'm thinking," Pyune said, refilling her own cup," if he doesn't get here fairly soon, Paula will get up in that pulpit and do the preaching herself."

Wiley gave his hee-haw laugh and shook his head. "Can you imagine that? Her red hair flying everywhere while she pounds the bible and tells everyone, 'You're goin' to hell.'"

Pyune slapped her hand on the table in a fit of laughter. "Then, her eyes would roll back into her head and she'd pro-claim the devil was in the rafters of the church, and unless we confessed our sins, we would all be lost." She groaned. "The sooner that new preacher gets here, the better."

"I hear Thursday," Wiley said, grinning. "Just in time to be settled and preaching Christmas morning?"

"Most likely," Pyune said. "Paula's got everything arranged. You know how she is."

Wiley tilted his cup, coffee spilling and Pyune tossing him a napkin. "Paula tells me she's organizing a big reception for him for Friday night."

Pyune narrowed her eyes at Wiley. "You and Paula seeing each other?"

"Oh, who knows, Pyune? That woman done yanked me all over the place. Keeps saying she wants to get married." Wiley wiped his hands over his face in frustration. "Being married to that redhead would be purely awful."

"Doesn't seem awful enough for you to stay away from her."

Wiley gave a sheepish look. "Well, now, cain't say it's all bad."

The twinkle in his eyes did not go unnoticed by Pyune. "Don't expect any sympathy from me if she dumps you."

Wiley drank the last of his coffee, which Pyune again replenished. "Don't you worry about me and Paula." He glanced at the stove. "How many of them biscuits did you make?"

Pyune found a potholder and opened the oven door. "I made enough. Nice and brown. Want gravy or just a piece of ham?"

"Just a slice of ham," said Wiley, leaning over and watching the slim but very healthy woman take the pan of biscuits from the stove.

Her hair lay close to her head and pulled back into a knot the size of one of her yeast rolls. Her profile was regal, a queen whose subjects were the throngs of people who ate her lemon pudding cake and pined for her succulent meatloaf with tiny bits of green peppers.

Her great grandfather was a Cherokee from high in the North Carolina mountains, and he'd married a daughter of one of Thomas Jefferson's slaves. If you saw anyone hereabouts with light caramel skin and laughing black eyes, most likely they were kin to Pyune.

She turned toward him, and he experienced the same butterflies in his stomach that he'd felt for years whenever he was near her. Their smokehouse dalliances had slowed, but his memories remained. Soft touches, smells of honeysuckle and fried tomatoes on her skin. Their friendship was comfortable, but the presence of Paula Jennings floated around the edge, taunting and causing a hint of malcontent – at times maybe more than just a touch.

"Coming by for lunch?" she asked him.

"Most likely."

Pyune handed Wiley a biscuit and looked down at him. Her hand lingered on his for a moment as she said, "I don't give a damn about Paula – but I do care about you."

It was the first time Wiley had ever heard Pyune cuss.

~~~ ~~~

Chapter 4

M onday's menu, scrawled on the chalkboard hanging by The Boardinghouse's double-oak doors, promised chicken and dumplings, along with turnips, mashed potatoes, rutabagas, carrot salad, candied yams and collards. "Turnips" was misspelled "turneps," but if anybody noticed no one said as much.

The table that faced the street next to the bay window in the front of the restaurant was known as the Paula Jennings's table. Right along with the scars of time, 30 years of gossip and secrets were engrained in the polished oak,

On this day, prim and proper, her back straight, her hands demurely in her lap, Paula – ever the starlet – was certain that everyone had eyed her when she arrived and also that they had admired the fur collar on the wool coat bought in New York City.

Her bright-red lipstick accentuated the smile she wore, perhaps a prelude to the exciting event that was about to take place: The new preacher was coming!

Paula's stature in Ivy Log was established when, years earlier, she'd voted no to the building of a Hardee's on the south side of town, not far from Ivy Log Creek, the spot where Main Street ended at hwy 129. Her stand had resulted in spats, accusations, and threats from those who felt she had no vision.

"I'm a conservationist," she had replied. And her faux charm had swayed the town council from authorizing the razing of a 160-year-old brick building with a façade displaying large pockmarks made by Union bullets and now holding the sign "Patton's Drugstore."

But, it wasn't about conservation – it was about money. Paula didn't own the proposed Hardee's property, but she did own two acres north of town, and she was willing to wait until the fast-food chain decided it was a better location.

And, now, through Paula's doing, the new preacher was coming, the man who would lead The Church of Ivy Log in its 145th year as the community's oldest place of worship. Sure, a hiring committee had been organized to find a replacement for the deceased Pastor Aldelpheus Cobb, but it was Paula who'd led everyone in the direction God had instructed her to follow. It was that simple. Everything she did was God inspired; therefore, questions were unnecessary.

She waved as each member of the selection committee entered the restaurant. And she called out, "Yoo hoo." But there was no need for her to act as though no one could find her. The table in front of the bay window had been hers for three decades, and she sat like a queen on this snowy, cold December day waiting to do God's work on behalf of the citizens of Ivy Log.

Paula caught Pyune's eye. "Hot coffee for everyone, Pyune."

Pyune didn't move. Instead, her gaze roamed the dining room and fell on the dessert table. The pound cake was about gone. Paula snapped her fingers, but Pyune ignored her once more and wandered over to Frank and Adela, who were sitting quietly and drinking coffee.

"Hi, folks," Pyune said, chirping the words. "What's got you out on this cold day?"

Adela laughed. "Why else would we travel nine miles over snow-covered, icy roads if it wasn't for your fried chicken livers?"

Pyune smiled wide. "Ah, they're good too. How about you, Mr. Frank? You like chicken livers?"

"Nothing can keep me from your chicken and dumplings. Let Adela have the chicken livers." Frank winked at Adela.

Pyune smiled at her. "We need to be thinking about your wedding cake. Tiny cream roses and a trail of soft green leaves all around?"

"Perfect."

"Naw," said Frank. "Make that cake with – "

The sound of snapping fingers flew across the room again as Paula's voice shrieked above the crowd. "Pyune, bring the biscuits and cornbread."

Pyune turned around and slowly wiped her hands on her apron, her eyes holding Paula's until the redhead looked away.

Adela patted Pyune on the arm. "You go on. Your food is always worth waiting for. Don't worry about us."

~~~

The members of the illustrious committee in charge of hiring the new pastor settled themselves in their chairs and waited for Paula to begin the informal meeting. Paula pursed her lips until she was assured she had everyone's attention; one eyebrow arched, heavy eyeshadow glittering from the overhead lights, her mascara the blackest of blacks.

"Thank y'all for coming on such short notice. I thought it best we meet one last time before our new pastor arrives."

Doyce Conley, Calvin Anderson, Harley Bradley, Dale Cochrane and Wanda Osborne, each a longtime member of the church, dutifully listened as Paula lowered her voice, a thing she did to draw her audience closer so they would be certain to take in her every word. "I received a call this morning from the Harvard Divinity School. *He's on the way.*"

Paula sat back in her chair and smiled as though a halo had appeared atop her red hair. She nodded slowly and swiveled her head so she could fully take in the approving looks.

She said, "All our hard work has finally been rewarded. Can you imagine? A graduate of the Harvard Divinity School is the new pastor of our church." Her voice rose as she spread her arms wide. "And not just a graduate of their divinity program — a doctor of philosophy as well!"

Doyce squirmed in his chair. "Well, I just wish we could've interviewed him."

"Now, Doyce, we did interview him." Paula's brow wrinkled, moving her thinly-plucked eyebrows closer together in a harsh line.

Doyce shook his head. "That wasn't a real interview. A tele-phone interview is not sufficient in my opinion." Doyce, a farmer in a rich valley five miles west of Ivy Log, was as docile as one of his cows yet mulish when it came to church matters.

"Right," said Calvin, his wispy gray hair moving whenever he spoke. "He's got all the credentials and everything, but I think a personal interview would've been the way to go."

Paula threw up her hands. "Just look at the others we interviewed. What about the pastor from Mississippi who was secretly a member of a nudist colony?" She took a quick breath. "And what about that fellow who was known for preaching all night long? Can't have any of that. And the worst one — the scallywag who stole $10,000 from his church's bank account and said it was a loan repayment. The background check on William Johnson showed him to be of impeccable character. Not one hair on his head was out of place. And he came highly recommended by the school, as well"

The committee members quieted.

With her words cajoling and her slight mountain twang a decibel higher, Paula could not be stopped. "A pastor is the lifeblood and center of a church. Even when there is a vacancy, there has got to be leadership — like a shepherd leading his flock. With the Lord's help, I've tried to lead this committee the best way I know how. We've looked at dozens of resumes, checked references and interviewed candidates. What more can we do?"

She lifted her hands, palms up, as if releasing the budding controversy like leaves into a passing wind. "The new preacher will be here at noon, Thursday. We've got the parsonage to clean and the food to organize for his reception. He's got to prepare the ceremony for Frank and Adela's wedding and preach on Christmas morning." She let out a huff of exasperated breath. "My goodness, can you believe it — Christmas is less than two weeks away."

There was a slow nodding of heads. Wanda leaned forward hesitantly, her blue eyes shifting to Dale and then back to Paula. "About the parsonage. With Pastor Cobb's sudden death, nothing has been touched in the residence."

"That's right," said Dale.

Pastor Aldelpheus Cobb was 83 years old at the time of his death, preaching at The Church of Ivy Log for longer than 40 years. He had left his church family with the next Sunday's sermon lying on his desk, his bible open to I Corinthians .

Paula, superb organizer that she was – and with a ven-geance for detail – demonstrated her leadership skills once again. "It's simple. Let's just go through his things, pack them up for donation, or maybe we could even have a yard sale in the spring."

She dabbed her mouth with a napkin, careful not to remove any lipstick. "No telling what all we'll find. Nobody's been in the parsonage for as long as I can remember."

~ ~ ~

Paula was a study in all the things insecure people did to tell the world they were important. Ignorant of this, Paula's image was orchestrated into what she believed portrayed the best of everything; hence, the Lincoln she drove, the coat with the fur collar she made everyone aware was bought in New York City, and the large antique diamond ring that wrapped around her manicured finger, a ring inherited from her mother on her 21st birthday.

Paula had been born Paula Louise Jennings, into what might be called one of the first families of Ivy Log, a first family that became a first family only when Paula's mother, Irene, married Herbert Jennings when she was pregnant with another man's baby.

The Jennings name brought with it respect and even a little bit of awe; awe for the money Herbert had inherited from his family's logging business.

In small towns, few secrets are kept. Years can go by, but the truth eventually prevails, and that's what happened with Paula. And, it was not only the single dimple in her chin that did it, it was also the red hair. Instead of whispers, these two distinguishing traits were what had elevated her to what she thought was as close to a blue blood as one could get. She was quite aware that Henry VIII was a redhead – and *of course* she had to be a direct descendant. It wasn't until she was older that she discovered the distinct dimple on her chin to be a trait of the Carberry's.

At 48, she had laid claim to the role of Ivy Log's richest res-ident. Richest, that was, until Frank Carberry returned to his birthplace after a 30-year absence. Everyone, but especially

Paula, noted Frank's return. Paula was particularly cognizant of the dimple on his chin – since she had one just like it.

Never married, she'd elevated herself as the titular matriarch of Ivy Log, overseeing the town as well as those she called the *little people*. Paula's shallowness was so great it was absurd – but in Ivy Log she ruled supreme.

~~~ ~~~

Chapter 5

Wiley made his usual rounds, delivering wood in Ivy Log, leaving Elizabeth Lindquist's woodpile and turning onto Main Street, past the town square where snow was piled along the curbs. There was no snowplow in Ivy Log, but Doyce Conley's big John Deere tractor, with its front-end blade did a good job of pushing the heavy snows off the busy street. The diesel fumes lingered from his early-morning scraping of the quarter mile main road that led in and out of town. The town paid Doyce $10 a year for his services, which was plenty, as nothing made him happier than the tractor huffing and puffing its way through town and him sitting high at the wheel.

Wiley slowed his truck and waved to Vallie Thomas, recognizable in her ratty, well-worn plaid coat, her round body waddling to Patton's Drugs where she'd find that special cough syrup with the most alcohol in it. Henry Patton told Vallie that a certain cough syrup was 40 percent alcohol, and this seemed to ease her mind as well as her persistent cough. The alcohol content was only 10 percent, but Vallie was happier thinking it was four times stronger. No matter, she couldn't read the label.

Wiley noticed that Patton's Drugs was missing the "D" in its sign, hence "Patton's rugs" blinked in dull blue letters. *Wonder if Henry Patton knows he's advertising rugs?*

Next to Patton's, a sign in the window at Drake's Hardware, one of the oldest buildings in Ivy Log, announced Santa's arrival. Every kid in Ivy Log who was old enough to walk and under the age of 12 would be there to receive a stocking jam-packed with hard Christmas candy, walnuts and a bright red apple. Wiley was certain that Haskel Drake had stuffed a shiny silver dollar in the toe of each stocking, too, just like he'd done for the past 40 years. Everyone who'd grown up in Ivy Log had been given one; Wiley's tucked away in an old sock that hung from a hook in his gun cabinet.

Dr. Washington Casteel's office was open, his sign "The Doctor Is In" hanging above the sidewalk next to James Stephen's sign with "Fresh Eggs, Worms and Chicken Manure" scrawled in faded, black paint. Unlike Dr. Casteel, James Stephens wasn't in, and he wouldn't have eggs, worms or manure until next spring, after he returned from a winter in Florida.

Most mountain folks refused to succumb to the call of southern beaches, places where flatlanders from all over gathered to bask in the tropical sun and talk about winter. It was well known that a real mountaineer's blood was different from most folks. Made up of more than red blood cells and platelets, it carried a certain allegiance that inured one to the rocks and streams and the special air that can only be breathed at a minimum elevation of 2,000 feet above sea level. If a person listened carefully, this rare blood also carried the sound of a heartbeat, a heartbeat that mountain folks believe will go on forever - for them alone.

The Boardinghouse's door opened and a rush of cold air swept the room as Wiley stepped inside, his nose red, a thick, wool stocking cap covering his head. He removed his gloves while his eyes searched the room. He found what he wanted when he saw Pyune, her back to him, her fingers moving deftly among the desserts lined up on a long table covered by a cloth with embroidered Christmas trees and snowflakes and an angel or two.

Removing his hat and uncovering his bald head, he nodded to most everyone and walked through the center of the room. To his left sat Paula, but he didn't acknowledge her as he went to the table where Frank and Adela were sitting.

"Howdy, folks," Wiley said. Before any conversation could begin, Pyune placed a bowl of chicken and dumplings in front of him. "Just what I need," he said, admiring her Christmas apron.

He picked up the peppershaker. "So, the big day is comin' up fast. Not too late, Frank. You could come with me, and we could hide you out in them there mountains. Nobody would ever find you." The peppershaker, almost empty, stopped in "mid-shake." Wiley squinted his eyes at Frank. "Why, we could even go huntin'."

Frank laughed and reached over and patted Adela's hand. "Nope. Don't want to leave this woman. Been looking for her all my life."

"That's right. Don't take my man away from me." Adela shook her finger at Wiley. "You just get him to the church on time. That's all I ask."

"I can do that, Miss Adela." Wiley scooped up some dumplings. "I imagine everybody in Ivy Log will be at that weddin'. Can't believe Frank asked me to be his best man."

"I'm proud you're my best man," Frank said. "Look how many years we've known each other; since first grade."

"How 'bout that? And who ever would a thought you and Miss Adela would get married?" Wiley stared across the room, his thoughts far away in a place called memories. "I miss ol' Andy. War is a terrible thing." Andy, Adela's young husband, had died in the first few weeks of the war.

Frank nodded, and they talked and ate until Pyune stepped from the kitchen and called to Wiley, "Ready for some pecan pie?"

"Cain't you tell, Pyune?" he replied, just finishing his last dumpling. "Don't you see my plate is empty and my hands are startin' to shake just thinkin' about your pie? Did you put a lot of vanilla in it?"

"Just like you like it," Pyune said, her forehead glistening from the heat of the kitchen. She placed the pie in front of Wiley and pulled out a chair. She turned to Frank. "Your son coming in for the wedding?"

"We were just talking about Andy. Don't believe he'll make it. Afghanistan is a long ways from here." Frank squeezed Adela's hand and found her watching him with that look a woman gives a man when she's in love with him.

Wiley took his first bite of pie said to Pyune, "Good pie."

~~~

Paula had watched intently as Pyune brought Wiley his pie and rested her hand on his shoulder, the ceiling lights reflecting off her face and her perfect white teeth whenever she'd smiled. Paula found herself perspiring. Her hatred of Pyune had begun long ago and would fester like poison ivy whenever she'd see Wiley and this half-breed enjoying the company of one another. Yet Wiley's interest in the woman was more than purely physical, and it was a mystery to Paula. What did Pyune have that she didn't.

She pulled her eyes away and said to Wanda Osborne, "I'll meet you at the parsonage at 8 o'clock in the morning. We've got lots of work to do." Paula turned to the men. "Doyce, I want you to get two big garbage cans from the church and place them outside the back door of the preacher's house. Calvin, we need some containers. Boxes. Can you round some up for us?"

Both men nodded as Paula pulled on her coat, then the soft leather gloves that were a gift from her Sunday school class on her last birthday. Her long fingers flicked at the fur collar that brushed her cheeks. Her parade across the restaurant was orchestrated and designed to turn heads. She eyed Wiley and gave him her most seductive look. He didn't smile or acknowledge her in any way. She hesitated a moment, then swung open the door and marched out into the frosty air.

~~~ ~~~

Chapter 6

Filled with Pyune's chicken and dumplings and pecan pie, Wiley pulled his old truck from the back of The Boarding-house and climbed a narrow mountain road with drop-offs that would cause a sissy flatlander to faint. His mood was reflective; maybe it was Frank and Adela's upcoming marriage, their devotion to one another and the companionship they shared.

Wiley had never married. His home in the dancing place of rabbits, as the poet Byron Herbert Reese had once said of the Appalachians, was a cozy cabin he had built during the summers when he returned from college. Made of spruce, he used the expertise of Scandinavian design to notch the corners of the round logs and build a foundation of stones from the creek beds. When he sat on the front porch watching a sunset, he'd often dream of just the right woman who'd want to sit next to him and grow old together.

Born north of Brasstown Bald and south of Lake Chatuge, high in the green hills, Wiley didn't stray far. The mountains framed his life – mountains so high he could even chase an angel if he wanted to.

"Where you from?" he had often been asked, his mountain talk indicative of some cove or valley where years before him families from Ireland and Scotland and Germany had come to till the fields and build the churches. They worked hard but found time to bask in unhurried living and perhaps even felt Godlike sitting atop the soaring peaks.

He'd never leave the clouded forest, the place where giant yellow birch danced with the mountain winds. He'd die there, his legs resting on the rail of his porch, his eyes looking toward the sun as it slipped behind a faraway peak.

He wondered about Paula. He admitted that the city girl filled a need he had, a need that exposed his weakness. While his core was solid, etched in his soul like the rocks in the mountains, there was a part of him that wanted more. He thought he had found it in Paula, in her unique ways, in her almost soap-opera character. She enchanted him, much like Delilah had charmed Samson.

In his secret mind, he had imagined himself married to her, taking the prissy girl to live with him in the place where the spirits of long-ago Indians spoke to each other. But, in the dark corners of those temptations, it was apparent she was not molded as he had been made — and did not possess the same motivation. He understood the purpose he served. And why he could not leave. And why he must honor what was true.

Sometimes he didn't obey the voices he had heard so many times, rising and becoming louder as he pursued what pleased him, without any thought of consequences. It was his conscience, of course. His desire for the redheaded woman was simple. They were the same desires men had felt for women since the beginning of time.

He recognized his weaknesses as if they had been painted purple and hung on a flagpole and waved to him every time he thought of the four-poster bed in her upstairs guest room. Sooner or later, he must decide if his affliction was curable, if he could remain in the mountains, away from the city girl and the fingers with the red polish that reached toward him and beckoned him closer.

~~~

Tom Keeling's horses heard his truck and paused at the fence. Wiley laughed out loud. He couldn't imagine Paula helping him shoe horses. She'd complain that she'd just had a manicure.

What was their common ground? They had none. Maybe he could call their mutual lust for one another common ground. But, how lasting was lust. He began to count on his fingers the

years they'd been together, soon realizing it was a lifetime —
since first grade when he'd arrived at Miss Proctor's classroom
and Paula laughed at him. Said he talked funny. Pinched him
on the cheek and then wiped her hands on her dress. "Your
face is dirty, mountain boy."

Even then, he couldn't take his eyes off her red hair. He had
never seen red hair before and even then wondered if it was
the sign of someone who was special or if the person had been
afflicted with a curse of some sort. He couldn't distinguish
between the two, only that when he looked around the
classroom he saw no one else with hair afire.

At long last, on the back side of 40, he was seriously con-
templating marriage. Trouble was, if he married Paula, he
could not remain a mountain man. She'd hinted at marriage,
especially since Frank and Adela had announced their engage-
ment.

Now, he'd have to tell her he didn't want to get married. It
wasn't that he didn't want to get married — he just didn't want
to marry her. Yes, he'd have to tell her and then run and hide
deep in the mountains under the biggest rock he could find.

On a rise high above the valley, he looked down at the
Keeling farm. Stretched in nature's special winter colors, the
edges, spiked with long, blue edges of shadows, crept out
across the snow and met the rolling pastures and the rosy glow
of a fleeting sun.

Tom Keeling's three horses galloped across the snow and
frolicked as if children, their tails held high as they ran, the
snow kicking up behind them. Smoke rose from the chimney
and he imagined Barnie Mae Keeling standing at her wood
stove, a bit of Smokey Mountain peach snuff in her cheek.

Tom and Barnie Mae Keeling were mountain people whose
understanding of life far surpassed his own. They felt the
closeness of the morning star, living a life in a place where
peace was theirs just for the asking.

He put his truck in gear and headed down into the valley,
thinking he must have a heart-to-heart talk with Paula —
dreading it more than anything he'd ever had to do.

~~~ ~~~

Chapter 7

E xcept for God, the Reverend Aldelpheus Cobb had reined supreme for 40-plus years in The Church of Ivy Log. A quiet man, except when he was in the pulpit, he spent long hours in his study, where the shelves sagged with books wrapped in covers with titles that touted its owner as a learned man. Books whose subjects related to Christology, eschatology, pneumatology and on and on.

The pages between the hard covers spoke of hermeneutical and homiletic principles from the minds of doctors of philosophy who lived in every country on earth and who had, in their own minds, answered questions that had been asked since the beginning of time.

Pastor Cobb had believed preachings from those books would ensure theologically sophisticated parishioners, but after 40 years in The Church of Ivy Log, he discovered his parishioners were no more sophisticated than when he first began his weekly sermons. He also discovered that simple mountain folks did not need all those fancy books to understand the love of Christ.

The books were musty, the dust in the pastor's study like thick pollen, but he read on. He forbade the hiring of a cook or a housecleaner after his wife died some 20 years earlier. He said the expenditure was frivolous, not worthy of the hard-earned money of his parishioners. When he was not in his study turning the pages of the Holy Bible, he was at church shaking hands, quoting scriptures and, best of all, singing the

Lord's praises in his soft, often off-key, tenor.

At 83 years of age, his death had been sudden but not unexpected. And although he was slight of build, he delivered his message with power and conviction. On Sunday mornings, Sunday nights and at Wednesday-night prayer meetings, he arrived fresh-shaven, smelling of Old Spice and wearing a tie he had owned since the '50s, always ready to minister passion-ately to his parishioners.

On the morning he was late for Sunday-morning prayer, Doyce Conley was dispatched to the parsonage where he found Brother Cobb sitting in his chair at his desk, his hand resting on his bible, precisely on I Corinthians, Chapter 15, his fore-finger placed on Verse 52. His body was cold, a slight smile on his face. He had gone to see Jesus.

An attorney in Blairsville handled his estate, what there was of it. The pastor was estranged from his only son, Sam, who was not mentioned in his will. His personal belongings were donated to The Church of Ivy Log, with the proceeds dir-ected to go to Foreign Missions. An unidentified individual became the recipient of an undisclosed amount of money. There was $832.11 in his bank account.

~~~

"Can you believe it?" Dale Cochrane threw one more pair of Pastor Cobb's pants on a pile in the center of the living room. "That's thirty- two pair and counting. I've never seen so much stuff in my life. Looks like he never threw anything away. By the style, these pants look like they're 50 years old."

Wanda, her blue eyes wide and unbelieving, shook her head. "We'll never get this place cleaned out before the new pastor gets here."

Paula pulled out a drawer and began raking out its con-tents. "We've got to. Just keep at it."

From the other end of the house, Dale called out. "You aren't going to believe this."

She walked hurriedly down the hall holding a box she had found underneath the pastor's bed. The box was the size of a large shoebox, old and frayed around the edges, its faded color a dark green, dust coating the box where the imprint of her fin-gers had smudged the top. She sat on the sofa, holding the box as though the contents were priceless and full of glorious wonders. And it was.

"What" asked Paula, who plopped down beside Dale and snatched the box from her lap,. "Let me see."

The letters were tightly packed together, their edges even along the top, ivory-colored envelopes with the sawtooth borders of stamps poking up like small treetops. Paula pulled one out and read the address: "The Reverend Aldelpheus Cobb, The Church of Ivy Log, Ivy Log, Georgia."

Dale leaned over. "Look at that fancy handwriting."

"My goodness. I love old letters." Paula took out an envelope.

Wanda came over and yanked the letter from Paula's hand. "No, we can't do that. This is Pastor Cobb's personal stuff."

"The pastor is dead and he won't care," Paula said, grabbing it back.

"But these look like private letters." Wanda shook her head. "This is an invasion of Pastor Cobb's privacy."

Paula gave Wanda a menacing glare. "Wanda, honey, there's no need to get pushed out of shape. We're here to clean the parsonage, and it's our responsibility to go through everything to determine its value. And that includes these letters."

Paula, her long fingers like the agile legs of a spider capturing a helpless fly, pulled open the flap and slid the letter from the envelope, her lips moving slightly as she scanned the page.

"Well?" Dale leaned in closer. "Now that you went ahead and opened it, who are they from?"

"I don't know. It's signed with a big round 'O' at the bottom." Paula looked up. "Wonder who 'O' is?"

"Look here," Dale said, pointing to the envelope. "It's postmarked Blairsville, Georgia."

There had to be whispers inside, sentences filled with words that led down endless roads — maybe even seductive, exposing secrets that waited, begging to be plucked.

Paula read on. When she looked up at Wanda and Dale, she grinned. "Well, I'll be danged."

"What?" Wanda asked.

"This letter is quite passionate."

Dale shook her head. "Passionate? The only time I saw Brother Cobb passionate was in the pulpit. No way there was a woman in his life."

"Now what makes you say that, Dale? Wanda thinks Brother Cobb was a private individual, so maybe there are some things we didn't know about. You know . . . like a woman."

"A woman!" Dale jumped up from the sofa. "I can't believe that!"

Paula dipped her chin. "Well, now, my dears, let's just read these letters and we'll find out."

Wanda sucked in her breath. "This is not the Christian thing to do. Brother Cobb had his own life and deserves respect in his death. I won't be a part of this." She picked up her coat and scarf.

"Just where do you think you're going?" Paula placed the box of letters on a nearby table. "We've got a job to do. The new pastor will be here on Thursday, and we have just two days to clean this place." She shoved the box to the side and picked up a broom. "Just forget about those letters."

Had Brother Cobb known Ivy Log's most renowned gossip would pilfer his treasured secrets after his death, perhaps he would have made certain his affairs were in better order. Had the pastor been known to curse — which, in his entire lifetime he never had done except when he used the words "hell" and "damnation" in his sermons — from his grave one could imagine hearing a feeble, yet distinct, "Oh, shit."

~~~ ~~~

Chapter 8

In the beginning, their courtship had been a tumultuous one. Who would have thought the cantankerous, retired major general would have wooed the widow as he did – cursing, threatening, hating, disparaging, reviling, and, finally, a slow succumbing to the joys of love?

He pulled her to him and smoothed her hair away from her face. "I can't remember – did I ask you to marry me or did you ask me?"

Adela narrowed her eyes. "Either way – we're getting married, Frank Carberry. Just be at the church on time and I'll be there waiting for you." She kissed his cheek. "Are you going to build us a fire?"

"Yep. Wiley brought some firewood by earlier. Seasoned oak."

"Good. I feel like snuggling. Snowing hard out there."

Frank placed several pieces of oak in the fireplace, then looked over at Adela. "Snuggling? It's 3 o'clock in the afternoon."

"And?" said Adela, as she slipped her sweater over her head.

~~~

Their lovemaking had been tender, their passion tempered by the profound realization that their love was nothing short of a miracle, although things had not always been exactly "lovely" between them.

Before Adela, Frank had been a recluse, a lover of solitude.

His return to Ivy Log after a 30-year absence was one of Ivy Log's delicious subjects of tittle-tattle that so absorbed the town. Because of his solitary life, some thought him mentally ill, perhaps he was someone who snuck out at night and howled at the moon. Andrew Morris swore he saw Frank running naked through a cornfield at midnight, flying a kite, and his dog, Cootie, following behind and chasing his bare butt.

As rumors go, however, nothing compared to Paula Jennings's claim that Frank harbored a harem of women inside his lake house, each one pleasuring him at his slightest whim.

"Who were those women?" someone asked Paula. "Well, I haven't seen Shirley Brechler for a few days," she had replied with certainty – and malice. But Paula was never wrong about anything. Just ask the women who trailed after her and supported her claims, regardless of their lunacy. Their upstanding membership in The Church of Ivy Log allowed them to sing in perfect harmony and smile at each other in their smug little way. Prunes for lips, when "Standing on the Promises" hit a high E, they could hardly open their prim little mouths.

Truth be told, no one really knew what went on in the Carberry mansion when Frank retired from his military career. The gate at the beginning of the lane was always locked, a sign saying "Keep Out" posted squarely in the middle of the road. And everyone knew Frank loved to shoot guns.

The old soldier had long ago admitted his frailties. His inability to recover from a deep wound of the heart and his inherent stubbornness united to make a man who, at 62-years-old, wallowed in a life of what-ifs. His many years in the confines of his military duties had made him a wooden man, shaped by endless forays into a world of clandestine missions that left him somewhat tainted by the brutal, imminent reality of his own mortality.

Frank Carberry had been a lost man; the umbilical cord to his position of major general in the army had been cut when he retired and, as a result, had cast him into a place of unknowns, a place where he floundered and questioned his ability to survive in a nonmilitary world.

Long before Adela, he had wondered about the power of love. Was it possible? Was there any validity in a touch or a kiss that made one powerless, made one succumb to the belief that nothing else mattered? Perhaps the whys of it were not known, just that it was there. And, once it was acknowledged, there was no letting go, no return to what was. Only love remained, regardless of circumstances or the laws of the universe.

His soldier's life had taken him to foreign places, to places where he lived in anonymity, a no-name who quietly infiltrated the world of top-secret operations, clandestine and most definitely dangerous. He lost himself among the darkness that comes with an undercover life.

When he could not regain the normalcy of civilian life, his mind conspired with his heart in a way that left him cold and untouchable, especially untouchable by love. Until Adela. She had taught him what the military couldn't. She had taught him the power of love.

~~~

The winter day faded and Frank and Adela lay in semidarkness in front of the fireplace, the oak wood flaming softly. He reached over and touched her cheek, his finger trailing to her breast. He pushed back the blanket that covered her and smiled. "I love looking at you."

Adela brushed her fingers across his chest and leaned back on her elbows, her breasts inviting him to lean over and find them with his lips. "I want more."

~~~ ~~~

Chapter 9

Snow hushed the streets of Ivy Log, a winter's town whose sidewalks ran down Main Street, past the darkness of John Reese's barbershop and the windows of Drake's Hardware, where a Christmas display showcased a bright red wagon. The merchants along Main Street had long since shoveled snow from their doorsteps to allow locals entry into their shops. The fragrance of spiced holiday tea continued to drift from store to store. And the piped-in songs of Christmas came nonstop, as did the snow upon the rooftops and the branches of the cedars that lined the square.

At The Boardinghouse, the lights were dim, the desserts put away and the smell of collards and ham only a memory. Long after dark, Paula left the parsonage and slowly walked to her Lincoln, her 4-inch heels making delicate crunches in the snow; she was too vain to wear snow boots. Her New York coat with the fake fur collar was wrapped tightly around her, a pair of leather gloves on hands that, to her delight, clutched the tattered green box found earlier beneath the pastor's bed.

"Hey, Paula!" She turned and saw Vallie Thomas slushing toward her, her wool scarf half hiding a face that was perhaps the plainest in the whole Appalachian mountain range. *Why wouldn't the woman at least wear mascara?*

"Hey, Vallie. You're out late." She tried to keep the irritation out of her voice, which was hard to do. Vallie was known for her rambling conversations, and Paula didn't want to strike up even a short chat on this particular evening.

"Oh, yeah. Had to leave a note on the door at the hardware store. Wanted Haskel to put something on layaway for me. Left him twenty dollars. Well, not exactly twenty dollars, I –"

"Have a nice night, Vallie. Got to go." Paula opened the door to her car.

"Hold up, Paula. I have something to tell you." She sniffed her nose and pulled a tissue from her coat pocket, a coat so old and worn that it should have been put in a dumpster long ago "I seen Wiley over at the jewelry counter at Patton's Drugs. You know Henry has some 'pensive stuff behind that counter." Vallie grinned, her nose red and in need of wiping again. "Reckon he was Christmas shopping for somebody?" Her grin turned sly.

Paula tossed her handbag into the car. "Wouldn't know, Vallie." She turned and without seeming too anxious, asked, "Did you see what he was looking at?"

"No, not really. Just saw Henry open the safe and take some things out. Heard Wiley say 'Wow,' real slow like."

The scarf Vallie was wearing fell down across her forehead. When she pushed it up onto her head, Paula saw her hair needed coloring, her roots white. She also smelled the wet wool of the frayed coat. Wiley? Jewelry shopping? How interesting. "Well, you take care, Vallie. Got to go."

"Now, just hold on a minute, Paula. I ain't through telling you everything.

Paula yanked her gloves tighter on her hands and blew out a breath. "Hurry up, Vallie. It's cold out here."

"I heard Wiley say the word 'marriage.' Vallie nodded her head up and down, smiling, pleased at herself.

"Marriage?"

"That's right. Sure did."

~~~

Paula found her stately home at the corner of Dellwood Avenue and Main Street dark and cold, the chill caused by more than the weather. Another Christmas alone.

In her living room, she turned on the lamps, took off her coat and gloves and slipped off her shoes, her thoughts on Wiley. At noon, when she'd seen him at The Boardinghouse, he had not so much as acknowledged her. And she could hardly ignore his warmth toward Pyune, her touching him on the shoulder, him reaching up and patting her hand.

Pyune Murphy was the perpetual thorn in her side, a lifelong reminder that their mothers had been close friends despite the black woman's being their maid, someone whose station in life was far below Paula's.

Sometimes Hattie Murphy had brought her daughter with her while she cleaned the Jennings's house, Pyune sitting dutifully at the kitchen table doing her homework, ignoring Paula, who took pleasure in prancing in and out of the kitchen, generally with a smirk on her face. Pyune's mother often told Paula that she acted too big for her britches.

For both women, the years had passed in the small, seemingly untouched town, their lives continuing as though there was nothing else to do but sing hymns in church on Sunday mornings, fry chicken for the preacher, and watch as the young moved away to the big cities. To most, Ivy Log was a big dish of boredom that no one wanted to eat. But for folks like Paula and Pyune, it would be home forever.

In her favorite chair, Paula held the faded green box with the letters to Reverend Cobb and smiled to herself. Oh, how she loved mysteries.

A woman, whose life is enriched by gossip, has skills that steadfastly fuel her desire to discover all she can about everyone and everything. Paula's vile curiosity was unsurpassed as she turned over every stone in Ivy Log as though her life depended on it. Her personality, along with a measurable mean streak, sustained her. She was a very big fish in a very small pond, and everything she did solidified her self-proclaimed position as high priestess.

She had her own secrets. Hidden, she thought. She'd had a wild affair with Aldelpheus Cobb's only son, Sam, when she was 17, and had tucked that little hush-hush away long ago. But, she still remembered the power in his body as if it were yesterday.

Thus, when she sat in her queenly chair and opened the green shoebox that contained the private property of Pastor Aldelpheus Cobb, for over 40 years the pastor of The Church of Ivy Log — and now deceased — she had absolutely no doubt of her entitlement to do so.

She removed the top and did what she always had when she embarked on a grand adventure: she smiled.

The envelopes, not the thin, cheap kind — but quality linen the color of a faded wedding dress — lay like dead soldiers, one after the other, each most assuredly filled with delicious secrets. The first one was postmarked September 15. The last envelope was dated March 13 — a year-and-a-half later. All were placed in sequential order. She counted them, her long red fingernails clicking along the tops as her lips moved in tacit rejoinder.

Sixty-three letters. And, now, as she opened one of the newest letters and read the first line, her smile widened. "My dear darling, Al," it began.

"My dear darling, Al!" she blurted. In her wildest imagination she could not conjure up an image of the scrawny, hawk-nosed pastor as "darling." But, there it was, "darling" in an unmistakable flowing feminine script. She tried to remember if she had ever received a letter that began with "My dear darling." No, she had not. She was certain.

Hardly breathing, she read the remainder of the letter, her fingers grasping the two pages as though they were the missing Dead Sea Scrolls. She turned back to the first page and smiled. "You have made my heart soar. I never dreamed I could feel this way. I am going to bed now and dreaming of you. Every time I think of you, my heart beats faster and faster."

Paula returned the letter to its envelope. Why, Pastor Cobb, you little devil, you.

~~~ ~~~

Chapter 10

Smoke from The Boardinghouse chimney raced east, pushed by winds that made it the coldest December on record, or so the thick hair on the wooly-booger caterpillars later indicated. The woodpile behind the restaurant's great kitchen seemed to disappear at an alarming rate; a constant fire in the mammoth stone fireplace, much to the delight of those who had braved the cold to savor hot soups and stews from the glorious kitchen.

The front door greeted patrons with a freshly cut cedar wreath — wrapped by a red ribbon tied with bells at the end — ringing cheerfully every time the door opened, and followed by the stomping of snow boots and the shudder of cold that seemed unending.

Inside, the wide plank floors of native oak warmed the room. Crown molding added a soft touch, its cream color accentuating the pale green walls, on which pictures of the Appalachians hung in polished wooden frames.

The noonday chatter addressed the height of snowdrifts along the town square, the crooked placement of the star atop the town Christmas tree, and the arrival of the new preacher on Thursday. At precisely Noon, Paula burst through the doors of The Boardinghouse, her red hair tangled from the wind, the end of her nose pink and her eyes afire with excitement. She smiled and nodded as she threaded her way around the room to her special seat at the bay window. With flair, she removed her coat and gloves and arranged herself so she appeared in majestic splendor.

Wednesday's menu: "Fresh Pork Roast and Sweet Potatoes, Beef Tips with Rice and Gravy, and Roasted Chicken with Sage Dressing." Paula studied the menu a moment before scanning the room to see who had ventured to The Boardinghouse on this raw December day. She saw Wiley leaning against the door of the kitchen in animated conversation with Pyune, his hands lifting and moving as though leading a choir.

Moments later, the doors opened again, and Dale and Wanda, red-cheeked, hustled inside and made their way to Paula's table, brushing snow off their coats. They stopped a moment in front of the fireplace and warmed their hands, both squealing when a log popped and sent out a few flying embers.

"Hey, girls," said Paula, her voice somewhat irritated. "Haven't been waited on yet. Pyune's too busy talking to Wiley." She looked back at the kitchen door and noticed the two were no longer standing together. Wiley had sat down with Doyce Conley and was no doubt talking about tractors.

"How late did you stay last night?" Dale asked Paula. She smoothed her hair and Paula noticed that the woman's nails needed polishing.

"Oh, I left about an hour after you two," Paula said.

Paula had checked everything before she went home, and Dale and Wanda had cleaned the parsonage from top to bottom; its furniture polished, the curtains washed and ironed, the rugs vacuumed, the refrigerator and pantry stocked, and clean linens placed on the four-poster bed. A Christmas wreath hung on the front door to welcome the new pastor, along with a lighted Star of Bethlehem in each front window.

"I bet you stayed up all night reading those letters," said Dale. "Come on — tell us everything."

"I'm dying to tell you. Oh, the stuff in those letters."

"Well, what did they say?" asked Dale. Wanda frowned.

Paula, eyes gleaming, red lipstick shining, said, "Oh, sweeties, Pastor Cobb had an admirer, for sure."

"An admirer?" Dale asked.

"Whoever 'O' is, it seems like she'd known him for quite a while."

Dale inched forward in her chair. "Who is she?"

"How do I know? In her first letter to him, she talks about

how excited she was that they found each other again. So, no telling how long they've known each other."

Paula leaned in closer to Dale and Wanda, and in lowered voice said, "I'm sure I'll find out when I read more letters, but it's obvious to me there was some hanky-panky going on."

"Hanky-panky?" breathed Dale in hushed tones.

"In the first four letters, she signs them all 'Warm regards.' But in her fifth letter, she signs it 'All my love, O'." Paula pulled back so she could see both women at the same time. "I'm thinking Pastor Cobb was not as angelic as we believed."

Wide-eyed, Dale whispered, "But why would he keep it a secret? What's wrong with having a woman in his life? His wife had been dead for years."

"Who knows?" said Paula. "In one of her letters, she said she would see him in church the following Sunday. That leads me to believe she attended The Church of Ivy Log."

The women all looked at one another. The "O" woman had been under their very noses, with no outward appearances that she was sweet on Aldelpheus Cobb.

"What about that woman who always sits in the third pew on the right, behind Linda Richardson? She's the one who wore that little red hat with the netting."

"Oh, no. That was Cathy Barnwell's sister. She sometimes visits from Atlanta. Besides, her name is Cheryl. No 'O' in her name."

"I'm certain the letters will reveal just who wrote them. Just wonder why the signature is not written out. Why in the world would someone just sign it 'O'."

Dale giggled and leaned over the table, her eyes darting back and forth between Paula and Wanda. "There's only one 'O' I know about - and that's orgasm."

Wanda yelped. "Dale! Please! Mind your manners."

"Oh, come on, Wanda. You know that's the first thing you thought of."

"Is not!" Wanda gave Dale a smug look. "'O' could be many names: Ophelia, Olga . . . ."

"Ha! See, not many 'O' names out there and — "

"Girls, girls." Paula held up her hands. "We've got more important things to discuss." She paused long enough to place her clearly in control of the conversation. "The esteemed Reverend William H. Johnson — and may I remind you he's a graduate of the Harvard Divinity School and will most assuredly raise our church to heights never before achieved — will arrive tomorrow at Noon."

"Where are you to meet him?" Wanda asked.

"He'll meet me here at The Boardinghouse for lunch. Afterwards, I'll escort him to the parsonage and show him where he'll be living. Later, I'll walk him to the church where he can be introduced to the entire committee. Be sure and tell Calvin, Doyce and Harley to be at the church at 1 o'clock."

Paula was in a self-imposed reverie, her eyes closed, a smile on her lips. Finally, she shook herself as if chilled. "Oh, the thought of it. At last, a progressive, highly-educated leader for our church. God has surely answered our prayers."

~~~

Wiley scraped his plate, the last of the pork roast mixed with a tad of rice and gravy. To the left of his plate, a bowl of warm apple cobbler waited, a swirl of whipped cream beginning to melt, a dust of cinnamon on top. His heart skipped a beat. There wasn't anything he liked better than Pyune's fresh apple cobbler. He had seen her peel the apples many times, carefully slicing and arranging them in a heavy pan, doctoring them with bits of butter, then sugar and spices. He began to smile the first moment the smell of the baking cobbler filled the kitchen.

It seemed his greatest happiness came when he sat in The Boardinghouse kitchen and watched Pyune cook. There was a settling of his mind; a peace, a comfort that most of his life he had only found in his beloved mountains. Yet, as he traveled down the winding roads to the streets of Ivy Log, another kind of peace awaited, a contentment ladled to him in bowls and plates and poured into cups. And when the time was right, in the smokehouse behind the kitchen, he and Pyune found another level of satisfaction.

Across the room, in her usual place, he saw Paula. The women from church had left and she sat and refreshed her lipstick. Even though he had known her for many years, she continued to baffle him about who she really was.

In the upstairs guest bedroom of her sprawling two-story

house on Dellwood Avenue, she unleashed a power over him. Maybe it was his lust for her that caused his confusion. When she pranced around the room, the nipples on her small but firm breasts poking toward the ceiling, his head became cotton. Later, on his long ride home to the mountains, his head cleared and he faced the realization that she lacked the humility and grace he desired in a woman — the very qualities he found in Pyune.

He remembered exactly when he and Paula had become more than just friends. He'd watched her raking leaves in her backyard, moisture glistening on her upper lip, the outline of her hipbones clearly defined by the blue jeans she wore. When she offered him a cool drink, he accepted, following her into the house and watching her round behind sway as she flitted around the kitchen and filled two glasses with ice. When she turned toward him, some buttons of her blouse were undone, exposing the tops of her breasts.

When he reached for the glass, he touched her fingers and felt the smooth skin of manicured hands - a city-girl's hands. They made love upstairs in her guest bedroom. He'd never forget looking at the wallpaper that first time; how the branches of magnolia trees and their large white blossoms were etched into the paper like a scene from "Gone With The Wind."

He also remembered her clinging to him and begging him not to tell anyone about their lovemaking. Of course he wouldn't, even though mountain men were not known for making love to city women. Anyway, not a mountain man by the name of Wiley Hanson. It was, however, his opinion that a city boy could never satisfy a city girl like a mountain man could. Even now, he could feel Paula's panting breath on his neck and deep moans as he whipped her into a lather.

Wiley caught Paula looking at him and nodded. He knew he'd have to go over to her table. How could he not? Lust? It was always lust. He was not immune to it but rather thrilled by it — and 100-percent weakened by it.

He picked up his bowl of cobbler and headed her way. She was wearing a purple sweater with silver buttons, earrings that dangled, and several gaudy rings that emphasized her long, thin fingers; fingers that ended with long red nails.

"Wiley, dear, sit down," she crooned.

"Believe I will." He slid out a chair and settled in, his back to the kitchen so he couldn't see Pyune.

Paula tilted her head. "You and Pyune were in quite a conversation over there?"

Wiley spooned up some cobbler and blew on it, the steam puffing around the hot apples. "Yep. She's anxious about that recipe contest."

Paula perked up. "What recipe contest?"

"Want some cobbler?"

"What recipe contest?" Paula persisted.

"That magazine one."

"Good Housekeeping?"

"No. Want some cobbler?"

"Woman's Day?"

"No."

"Good golly, Wiley. Can't you remember what contest and what magazine?" Paula shook her head and thumped the table with her hand, now balled into a fist.

"Well, I reckon I could if I was a cooking for it." He scrunched his brow. "Believe it was a baking magazine. Twenty-five thousand dollars for first prize."

"Twenty-five thousand dollars? And Pyune entered it? I haven't heard a thing about it."

"Well, you know Pyune. She's so private about things. Anyways, she entered a recipe, and it's down to the top five entries, and she's one of 'em."

Paula narrowed her eyes and looked toward the kitchen. "What recipe was it?"

"Lemon pudding cake, I think."

"What?" Paula screeched. "She can't enter that recipe. That's my recipe." The skin on Paula's neck flushed red and the freckles across her cheeks became as big as pencil erasers.

Wiley pointed at her with his spoon. "Now, Paula, you know darn well that recipe was Pyune's grandmother's."

"You have got to be kidding."

Wiley, exasperated, placed his hands on the table. "That can't be your recipe. I sure ain't never known you to cook a lemon pudding cake."

"Listen here, Wiley Hanson, that was my mama's recipe."

"Yes, and your momma got it from Pyune's mamma, so hold onto your horses."

"You've got your facts all wrong. My mama gave that recipe to Pyune's mama when she worked for her some thirty years ago."

"Well, too late now. Contest is over. They're going to announce the grand-prize winner on Christmas Eve."

Paula jumped up and grabbed her coat. "I'll tell you one thing — if Pyune wins that twenty-five thousand dollars, she'll never see a penny of it. I'll take her to court for stealing my recipe." Paula stomped out of The Boardinghouse, the bells on the front door clanging loud and long.

~~~ ~~~

Chapter 11

Ivy Log's streetlights popped on in the early evening as a "closed" sign hung on The Boardinghouse. With the room now dark and empty, a few hot coals remained aglow in the main dining area's large fireplace. In the back of the 100-old house, the kitchen ovens continued to burn bright as Pyune pulled the last cake pans from the racks. On the counter, other cake rounds cooled, while icing, whipped and smooth, filled bowls that were lined up in a row like children waiting to see Santa.

At 9:30, Pyune refilled her coffee cup. Another late night. It would be midnight before the last cake was frosted and the last piecrust rolled, and 1 a.m. before the kitchen was cleaned and ready for Thursday's breakfast, lunch and dinner. Her kitchen help wouldn't arrive until 7.a.m., long after her "official" day had begun.

Outside, a silent snow fell. The wind had died at dusk, a welcome reprieve since the beginning of the storm on Sunday. A noise at the back door told her the cats were hungry. From the large stockpot at the back of the stove, she took a few scraps and placed them in an old pan and opened the door. A rush of cold air streamed into the room — and behind it, a fuming Paula Jennings, who huffed her way past Pyune into The Boardinghouse kitchen.

The redhead charged into the room like a runaway freight train, swirling her coat around as if it were a shield and she was preparing to do battle. Her 4-inch heels and teased hair pushed her height to nearly 6 feet — rendering her a formidable foe when compared to the petite Pyune Murphy.

"Pyune Murphy, how dare you?" Paula hissed as she stomped toward Pyune. "You took my family's prized lemon pudding cake recipe and entered it into a contest. Why, that is pure and simple fraud." She took a quick breath. "I'll see to it you are sued all over this town and back." When she stopped shouting, her face was inches from a stricken Pyune.

Pyune gave her a nonplussed look but said nothing.

Paula started in again. "Do you hear me?" Her lips twisted and curled menacingly with each word as she repeated, "Do you hear me?"

Pyune, her Christmas apron smeared with frosting, shook her head slowly. "Can you tell me how many eggs are in that cake?"

"Eggs?" Paula stammered. "As many eggs as I want to put in the recipe, you recipe thief you."

Pyune sat on a stool and folded her arms. "How could you know how many eggs, Paula? You've never even baked a lemon pudding cake." Her black eyes narrowed, a calmness spreading over her as she stared at a fuming Paula.

Paula drew herself up, took in a deep breath and scowled. "Pyune Murphy, you know darn well that was my family's recipe, and your mama stole it."

Pyune jumped from her stool and threw her thin body in front the woman with high heels and riotous red hair, whose vitriol this evening was supercharged.

"My mama didn't steal anything. For thirty years she worked for your family and baked that cake for every Sunday dinner for you and your mama. And the day she quit working for your family, she gave your mama a copy of the recipe. She did it out of love."

Paula folded her arms across her chest, a blatant haughtiness in her words. "Ain't nobody ever been given that recipe, because it was always my family's."

"That's not so," Pyune said and started to turn away.

Paula stepped forward and wagged her finger in front of Pyune's face. Her voice ebbed low and husky as though the devil rested on her vocal cords and sat smiling, prompting her on.

"My dear, dear Pyune," she said, capering around the kitchen, her New York coat wrapped tightly around her, the corners of her lips moving upward as if to her ears and her red lipstick gleaming against her pale skin. "Your naiveté amazes me. Why, your mama stole that recipe and I can prove it." She nodded her head several times. "You better pray you don't win that baking contest. Because, if you do, I'm taking you to court, and I'll get every single penny of that prize money."

Pyune shook her head but held her tongue.

Paula marched toward the door, laughing all the way. "You poor girl, nothing but a cook, just like your mama.

~~~ ~~~

Chapter 12

A blast of cold air swept through the kitchen as Paula opened the door and rushed into the night like a witch on a broom.

Pyune stood in the middle of the kitchen, a roaring sound in her ears. She felt the beginning of anger. Of course it was her grandmother's recipe, then her mother's, and now hers. She would not give up that easily, even though the redhead had done her best to spook her.

She closed the back door and walked slowly to her worktable. When she laid her head on the warm wood, she closed her eyes and thought about the many times she had made that cake. Then, a quiet giggle, the kind of sound that softly rumbles around in one's chest and won't go away.

The *recipe. How many eggs are in that cake, Paula?*

You do know how to crack an egg, don't you?

Giggle.

Measuring spoons? You know, those little spoons that read one-half teaspoon, one tablespoon.

Giggle.

Baking powder? You know, that's the thing that makes a cake rise.

Giggle.

You separate those eggs, you know.

How do you do that? Why, Paula, you've never separated an egg?

Giggle.

Girl, you take off that New York coat and I'll show you. It's real easy.

Giggle.

~~~

Pyune's soft breath came in puffs, slight movements that caused her lips to gently putter. Sleep came quickly and unexpectedly, her head resting on the table, her fingertips on the edge of a cake pan.

~~~ ~~~

Chapter 13

Oh, the delights Paula found in the old green shoebox that had been discovered under Pastor Cobb's bed. She read the letters slowly, the words falling from the pages like a Shakespearean sonnet.

The woman, this "O," whoever she was, had obviously been enamored with Aldelpheus Cobb who, most likely, would not appreciate the reading of his private letters were he able to express himself accordingly.

The "O" woman, judging from her warmly expressed adorations of Pastor Cobb, appeared to be a sensual woman who had no inhibitions about expressing her feelings for the pious man. By her intimations, it seems he wrote letters to her — to which these were her responses in kind.

Hallelujah for both of them. It was becoming more and more evident to Paula that the two had known each other all their lives, and without a doubt they had rekindled a long-held affection for one another. It was apparent that right under the noses of his parishioners, the pastor had preached his sermon while the "O" woman had sat primly in the pew in front of him.

Paula tucked away letter #38, written right after Valentine's Day and filled with loving words; but, of greater interest, a hint of an upcoming "union."

Paul's thoughts swirled. A union? Who was this "O" woman? She jumped up and opened the drawer that held the church directory. There were 213 names listed in alphabetical order, and this included past board members. Paula had been on the church board for the last 24 years and knew every member of The Church of Ivy Log. There was no way a woman with the initial "O" could get past her. Maybe the "O" was a pet name, a secret code.

But the woman lived in Blairsville. Could she be a church member who lived in Blairsville? No, there was no one in the directory who lived outside of Ivy Log.

Frustrated and even more curious, Paula returned to her reading chair. She picked up letter #39. It contained a brief message, only one paragraph. But, it was the most revealing thus far — since it mentioned Paula.

~~~ ~~~

Chapter 14

W hen the soft gray of daylight eased over the tops of the Georgia mountains, Pyune poured her third cup of coffee and nibbled on a cold biscuit. Iron skillets sat, warming on the gas burners, waiting for sausage fresh from the Keeling farm. From the ovens, the smell of baking biscuits wafted into the dining room, with apple butter on the tables right next to butter mixed with a dollop of honey and cinnamon.

She heard Wiley stacking logs on the woodpile outside and poured his coffee. When she looked out the window, he waved to her with a gloved hand. She watched white puffs of breath around his face and knew the temperatures had not risen above freezing. When the door opened, Wiley huffed and puffed himself into the warm kitchen.

"You better stomp off that snow 'fore you come into my kitchen."

"Ain't never seen anything like it. Believe it snowed all night." He shuddered and took off his gloves. "Where's that hot coffee you always got made?"

Pyune stepped to the side of the cup she was blocking from his sight and pointed to it. "You gonna build me a fire out front? That fireplace is stone cold."

"Give me a minute, woman. I been up since 5 a.m. gettin' your wood so this place would be warm." He sat on the stool beside her and pulled off his scruffy wool hat. He blew into his coffee and noticed Pyune had used Roy and Trigger's cup. *Hello, Roy.*

"Today's the day the new preacher comes, ain't it?" Wiley asked.

"Noon, from what I understand. Paula is meeting him here, then taking him over to the parsonage." She paused and sighed. "Poor fellow. He doesn't know what he's in for."

"Why do you say that?"

Pyune shook her head and raised an eyebrow, surprised Wiley could even ask such a question. "Are you kidding? Paula, for one thing. She'll toss him all over the place like a sack a flour. Man won't know what hit him."

Wiley's horselaugh filled the room. "You got that right. Maybe he's the type a feller who's his own man. Know what I mean?"

"Perhaps. But, I doubt there's any man who can survive her." Pyune stared into her coffee cup a moment, a grittiness coming to her voice. "She came by here last night."

It was Wiley's turn to raise an eyebrow. "What for?"

Pyune held her tongue. "Says I stole the lemon pudding cake recipe, and that she's gonna sue me."

"That woman. Now, why would she do that?" Wiley hung his head.

Pyune fiddled with her apron ties, her fingers nervous and searching for something to do. "Says it was her mama's recipe." She looked at Wiley. "That woman thinks she owns this town and everything in it, including my recipe."

Wiley placed his hand on Pyune's shoulder. "Don't you worry. I'll talk to her about it. She gets hot about something without even thinkin' and then won't turn loose."

"Won't do any good. She's got her mind made up that it's her family's recipe." She glanced around the kitchen, her face pained, her throat now trembling. "You reckon maybe that recipe isn't mine?"

"Course that's your recipe." Wiley rubbed his chin. "Didn't you tell me you had a copy of it in your grandma's handwritin'?"

Pyune frowned as she inspected her hands, flour and chocolate stuck beneath her nails. "My grandmother couldn't read or write."

~~~ ~~~

Chapter 15

Turquoise eyeshadow, black eyeliner, and face powder lay in a neat row across the top of Paula's dressing table. She applied her makeup just like the magazine article instructed, black mascara curling up her lashes. Her lips pouted red, coated shiny with clear gloss. Massive round hair rollers lined the top of her head, each one held by a metal clip. She picked up a perfume bottle, Shalimar by Guerlain, and sprayed it heavily across her bosom.

She leaned back and studied herself in her wide mirror, Hollywood lights rimming the top and sides. "You gorgeous thing, you," she said playfully — but seriously.

She decided her green Chanel suit, the one with the faux fur cuffs and collar, was the perfect outfit to impress the new preacher. She loved the tiny gold buttons that ran across the front, meeting the elegant V-shaped cut of the lapel. Her only indecision was what blouse to wear. A hot pink under the green might be too flamboyant; but, why not?

Her appointment with the new preacher, the esteemed William H. Johnson, graduate of the Harvard Divinity School, was only two hours away. Most everyone from town would squeeze into The Boardinghouse just to get a peek at the man who would stand next to the pulpit on Christmas morning and preach his first sermon at The Church of Ivy Log.

Paula shivered. His arrival promised to be a grand moment for Ivy log. And, she, Paula Jennings, would be the hand that reached out first to welcome him. She could see it now — the people holding their breath, their mouths open in awe, eyes bright with anticipation. Oh, how she deserved the limelight.

She looked into the mirror once more. She needed more blush. Then, what jewelry should she wear? Her mother's pearls? Yes, the perfect touch.

Quickly, she removed the rollers and brushed her hair. She chose a classic French twist for a chic look befitting the position of importance she wanted to project. After all, how often did she meet someone with a Harvard doctorate who possessed such a renowned reputation as a man of God?

She slipped on her Italian leather pumps and looked at herself in the wall mirror. *Perfection.*

Her position on The Church of Ivy Log's Board of Directors would be up for reelection at the end of the year. It was her 12th two-year reign on the board, a distinction she relished. And hiring the Harvard Ph.D. sealed her designation as president of the new Board.

~~~ ~~~

Chapter 16

Every table at The Boardinghouse, excluding Paula's, was filled. Lawrence Jacinto, the church pianist, sat with Karen Perkins, the choir director, as they discussed the music for the Christmas services. The church was thrilled to have such a talented pianist perform for them, not only on Sundays, but also at every special event held at the church. His piano, a majestic Steinway grand, the prized B model, had been bought with special funds raised by the church ladies through bazaars and cake sales, Pyune's lemon pudding cakes bringing more dollars than anyone else's efforts.

Conversations at each table hummed with excitement as forks clattered on plates, chairs scraped across the floor, logs popped in the fireplace, and the smell of pumpkin pie filled the air. Hot biscuits hid in baskets beneath red and green linen cloths — alongside a small dish of butter sweetened with confectioner's sugar and grated orange peel.

The front doors flew open with a flourish as Paula made her grand entrance. She glanced around the room and pulled at the fingers of her gloves. She saw heads turning and heard conversations drop as she walked slowly to her table by the bay window. She made eye contact with no one, removing her coat and lingering long enough to assure that everyone got a good look at her Chanel suit before she sat down. Her heart skipped a beat when she glanced at her watch and saw it was 11:59, only moments away from William Johnson's arrival.

At precisely 12 noon, the doors swung open, the chimes on

the wreath unusually loud, as if God's angels had announced the arrival of one of its own. There, in a cashmere overcoat with a plaid wool scarf, stood a tall man whose hair was the color of newly poured asphalt. His smile was wide, revealing teeth that were as white as the snow that stuck to his boots – a smile framed on one of the blackest faces Paula Jennings had ever seen.

Holding a glass, Paula's hand froze in midair. Her jaws clenched, her lips quivered, each an involuntary action. As for the rest of her, she could not move. Could not stand and greet the man who paused and nodded to Pyune Murphy, who, observing him, leaned on the doorway to the kitchen.

Paula commanded herself to stand, to walk gracefully across the restaurant and extend her hand in greeting, but found herself unable to obey. Perspiration formed on her forehead and dampened the hair at the back of her neck as she willed herself not to faint. The man was black, a Negro, a colored man, an African American, a man who had sounded white in their telephone interview; whose resume lauded him a renowned deliverer of God's word — but said nothing about his color.

Pyune nodded at William Johnson and pointed to Paula's table, pointed to the woman in the Chanel suit with the pearls at her neck.

Paula steeled herself as she waited for The Church of Ivy Log's new pastor to reach her table. Her heart thudded in her chest as she slowly pulled herself up from the table.

In the 145-year history of The Church of Ivy Log, there was no record of a pastor whose skin was any darker than Linda Richardson's climbing cream roses. The church's pastors had come from Ireland and Scotland, had declared the ground holy, had sung praises and baptized parishioners' children in the name of the Father, the Son and the Holy Ghost. And, as the angels trumpeted above them, they surely had not said anything about a black man preaching the gospel in Ivy Log's most-blessed church.

Paula stood erect, her eyes hard. Her freckled skin had paled, the bright red lipstick she had meticulously applied had dulled into a muddy smear. Her winter-cold stance matched the coldness of the snow that fell softly outside the bay window. Her voice cracked as she forced out, "How do you do? I'm Paula Jennings."

William Johnson, a warm energy in his voice, extended his hand. "How wonderful to meet you at last, Ms. Jennings."

Ignoring his hand, Paula sat down, adjusted her pearls and looked across the room to the faces that were all turned toward her table. She cleared her throat, sipped her water and placed her hands in her lap, looking down at her plate. She said nothing.

William removed his coat and scarf and pulled out a chair. "Ms. Jennings, how kind of you to meet me in such awful weather." He indeed possessed a preacher's voice, a bass that emitted wisdom and depth. There was also a slight air of formality; after all, he was a Harvard Ph.D. His fingers found the edge of his napkin, and he placed it carefully on his lap. Behind him, every eye was on him, studying his cashmere coat, his bright scarf — his black skin.

With her gaze traveling from the top of her table to the tall man who sat across from her, in a barely audible voice, Paula spoke. But her lips were stuck, as the words seemingly came from somewhere else. "Your . . . your appearance is . . . surprising, Mr. Johnson."

William raised his eyebrows, which matched his skin. "Oh? In what way, Ms. Jennings?"

Paula eyes held his for a long, vacant moment. "There was no mention of . . . of your . . . color."

William's smile widened. "Ah. My color. And should that have been mentioned?" His expression was quizzical, a touch of a frown forming between his eyebrows as he waited for her answer.

Paula stuttered, her words jumbled. "Well . . . I . . . it's just that — "

He interrupted her, his voice quiet and soothing. "Ms. Jennings, sometimes small towns and the churches in these communities do not like change. I understand that." He leaned forward and placed his elbows on the table. "I will assume you were not expecting a black pastor to lead your church."

"That is correct, Mr. Johnson," she crisply replied.

"Tell me, Ms. Jennings, were you expecting a man of God, a pastor who preached about Christ and everlasting life?"

His question flustered Paula. She raised her hand in a "stop" motion. "Please, Mr. Johnson. There is no need to discuss the matter. There has been some mistake. I'll contact the Church Board and we'll resolve the issue in the best way possible. I'm so sorry you've been inconvenienced." She began to rise from the table when Pyune stepped over and refilled her glass.

"Hello," said Pyune brightly. "You must be the new pastor. Welcome, and how about some good hot food?"

William grinned. "I'm always ready for some good hot food, especially on a day like this one."

Pyune set a carafe of coffee on the table and reached out her hand. "I'm Pyune Murphy, and I do all the cooking around here. I've got hot cornbread, pork chops, collards with ham hocks, and any pie you want for dessert." She paused. "And if you don't like any of that, I can whip you up some grits and eggs."

William leaned his head back and laughed, the sound rolling through the air and bouncing off the bay window in front of him. "Why, Miss Pyune, I'll do just fine with pork chops, thank you. Got mashed potatoes?"

Pyune nodded and turned to Paula. "By the way, I've got two cakes and three pies for the reception tomorrow night. That plenty?"

Paula cringed, her hands crushing the napkin in her lap. When she looked at Pyune, darkness had spread over her face, a picture of malevolence that decried her presence in the company of William Johnson. "It's possible . . . the festivities will be . . . postponed."

Paula rose. "Excuse me. I believe there are a few things that need my attention." She grabbed her coat, almost fell over herself, and made a beeline for the door.

~~~ ~~~

Chapter 17

The loving and generous spirit of the holiday season was nowhere to be found in Paula as she marched the two blocks from The Boardinghouse to The Church of Ivy Log, the members of the hiring committee waiting for her and the grand introduction of their new pastor. She hunched forward as the snow blew down Main Street, ignoring a greeting from Vallie Thomas, who rang the Salvation Army bell in front of Drake's Hardware as if she were calling the cows home. Paula moved so quickly that she almost tripped over a row of freshly cut Christmas trees that were leaned against the building.

Paula's grand design for The Church of Ivy Log did not include a black pastor. Her vision was for a traditional, almost formal, church — a church held in high esteem by the same God who had made Paula the moving force in the congregation in the first place. It was she and she alone who had guided the church all these years and assured its goals had been nothing short of holy and divine.

She burst through the doors of the church like the devil was chasing her. Her hair, now matted with wet snow, formed a flat wedge across her forehead. The members of the hiring committee gasped at the sight of her, shrinking back as though the very demons they rebuked had somehow found their way into their sacred place, hot on Paula's trail.

"We have been bamboozled," Paula wailed, her voice in the decibel range of a screeching banshee. She threw her handbag on the floor, fell into a pew and began removing her gloves, pulling the fingers as though they were on fire. "Yes, siree! Bamboozled is what I call it!"

"Whatever do you mean, Paula?" Dale Cochrane moved closer. Nearby, the hiring committee stared at the frenzied woman, each person wide-eyed and ashen.

"I'll tell you what I mean. Those Harvard people sent us a black preacher." She caught her breath. "And I mean *black*. We're ruined. I say, *ruined*."

"Now, now," Doyce said. "It cain't be all that bad. If God sent us a black preacher, then we must spread our arms wide and welcome him wi — "

"Shut up, Doyce! There's not going to be any welcome for William H. Johnson. Ph.D. . . . and his *soul train*."

Paula jumped up from the pew and walked around in a blind panic, up the aisle, around the vestibule and on the stairs to the choir section. When she stepped back down, she paused in the pulpit, at the lectern where a spotlight from above framed her head and shoulders. It was as though the shining light was a sign. Yes, it was! It was a sign from God — now as clear as could be as she caught a reflection of herself in the far windows of the church.

Her voice calmed as she raised her hand to the heavens. "Brothers and sisters, I do not believe God wants a black pastor to lead us. Never in the history of The Church of Ivy Log have we been led by anyone other than . . . than . . . well, you know. I, for one, do not intend to listen to soulpreaching, hearty amens yelled by the congregation, and Africa music shaking the rafters of this church." Out of breath, she stepped down, the pearls around her neck bouncing. "I would hope that everyone on this committee agrees with our need for a more . . . more traditional pastor to lead this church."

Harley cleared his throat and shuffled a few steps toward Paula. "We ain't even heard this new pastor preach yet. Let's go ahead and give him an opportunity to prove himself." He paused. "We can't just throw him out."

Paula pounded the lectern with her fist. "Throw him *out*! He's not *in* as far as I'm concerned. He has misrepresented himself, and I say he doesn't deserve our consideration."

The group quieted, their thoughts seemingly circling the room. Calvin, who'd also gotten up, slowly eased his body into a pew. "I think Harley's right. It wouldn't be right to turn him away just because he's black."

Paula threw her hands to her face and spoke through her fingers. Her words shot out like bullets. "Enough! We are dealing with a dishonest man. He should have told us he was black."

Sitting on the first pew, Wanda looked at Calvin, then at Paula. "Why should he have told us he's black?"

Paula's hands uncovered her face as she looked at Wanda. "How many times do I have to tell you people, we did not sign on for a black preacher."

~~~ ~~~

Chapter 18

That evening, the fire in The Boardinghouse popped and sang as Wiley poked the logs and laid a large piece of oak to the back of the grate. The restaurant was empty of patrons except for William Johnson, who had left early in the afternoon and returned just before the restaurant was to close. He sat at the table by the bay window, eating a bowl of apple cobbler. Pyune sat across from him and watched Wiley stoke the fire.

"My, my, Pyune, this is the best apple cobbler I've ever eaten. If my mama and grandma were still living, I'd tell them all about you and your wonderful restaurant."

"What kind words, Pastor Johnson. Thank you." Pyune studied the minister's face, saw evidence of a lack of sleep. In his eyes, she also saw sadness. Perhaps it could also be called rejection. His Harvard degree was not enough to overcome the small minds of those who could not get past color — not enough to combat those like Paula Jennings.

Though her own skin was light, Pyune, too, was the recipient of the prejudices that came with a woman of color. William Johnson did not need to tell her that the head of the hiring committee had rejected him as their new pastor. She could see it as he looked across the almost empty dining room.

The citizens of Ivy Log were cozy in their day-to-day lives, their remote mountain town safe and secure from outside influences for the most part, their intellects shaped by their own narrow perspectives of anything new or of anything possessing the slightest element of change.

Wiley pulled out a chair across from William Johnson and next to Pyune. He began discussing the church when the pastor told him what had occurred. "So, let me get this straight," Wiley said. "You're not gonna stay here in Ivy Log? All because you're black?" He shook his head. "That don't seem right to me."

Pastor Johnson smiled, a smile that implied resignation, perhaps, and which promised no challenge to those who made the rules. "I think it's human nature not to stay where one is not wanted."

"Pastor Johnson, what are you going to do?" asked Pyune.

He pondered her question a moment, clasped his hands together and leaned his forehead on them. "I'm not sure. I'll contact the board at Harvard Divinity School and see what their advice is. Legally, I don't know if there is anything I can do . . . or would even want to."

Pyune said, "I say let's go ahead and have the reception for you at the church as planned. Who knows who all will come, but I can promise you one thing, there are folks who will be delighted to welcome you."

"What about the committee?" William Johnson asked. "And Paula Jennings?"

Wiley laughed, his bald head shaking back and forth. "Unless Paula is standing at the church door holding a 12 gauge, I reckon you can be at the church at 6 p.m., a bible in your hands."

Pastor Johnson rose from the table. "I'll say goodnight. I'll check in with you folks tomorrow. At breakfast?"

After the pastor left, Pyune and Wiley turned out the lights and locked the front door of The Boardinghouse. "Seems like a good guy." Wiley said.

Pyune nodded. "I think so too." She looked out the window and watched William Johnson's car ease down Main Street. "I didn't even ask him where he's staying tonight. Reckon he's gonna drive all the way to Blairsville in this weather?"

~~~ ~~~

Chapter 19

Pyune put the last of the sweet potatoes in a slow oven, turned out the lights in the kitchen, and sat at the bay window in the winter darkness. She gazed at Ivy Log's Christmas tree, dotted with lights and a star on top. Doyce Conley was right — the star was crooked. It lay leaning toward Brasstown Bald as if pointing the way to something holy; a reason for traveling up the frozen rocks to a place where someone could stand high and closer to heaven.

Her eyes traveled down Main Street, the stores closed and quiet, their display windows bright with smiling Santas and Rudolph's red nose. In the town square lay the nativity, a manger, and in it the baby Jesus portrayed by a plastic doll. The steeple on The Church of Ivy Log poked up behind a row of snow-draped liberty oaks that had been planted in 1919 at the end of World War I, each one in the name of a lost but not-forgotten soldier.

She pulled her chair closer to the window and propped her elbows on the edge and observed the soundless snow catch the glass. So every snowflake is different — no two alike. Unique. Just like people — supposedly.

Down the block a ways, William Johnson's car traveled slowly on Main Street, coming in the direction of her restaurant. She jumped up and swung the door open, the cedar wreath flapping wildly. She waved and waited as he pulled the car to the curb and his window came down.

"Where are you going?" she called out, the sudden cold

burning her lungs and taking her breath away.

Through the falling snow, William held his eyes on hers for a long moment. "I don't really know."

Pyune opened the door wider. "Well, I do. Get in here where it's warm."

~~~ ~~~

Chapter 20

High in the mountain sky, the snow clouds spoke to each other, fancied themselves the ruler of the heavens and floated apart, revealing the galaxy that Galileo had named the Milky Way. It lasted only a moment, but that brief moment in time fell on William Johnson as he trotted through the snow and onto the doorsteps of The Boardinghouse. He shuddered with cold while he kicked the snow from his shoes and then stepped inside and breathed the lingering smell of Pyune's coffee and sweet potato soufflé.

"Ah, lady, it's much warmer in here than outside." He pulled the wool scarf from around his neck and hung it on the back of a chair, snowflakes falling to the floor and melting.

"Guess you haven't found the parsonage yet?" A wry smile caught her lips.

He chuckled. "Ms. Jennings and I did not discuss my sleeping arrangements for this evening. She was in too much of a hurry to end our conversation. And, I just assumed I'd be staying in the parsonage — you know, the new pastor . . . I." He paused, sadness in his eyes but perhaps a twinkle too.

They both laughed, falling into a comfortable camaraderie that eased the flagrant dilemma that awaited the eminent pastor, a graduate of Harvard Divinity College, a black man whose credentials meant nothing to the woman who headed The Church of Ivy Log's Hiring Committee as well as controlling the powerful church board.

They sat in the dark at the bay window, drinking coffee, the silence between them full of questions that neither could answer. When William looked at Pyune, he saw someone like himself, an individual who considered the motives of others, questioned neither with hostility nor condemnation but with a yearning for understanding.

William watched snowflakes swirl under the street lamp. They lifted and swirled, fanciful and free. In his mind's eye, he saw a musical note on each one, a song playing in the night air, until the flakes found a place to rest in a snowdrift. He spoke softly, as if talking to himself. "All I wanted was a small church, a small church with folks who wanted to hear the word of God."

Pyune refilled their cups. "Why a small church?"

"Burned out," he said, stirring his coffee. .

"Burned out? I don't understand."

"My prior churches were quite large. Congregations of about three thousand each. It was easy to get lost in all the numbers and names."

Pyune studied William's face. "What exactly are you saying?"

William Johnson's eyes became dreamlike, and he searched the air before they rested on Pyune. "I wanted a small flock. A church family where I know all the names. The birthdays. The anniversaries. What the kids wanted to do with their lives." He sipped his coffee and frowned. "I'm sorry. I'm being unrealistic. Why would The Church of Ivy Log want a pastor who is black? Such a change from what a small town is used to is obviously too much to expect."

Pyune, her fingers playing with her napkin, leaned forward and cleared her throat. "Pastor, did you ever consider that you might be just what this town needs?"

~~~ ~~~

Chapter 21

Around 11 p.m., as folks in Ivy Log lay warm in their beds, Pyune Murphy made a decision. She left the table where she and Pastor Johnson had discussed the woes of the world, as well as his own unpleasant predicament, and pulled on her coat. "Come on, Preacher. We're going to get you settled in the parsonage so you can get some rest."

"Parsonage?"

"That's what I said. It's your home now."

He hesitated, his towering frame a dim shadow in the dining room where the fire had died and the restaurant lay in darkness except for the streetlights from outside.

"Whoa!" he said, holding up his hand. "It was quite clear to me that Ms. Jennings was unreceptive to my being here at all, much less in the pastor's house."

Pyune pulled on her gloves. "Oh, really? I have me a key to the parsonage, it's bitter cold outside, and the last time I checked you were The Church of Ivy Log's new preacher." She clucked her tongue. "Get your coat on and let's go." Without another word, she threw open The Boardinghouse doors, the wreath slapping in the wind, and braced herself for the onslaught of arctic cold.

William pulled on his coat, laughing the entire time. He knew when to obey a woman with purpose. He followed her to his car and opened the door for her. "Where to?"

"Two blocks down Main. Turn left. Church is on the left."

"And the parsonage?"

"Right side of the church."

The tires crunched slowly through the snow, the tracks deep and leading to the grand church whose steeple rose high into the midnight sky. They parked in the driveway of the parsonage, a small cottage-like structure made of neat red brick, its eves painted a soft green. The windows were long and narrow, the mullions providing a warm quaintness. The little house appeared inviting, a place where men of God read their bibles and prepared for encounters with the Holy Spirit.

"There's a light on," said the pastor. "Reckon someone is there?"

"Naw. There's always a light on in the parsonage. Just tradition in case anyone needs to pray with the preacher. That light keeps shining even though Brother Cobb's dead." She looked over at him. "You got to keep your light shining. No matter what."

William Johnson nodded slowly. Her words were wise, full of strength.

They entered the parsonage, a rush of warm air greeting them. Then, the distinct sound of a door slamming from the back of the house made them both hesitate.

Pyune placed her hand on the preacher's arm. "Not sure what that was."

She ran through the house, ending up in the kitchen, where the back door was partially open. Shoe prints in the snow led away from the parsonage and around the corner of the church.

Pyune shrugged her shoulders. "Well, looks like this home was a refuge in the storm for someone else." She closed the back door and they both peered through the window.

"Wonder if the person needs a place to stay, just like me?" Reverend Johnson asked.

"Don't know. If he comes back, you can decide if you want to let him in." They laughed. After a half-minute of nothing happening, she motioned and said. "Let me show you the residence."

They went through the small rooms, ending up in the main bedroom, with a four-poster bed piled high with quilts and pillows. "You'll be comfortable here, preacher. If you need anything, just let me know tomorrow. Come over for breakfast around 8 o'clock. Special is sausage and cheese grits.

"Please call me William, Ms. Murphy." He looked around the small room and suddenly found himself weary, a weariness that was more than his body. "Thank you for giving a stranger a warm place to sleep."

"Stranger?" Pyune laughed. "You're our new preacher."

~~~

William dropped Pyune at The Boardinghouse, watched her replace the wreath the wind had blown down and then enter the dark restaurant. He turned the car around and eased back into the same ruts that led him to the parsonage earlier. He looked toward the town square and saw the giant blue spruce, its branches swaying. He noticed the crooked star. At an angle or not, the star seemed to be watching over the manger and the baby Jesus and the Three Wise Men. He slowed his car before he turned toward the parsonage, where he would sleep in the four-poster bed, get up before daylight, and leave the little town of Ivy Log before Pyune had finished frying her first batch of sausage.

~~~ ~~~

Chapter 22

Paula Jennings pulled free of her outercoat, muttering to herself all the while as she then kicked off her shoes. Then she removed the jacket of her Chanel suit, as well as her mother's pearls, tossing the matching earrings on a nearby table. She took a seat in her living room, all the lamps out, the only illumination coming from a nightlight near the stairs.

She had left a message for the Harvard Divinity program director to call her. It was 10:20 p.m. and the telephone sat silent. Her message had been on point: The Church of Ivy Log was not interested in the pastor they had sent. If she had not heard from them by 9 a.m. the following morning, she would drive to Atlanta and take care of the matter without so much as a howdy-do. How could they recommend an African American, a Negro for their church? It was not what the church fathers had intended when they began the church almost a century and a half ago. She was not saying God had messed up in His sending the man. Oh, no. It was Harvard Divinity's fault, their oversight, their negligence that had caused the dilemma in which they found themselves. And it was she, Paula Jennings, who intended to straighten out the matter.

The hiring committee had huddled for an hour in the church office and discussed William Johnson. Dale Cochrane felt the new pastor should be given an opportunity to preach and then they could make a decision on whether he should stay or go. Wanda Osborne stated they were acting too hastily in their rejection of the Harvard graduate. Of course, their opinions were overruled by Paula, who declared there was a grand conspiracy to infiltrate the church with a black pastor, who would then undermine the traditions of the church with his own style of . . . of religion. Yes, that was it. His own religion. Nobody wanted that. No, not one person in the church would want 145 years of tradition uprooted and scattered to God knows where.

The ringing telephone jarred Paula from her chair. She switched on the lamp and grabbed the phone.

"Hello." she said.

"Ms. Jennings?" A smooth, soft voice asked.

"Yes. This is Paula Jennings. Is this Mr. Mager?"

"Why, yes. I'm returning your call." Raymond Mager paused. "I know it's late, but your call sounded urgent. What can I do for you?"

Paula took a quick breath. In an almost bellowing voice, she spoke. "Mr. Mager, the pastor recommended by your facility has arrived and I'm afraid he won't do. The Church of Ivy Log is not interested in . . . in a . . . in hiring him." She paused. "I . . . we think there has been a terrible mistake."

A few seconds of silence. "What kind of mistake, Ms. Jennings?"

Paula didn't hesitate. "What kind of mistake? You know very well what kind of mistake. William Johnson is black. You sent us a black pastor. You never said one word about him being black, and neither did he say anything in his telephone interview with the hiring committee." Paula felt her voice rising. "Not one word."

Raymond Mager was a good man, a man renowned in religious circles for his unending work on behalf of poor and neglected children in the West Virginia mountains.

"My goodness, Ms. Jennings, I've known William Johnson for years. Why, I've listened to him preach, prayed with him, heard him sing "Sweet Hour of Prayer" a cappella in front of thousands of people, and not once noticed he was black."

A slow flush crept up her face, and she felt every quarter-inch of its movement. Her fingers squeezed tightly around the telephone. "How convenient of you not to notice, Mr. Mager. I, however, did notice Mr. Johnson was black. And, I will be unable to use his services at the Church of Ivy Log." Her words were steel-hard, bitten off at each syllable like a dog chewing a bone.

Raymond Mager was not affected in the least. "I understand, Ms. Jennings. But may I remind you that this is the twenty-first century. And, as such, you are obviously unaware of exactly what your decision might mean for your church and to your town of Ivy Log. May I also remind you that God sent William Johnson to Ivy Log, and it is His decision and not yours as to whether or not he stays."

Paula rose from her chair, her jaw tightened while hardness formed around her lips. "Mr. Mager, perhaps we should let Mr. Johnson make the decision on whether or not he wants to stay in Ivy Log."

She hung up the telephone, turned out the lamp and walked upstairs, every step deliberate and forceful. Paula Jennings was tougher than week-old biscuits, stronger than Granny's moonshine — and one of the most ruthless women on the face of the earth.

~~~ ~~~

Chapter 23

The stairs were hidden in the back of the kitchen, behind a large wooden pantry that housed heavy bags of flour, sugar, and hundreds of the items needed for the running of a restaurant. In the dark, Pyune climbed each step slowly, her thoughts in many places, all jumbled up. Fatigue had settled in her mind as well as her body, and everything about her was demanding rest.

Her little rooms were cozy and warm from the heat of the kitchen below. The fragrance of yeast and cinnamon rose upward and found places to hide among the many crooks and crannies that made up the ancient two-story frame house.

At the high window, she looked out into the snowy night and saw the lights of the town Christmas tree. Across the way, the towering steeple of the church nudged the sky, and down below was the parsonage, dark except for a small light in the window in the sitting room. She'd told the pastor that the light was a tradition, a beacon for the lost who perhaps wanted to pray with the resident pastor. His car sat in the driveway, gathering snow on its top, the tire tracks already covered by heavy flurries that seemed unending.

Pyune turned from the window and pulled out a dresser drawer and removed a small book, its cover worn, the pages thin and crisp with age. Between pages 73 and 74, a yellowed piece of paper lay folded, its edges stained like her kitchen's cookbook. It was a letter from her grandmother. She studied the handwriting. If her mother and grandmother couldn't read or write, whose handwriting was it? She rubbed the paper with her thumb. Was she eight or ten when she'd received it? She closed her eyes and saw her grandmother's ramshackle little house in a holler near Brasstown Bald. She saw her hovering over her wood stove, humming "Little Brown Church in the Wildwood" as she stirred a pot of chicken soup. *Who wrote this letter for you, granny?*

Pyune folded the letter carefully and returned it to the book, again between the special pages. She wondered what it would be like to win $25,000 for her grandmother's recipe. Were she alive, her grandmother would dance on her front porch until dawn and tell Pyune to spend the $25,000 on worthy things. She was a poor but practical woman, used to simple things — simple things like lemon pudding cake on Sundays after church.

Pyune's chance of winning the grand prize was a remote possibility as far as she was concerned. Yes, she was one of five finalists, but the likelihood of first place was, in her mind, something black women were not privy to. For an instant, she saw the long fingers of Paula grasping the money out of her hand and shrieking, "Mine!"

She shuddered at the thought.

Pyune pulled back a quilt her mother had made — a Dresden Plate pattern with lovely corals, greens and yellows — and eased her tired body into bed. In just a few hours her kitchen help would arrive to assist her in preparing for a hungry Friday crowd. Despite the weather, folks came for her hot sausage and grits with buttermilk biscuits and apple butter. They filled their plates like truck drivers and drank gallons of hot coffee. What else could they do during a mountain winter other than eat and talk about the local news of the day. Especially with the arrival of Christmas — and of course the new preacher.

She yawned. Her last thought before falling asleep was of Pastor Johnson. She liked his calmness, his thoughtful way of speaking. But could he possibly be wise enough to change a person like Paula Jennings?

~~~ ~~~

Chapter 24

Well before daylight, Wiley drove down a deserted and silent Main Street. The lamppost lights stood like sentries in the night, their warm light welcoming. The red and green of Christmas filled the storefronts across from the town square. No doubt shoppers would keep the sidewalks busy despite the weather. After all, Christmas was just a little over a week away.

When daylight eased into the eastern sky, it was no surprise to anyone that this day was no warmer than the day before. It seemed the mountains lured the northerly winds with malice, their rugged crags like icy fingers that wrapped around the little town and kept its inhabitants winter prisoners.

Behind The Boardinghouse, the woodpile cats puffed up their fur, squinted their eyes and waited for the kitchen door to open. Their gazes never left the door, as any moment Pyune would provide them with breakfast.

The smoke from the chimney billowed gray like the clouds that raced overhead. Wiley's movements were stiff as he stacked firewood, occasionally disturbing the cats. His bright-red stocking hat was snow topped; the ends of his scarf wrapped around his neck and flapping in the wind. He believed he'd never be warm again.

From the restaurant woodpile, he drove his truck to the parsonage, carefully navigating the snowdrifts. He had seen the preacher's car parked in the driveway when he drove through town earlier and wanted to unload some dried oak for him as soon as he finished at The Boardinghouse. A nice fire would feel good in the little residence on a day that would have temperatures plunging into the low teens if not the single digits.

On Church Street, he pulled his truck behind the pastor's car just as William was coming down the steps of the parsonage.

"My goodness, Pastor Johnson, you're up mighty early." He noticed the luggage in William's hands. "Breakfast ain't even ready at the restaurant." Wiley paused and found himself more than curious. It was only 7 a.m. What fool would be out this early unless he was delivering firewood? He stepped closer. "Can I help you with anything?"

The preacher hesitated a moment before stepping into the snow-covered driveway. He seemed bewildered, a frown across his brow, his eyes downcast.

Figuring it out, Wiley asked the tall man with the long coat and red and green scarf, "Leaving us?"

"Don't see that it would do anybody any good to stick around. A little town like this should be united; its church even more so." Warmth emanating from his kind face, he shrugged. "It's not all about me."

"I understand that." Wiley cleared his throat and pulled his hat lower on his forehead and over his ears. "Can't believe you'd run out on Pyune's sausage and buttermilk biscuits, though." He grinned. "She'll have her feelings hurt."

The reverend turned his face to the dark charcoal skies and watched the swirling flurries and the heavy clouds. He looked up and studied the lofty steeple of the church, its white cross and the soft green of the copper trim. From there, his gaze found the stained-glass windows. St. Mary, Star of the Sea, depicted water churning around Mary, who sat on a rock holding the baby Jesus while cherubs hovered above. The artist had captured perfectly the warmth and sublime grace in the youthful mother of the Christ Child.

He pulled his gaze away and looked at Wiley, his eyes glistening. He blinked several times. "That's the last thing I'd want to do. What time you say is breakfast?"

~~~ ~~~

Chapter 25

Paula went downstairs, poured herself a cup of coffee, sat in her Queen Anne reading chair. When asked, she would reply that she'd inherited the antique chair from a wealthy relative who was a distant cousin to the King George II. The truth was not quite so fascinating or alluring. The chair, while indeed a quality reproduction, had been purchased at a second-hand store and re-covered with fabric she'd found at an estate sale in Atlanta.

She had managed to fall asleep — albeit fitfully — tossing and turning and cussing and muttering, all because of the Harvard Divinity School graduate who had slipped into Ivy Log as if God and all his angels had called him. Well, she knew better.

The conspiracy was blatant as far as she was concerned. The new pastor was destined to spread the gospel by bible-thumping, rip-roaring "amens" and "praise the Lords," along with stomping, whooping, and hollering and a calling of the devil to show himself so he could be kicked back down the road to hell.

Not a chance. Not a chance as long as she had anything to do with it.

She had phoned all the members of the hiring committee at 7 a.m. and scheduled a meeting at 10 a.m. that morning at the church office so the unpleasant issue could be settled once and for all. And, settled to her liking.

She'd also made a mental note to call her attorney just in case Pyune won the recipe contest. Fraud? Was that what you called it when someone stole someone else's private information? She was certain Pyune would never touch a dime of the money, should she be lucky enough to win it.

Paula sipped her coffee and reached down beside her chair and placed the green box of letters that were written to Aldelpheus Cobb on her lap. Love letters? It was beginning to look that way. The words were certainly loving, if even somewhat passionate, definitely composed with the intent of beguiling their recipient.

Whomever "O" was, she had known Pastor Cobb for a number of years, had recalled previous rendezvous, had most certainly planned future trysts.

Paula had read over half of the letters, beginning with the first one. It was clear Pastor Cobb and "O" had been a couple. They had met in some city where they spent the weekend sightseeing. Paula tried to remember a weekend when Pastor Cobb had missed his Sunday sermon. Yes, yes, there was a four-day period back in the summer; a church conference hosted in Atlanta.

She picked up the next letter and began reading. She was positive she would discover "O's" identity. There would be some clue; a tidbit of information she could connect with someone she knew in the community - and then she'd have it. She'd be onto what Aldelpheus Cobb had been up to, but better than that, she'd know with whom.

It was 9 a.m. when she read the last letter, taking in the fancy design along the borders and the scent of the perfume on the paper one more time, as well as the flowing script of Pastor Cobb's lover's handwriting. *Yes, Pastor Cobb's lover.* Paula was elated. Numerous clues had come to the surface that, at long last, would solve the mysteries held within the green box.

She tucked everything away and walked upstairs to her dressing table. She sat in front of the mirror, admiring how very pretty she looked, primping herself for breakfast at The Boardinghouse before her 10 a.m. meeting with the hiring committee. It was going to be a good day. After all, she was in charge. And with God's blessings, of course.

~~~ ~~~

Chapter 26

The bells rang with a fury as Paula opened the doors to The Boardinghouse, and with orchestrated fanfare twirled the green scarf from her neck and stepped toward her table. In an instant, a gasp left her lips and her smile vanished. Heard as far away as the dessert table, her intake of breath seemed to suck all the air from the room and hold it as though the earth had stopped spinning.

"How dare they," she whispered in a hiss. She narrowed her eyes, raised her chin and rushed to *her* table, which had been hers alone for 30 years, where William Johnson and Wiley Hanson now sat eating Pyune's renowned sausage and grits, each man holding a buttermilk biscuit in his hand and talking about the desired qualities of a good coonhound.

"Outrageous," Paula muttered as she pushed aside Leroy Varner, spilling his coffee on Penny Capps and her new winter coat. She bumped into Pyune, who was carrying a tray of fried eggs, and stepped on the toes of Dr. Casteel, whose long legs stretched out from under his table.

When Paula reached her table, she was panting, her eyes feverish. She leaned over the table and into the faces of the two men, her breath hot.

She looked directly at William Johnson, her words spewing from her mouth like venom. "I do believe you're sitting at my table." Her head whipped around to Wiley. "Just who do you think you are, sitting at *my* table, Wiley Hanson? You've got a lot of nerve."

Wiley, the mountain man, the man who feared no one, leveled his eyes at Paula. There were biscuit crumbs in his beard. His blue eyes were clear and thoughtful as his gaze swept Paula's red hair, her powdered freckles and the fake beauty mark by her left eyebrow.

His voice, somewhat raspier than normal, eased into the words. "Listen here, you gorgeous redhead, settle yourself down with us and have some of Pyune's biscuits and apple butter. I can't think of a better way to start the morning on a cold day like today."

Paula raised her eyebrows, the beauty mark distorted by a deep crease in her forehead. "Evidently, you have gone deaf. You're at *my* table, and I don't particularly like it since you're sitting with a . . . bla . . .stranger." Her head jerked in William's direction. "I don't like . . . strangers sitting here."

Wiley pulled a biscuit from under the cloth napkin and slowly began spreading apple butter across the top. "Well, here's what I'm thinkin', Paula. You can either sit here and be nice." He licked his finger. "Or you can go over yonder and sit with Frank and Adela, since all the other tables are taken." He bit into his biscuit and chewed mightily, his voice dropping into a semi-whisper. "I hope you join us for breakfast, 'cause we ain't moving from this here table."

The look Paula gave Wiley would have stopped the devil in his tracks. Her chest heaved inward, a swallow of breath held there, unmoving, like the frozen frame from a broken strip of film. Across the restaurant, every eye was turned toward the table; *the* table that had been the titular property of Paula Jennings, a claim she'd staked when she was 18, thirty years ago.

However, on this day, a mountain man, who spoke no differently than his hillbilly ancestors, challenged that claim.

Paula blinked several times, her lashes fluttering like butterfly wings as she recovered from her frozen state. The long moment got longer. Then, as if an angel had thumped her head and said, "Be nice," she smiled sweetly at Wiley; smiled sweeter than the apple butter on Wiley's biscuit and wider than the rim of his coffee cup. She threw her head back and laughed out loud, a throaty laugh as though she had heard a bawdy tavern joke. The sound rumbled up her neck and spilled out into the watching restaurant.

Paula Jennings was not about to lose face.

She said, "Why, of course, I'd be delighted to have some of Pyune's sausage and grits." She waved toward the kitchen. "Pyune, darlin'. Can you bring me some coffee?"

She removed her coat while Wiley pulled out a chair.

Wiley watched Paula spread her napkin on her lap. He had known the woman since grade school, had made love to her in her upstairs guest room, had talked about marriage, had said the word "love" on several nights as they lay naked on a feather mattress. Even so, he felt far removed from her, as though something would always be missing.

Her smile lingered, but her eyes betrayed her. They burned as they moved from Wiley to Reverend Johnson and back again. It was clear that neither man knew the line they had crossed: *The table.* It was all about *the table.*

~~~

Pyune served Paula's coffee from the right, just like her mama had taught her so many years before. She smelled Paula's perfume, noticed her long red fingernails and the purple earrings that were so heavy they pulled her earlobes into the shape of oblong pancakes.

"Want the special?" she asked Paula.

"That I do." Paula looked up and squinted her eyes. "Pyune, how's that recipe contest coming along? Heard anything?"

Pyune looked at Wiley when she answered, "No."

Paula sipped her coffee daintily. "Well, please let us know the outcome. We're dying to find out if you win."

Wiley watched Pyune leave the table and return to the kitchen. He stirred sugar into his coffee, the spoon making deep ripples. He leaned back in his chair. "Your interest in Pyune's recipe is misplaced," he said to Paula. "Please do not deny her this bit of happiness." His words were as soft as teacakes, but whatever Wiley Hanson said was never frivolous.

"Oh, my gracious, Wiley," Paula dragged out Scarlett O'Haralike. "I didn't know you were so involved . . . so interested in . . . recipes."

Wiley eyed Paula evenly. "You know exactly what I mean."

The little bit of light in Paula's eyes dimmed, anger gathering in her face. "Yes, I believe I do." She left her gaze on his for a long moment. She would handle him later — when she knew he'd be at her door. She well understood his desire for her, a city girl whose lust for a mountain man was just as strong. In public, they tolerated each other, a relationship much like moonshine to a bible-thumping populace; not discussed with ardor in general conversation but relished in private.

"Well, now, Mr. Johnson, where are you off to?" she asked, Wiley ignored and left to eating his biscuits.

~~~

William Johnson studied Paula's face. A chameleon. An actress. She was a woman whose sole purpose was to control, to manipulate anyone and anything to her liking; someone whose identity was forged by her power over others. She was manipulating him right now. *Where was he off to?* The message was clear.

The pastor said, "At the moment, I'm going to have another cup of Pyune's delectable coffee. Afterwards, I believe I'll get unpacked and settled in. Got to prepare for the Christmas morning sermon."

Paula looked at him wide-eyed. "Settled in? Where?"

"Why, the parsonage, of course. Slept cozy and warm last night. Felt good after that drive from Atlanta."

"You . . . you . . . you slept in the parsonage?" she croaked, her words sounding like an engine needing oil.

"Absolutely. Felt quite at home too." The preacher's voice had boomed, every ear in the restaurant now tuned in to the conversation at *the* table. Reverend Johnson grinned sheepishly, appearing embarrassed. "Never slept in a four-poster bed before."

Paula said nothing, but her mind traveled at warp speed. *A squatter. That's what the new preacher was. A squatter. He was in the parsonage, and neither hell nor high water will get him out.*

Pyune returned and served Paula grits and sausage, once again from the right side. She placed a basket of fresh biscuits in the center of the table, within reach of Wiley, who promptly peeked under the red napkin and picked up two with one hand, the apple butter with the other. "Get you a hot biscuit,

William – 'fore somebody else comes along and gits it."

The pastor didn't hesitate. "Pyune, I don't know how you do it. Everything you cook is wonderful."

"Thank you, William," said Pyune over her shoulder as she returned to the kitchen.

William? Pyune's calling the Harvard seminary graduate William. How lovely. Paula's smirk set firm on her red lips.

"I'm surprised you were able to find the parsonage . . . and get inside," said Paula, cutting her eyes sideways at her nemesis as she began eating her grits.

William split his biscuit. "Well, it's like this. In the midst of that awful snowstorm out there, an angel appeared." He grinned around the table. "Her name was Pyune."

"Pyune?" Paula wrenched her head toward the kitchen, then back to William.

"That's right. We rode over to the parsonage together. Barely got through the drifts. Then, I saw this soft glow in the front window of the house and I knew I'd find warmth and comfort inside." He bit into his biscuit. "And I sure enough did."

Paula listened attentively. "I'm wondering . . . I believe the parsonage was locked, wasn't it?"

"Sure was. But Pyune had a key."

"A key?" Paula looked dumbfounded.

"Thank goodness she did or I don't know where I would have slept. No motels around here. Couldn't have gotten very far in that weather." Another dollop of apple butter.

Paula ate quietly for a moment. *The squatter has settled inside the parsonage and even has a key. A key Pyune had given him. How convenient.*

"Mr. Johnson, I wouldn't get too cozy in the parsonage. As head of the hiring committee, I've called a meeting for 10 o'clock this morning to discuss . . . the issue."

Without missing a bite of his biscuit, William looked up. "And what issue would that be, Ms. Jennings?"

Wiley placed his hands across his stomach, his eyes alert. "I'd kinda like to know that myself."

Paula swiped her mouth with a napkin, lipstick smearing on her chin. She took a deep, agitated breath and looked across the table at the two men. "Please! This is a church matter, and as president of the church's board of directors, I am sworn to uphold the church bylaws. Mr. Johnson, your tenure as The Church of Ivy Log's pastor has to be ratified. And, until that happens, you are not the pastor of the Church of Ivy Log."

So there. Said and done. Paula's forced a smile so obvious it strained her face. She straightened her back and looked across the room.

Wiley's eyes were wide, a frown on his forehead. He leaned forward, pushing the basket of biscuits out of the way. "Gosh, why wouldn't you ratify this fine man — a doctor of philosophy in theology?"

Paula stared at Wiley. His flannel shirt was missing a button, he'd gotten apple butter on his knuckles, and a wisp of hair lay at the end of his cuff. This reminded her of where he came from - his life in the mountains and his simple ways. *How dare you question the authority of the Board? Of me?*

She ignored his question and turned to the pastor. "I think I'd like to have the key, Mr. Johnson."

The parsonage. A haven to most pastors. A place to pray in the quiet of early mornings when God seemed to be less busy, not as occupied with the woes of the world and better able to hear prayers. Perhaps a place to converse with angels as they sat atop a bookcase nearby and hummed sweetly, while the pages of the bible seemed to turn on their own and verses were read with lips moving but in silence.

Paula repeated. "The key, Mr. Johnson?"

William's handsome face seemed to take on an angelic mien, the minister now preparing to do what he excelled at, in the most gentle of ways cajoling others into revelations about themselves by massaging the heart from the outside with words alone. He said, "Now, Miss Paula. The key? What key are you talking about? The key to knowledge? The key to the city? The key to my heart?" He grinned, his eyes shining, an infectious laugh lingering, waiting to be expelled. He tilted his head and looked expectantly at her, his eyes searching her face.

"Nonsense, Mr. Johnson. You know very well what key I'm talking about. The parsonage key." Her freckles had darkened — a sure sign of her anger. *"Never make a redhead angry,"* the song said.

"Wish I could oblige, but Pyune never gave me the key."

Paula glanced toward the kitchen. "Pyune!"

Wiley reached over and touched Paula on her arm. "The key stays with Pyune. Pastor Cobb gave it to her years ago." His eyes softened. "A key has always been kept at The Boardinghouse. It's tradition."

"Heck if that's so," Paula shrieked. "Pastor Cobb is dead, and there's no need for Pyune to have the key."

Wiley placed a silent fist on the table. "You know very well that The Boardinghouse has had a key to the parsonage. Had it for years. Pyune fed Pastor Cobb just about every day, and when he was out ministering, she walked a plate down and left it in his refrigerator."

"We'll see about this." Paula jumped up and yanked her coat from the back of the chair.

Without another word, she slammed a $5 bill on the table, left her grits and sausage and flew out The Boardinghouse door. She streaked past the bay window and *the* table where Wiley and William sat. They watched the wind catch her hair and the snow attack her scarf; the hot wrath of the redhead sizzling in the cold air.

~~~ ~~~

Chapter 27

The steeple pierced the sky, rising up white against the cold dreariness, sending a message that anyone could pray, sing God's praises and find fellowship in the building below.

In a church there will be those who clutch their bibles and cling to the belief that they're going to heaven. But, when Paula burst through The Church of Ivy Log's doors, she was not clutching her bible nor was she thinking about heaven. She was consumed with thoughts concerning the Reverend William H. Johnson.

"That preacher!" she hollered as she pulled the scarf from around her neck and put her hands on her hips and faced the hiring committee. "He spent the night in the parsonage. Can you believe it?"

"Well, heck, where else could he sleep?" Calvin asked. "Ain't nobody wants to travel in this weather."

Paula paced back and forth. "Who cares where he sleeps, just not in the parsonage. To my way of thinking, he as much as committed breaking and entering. We'll never get him outta there."

"Hold on," said Doyce. "I think you're bein' too hard on the fellow. Something else is goin' on?"

"Pyune Murphy! That's what going on!" Paula took a quick breath and pounded the air when she pointed in the direction of The Boardinghouse. "*Ms. Murphy,*" she strung out sarcastically, "had the nerve to open the parsonage with her key. An *entrusted* key, I might add."

"Okay," Doyce said, coming a little forward in his seat. "What's the problem with that?"

Paula's fuming fingers moved quickly down the front of her snow-wet coat, popping buttons all the way. "Why, that man slept in Pastor Cobb's antique four-poster bed as if he were royalty. Slept there *illegally*, I'd say."

"There's no harm done," said Dale, timidly and without any eye contact with Paula.

"No harm done? Look here." Paula came to a stop and pointed her finger at the committee. "William Johnson is not the man we hired."

Doyce said. "Course he is. We just didn't know he was . . . was of . . . African descent. Now that we know, what's to be done about it is up to us." The others nodded their heads in agreement.

"That's exactly right!" Paula clapped her hands together. "I say we boot him back to Atlanta. He has misrepresented himself."

Wanda raised her hand as if in grammar school, asking to speak for the first time. She straightened her skirt and licked her lips. "It's . . . it's Christmas. It wouldn't be right to send him away."

"What would be so bad about having Mr. Johnson stay a while?" asked Dale. In a whisper of a voice, she added, "Mr. Johnson deserves our charity."

Outside, a cardinal tapped on the glass, its feet hidden in the snow covering the windowsill. Five members of the hiring committee looked at one another and then at Paula. She circled the desk, putting a balled fist under her chain.

"I am shocked at all of you," she ranted. "We aren't the Salvation Army. This is a business. We are employers." She nodded her head several times, as if moving her every thought into its proper place. "You people just aren't thinking right." She squinted her eyes and breathed heavily through her nostrils. "We've got us a black preacher all right. But, that's not all we've got. We've got a heap of trouble. Pretty soon we'll lose our identity, our place in this town, and most of all our long-held traditions. Traditions, I might add, that don't include a . . . a Negro."

Paula turned her back on the committee members and

watched the cardinal at the window. She turned around slowly, her words firm. "His welcome reception is at 6 o'clock tonight. We've got a lot of work to do until then. He can stay until after Christmas morning's sermon, and then he's outta here. And that's final."

The committee eased to the door, one by one, staring at Paula. They'd never defy her, never override her wishes. It had always been that way, even since grade school when she dominated them as though they were her subjects, sworn to loyalty and devotion. If they didn't, there would be hell to pay.

"Wait just a minute." Paula folded her arms across her chest. "Let's take a formal vote on whether he goes or stays."

"A written vote?" asked Harley.

"A written vote," said Paula with conviction.

Everyone retook a seat and she handed out paper and pens. She said, "Vote yes or no; yes to stay, no to go."

Doyce held the blank piece of paper and stared at it, his lips clamped together. A flush of red crept up his neck and soon covered his face. "I ain't votin'. I abstain."

"Abstain?" hollered Paula. "You can't abstain. You've got to vote. This is serious, Doyce."

Doyce slowly folded the piece of paper and stuck it in his pocket. When he looked up at Paula, his eyes watered, the lids drooping slightly over his bright blue irises. "Remember when your mama was too sick to make your prom dress and my mama made it for you? She worked on it three nights in a row, all night long. Even after she done took care of all us younguns." His voice broke and his words sounded like a frog that hadn't learned to croak. "I said to mama, 'How come you made that Paula girl a prom dress? You know she's the meanest gal we ever met.'"

"What's your point?" Paula asked, shifting in her chair.

A single tear rolled down his worn cheek. Doyce pulled out his handkerchief and blew his nose. "Know what she said? She said she done it for Jesus." He paused and cleared his throat. "I asked her what she meant by that, 'cause I didn't quite understand. I was so young and all." He carefully folded his handkerchief and put it back in his pocket. "I never forgot what she told me. She said, 'You 'member this, Doyce, even if you don't remember anything else I've said to you before I go see Jesus. If you have trouble doing something nice for someone you don't like, do it for Jesus.'"

"So?" Paula asked, holding a cruel glare on him.

Doyce zipped up his jacket and looked at Paula for a long moment. "'So,' you ask. I'm doing this for Jesus."

In the quiet of the room, Paula let out an exaggerated sigh. "Oh, Doyce, what the heck does a prom dress have to do with this preacher? Just get over it. Even if you don't vote, the majority will vote with me." She looked around the room. "Right, everyone? I mean, we've got to make this an official decision."

Harley, the most widdle-waddle of a man when it came to decisions, raised his hand, his forefinger extended as he shook his head. He was a stickler for rules and regulations. "Well, now, Paula, let's discuss all this a little further."

A strange conveyance occurred, as though from another world, leaving Paula both stricken and tongue-tied. A mug shot of the FBI's most wanted criminal could not have been more intimidating than the expression on her face. Silence soon took up the empty space in the room, creating a stillness so great it was as though breathing itself wasn't allowed by those in attendance. The shock waves that followed were noiseless, penetrating like alien amoebas which grasped a person's body and turned it to stone. Any moment, Paula would levitate above the desk, melt into a blood-dripping creature, and kill them all.

Doyce was the first to speak. "I move we adjourn this meeting until after Christmas."

"I second the motion," said Calvin, so fast he barely gave Doyce time to finish.

Both Dale and Wanda nodded their heads and said in unison, "Agreed."

Harley nodded, too, albeit slowly; no way he'd voice his position.

Paula's lips moved, but the words might as well have been chiseled out one by one with cold precision, since she sounded like a bailiff. "Let the minutes of this meeting show the issue of William Johnson as unresolved, and the meeting has been adjourned until December 26."

"Can we go now?" Doyce asked, making it clear by his tone

that he'd had enough.

Paula's eyes canvassed the faces of the hiring committee members. "Not only have I been bushwhacked by the preacher, but it looks like all of you are victims of the same thing." She stepped away, then turned back to the committee, her fingers slowly buttoning her coat. "If I were any one of you, I'd say some extra prayers tonight."

~~~ ~~~

Chapter 28

Perhaps it was just happenstance, or then again it could have been an orchestrated movement in the universe, a slight wobble of the planet, or even a whisper of something unknown. It came as though a hand had parted the snow-laden clouds and declared a moment of glorious sun — so bright the snow seemed to be on fire. And with this, Ivy Log's bitter cold abated, as if in one collective moment a soft, warm breath had been blown out into the winter air, across the town square, up and down the streets of the small mountain community.

At The Boardinghouse, the fireplace ashes glowed dimly. The dessert table was empty, the pans of barbecued chicken long gone, as were the hungry folks who devoured the turnip greens and ham and left only crumbs on their plates.

In the kitchen, Pyune rolled pie dough while pecans toasted in the oven. On the stove, a pot of black-eyed peas simmered; a bowl of cinnamon and nutmeg nearby for apple pie. Wiley sat on a stool at a large wooden table and sipped his second cup of coffee and listened to her hum. He watched the sureness of her hands as she pushed the rolling pin, swiftly pulling back and forth and then across the dough. Flour dusted her hands; a small piece of dough stuck between two of her fingers.

Could she sense him starting at her? It wasn't likely, her thoughts perhaps in a faraway place, maybe with her grandmother when she had meticulously instructed her on the intricacies of making perfect piecrusts.

He felt the warmth of the kitchen, smelled vanilla, and in a squeezing of his heart, sensed the joy of simplicity. He found himself savoring the little things about Pyune, her movements, her deftly folding pie dough into baking pans, her crimping the edges into tiny flutes. A masterpiece was in the offing, and all with just shortening, flour and water, a pair of magic hands. He even marveled at the precise way she spooned red cherries into a pie shell. Mesmerized by her actions, he laughed softly and began humming an obscure melody from his childhood.

From across the kitchen, Pyune looked up and gave him a pearly grin, her eyes shining just as brightly as her teeth. "Don't believe I ever heard you hum, Wiley. What's got into you?"

"Oh, I don't know. I reckon it's the holidays. You know, tidings of peace and joy, that Christmas apron you got on, Santa Claus."

"Santa Claus?" Pyune held the rolling pin out in front of her.

"That's what I said, Santa Claus. Ain't nothing wrong with that, is there?" He held her eyes with his, and in his mind he visualized her as a gem sparkling alone in a field on a bright moonlight night. Then, deep inside her glistening black eyes, he sensed loneliness. It had settled there, unmoving. He reached out his hand.

Sensual, captivating Pyune Murphy — gentle and without an ounce of pretense, as well as the maker of heavenly cobblers — seemed confused.

His rough fingers, bending slightly, signaled her to come closer.

Her gaze left his hand and traveled slowly to his face. Her lips quivered as she found his eyes again. She took a small step forward but stopped.

"Come," he said, almost at a whisper.

"I . . . I want to . . . ." Pyune felt her throat tighten. "But, I — "

"But, you what?" He grinned. "All I want to do is wipe that flour off your nose."

Pyune's eyes widened. She pulled back a step and pressed her hands to her face, the flour dusting her warm skin.

Wiley's face softened, his heart beating slow and sure. "Forgive me, Pyune. Somehow, someway, I feel as though I have . . . come home. And, there you are . . . waiting for me."

"Waiting for you?"

Wiley nodded. "Yes, waiting for me."

His eyes kept hers. Not looking away, he stood from his chair, a weakness in his legs, a small knot in his stomach. The room stilled, the simmering pot the only sound.

She took Wiley's calloused hand and kissed it, whispering, "I've always waited for you."

~~~ ~~~

Chapter 29

Along Main Street, at Drake's Hardware, in Patton's Drugs and along the sidewalks, last-minute shoppers scurried in and out of stores, their packages and bags heavy in their arms, while in the town square a group of carolers from The Church of Ivy Log sang *O Come All Ye Faithful*, Vallie Thomas's soprano voice rising high and dreadfully off-key.

At the church, the snow from the sidewalks had been shoveled into a large mound, on which someone had placed a tattered hat, a broom, and eyes and buttons created by rocks. Not the world's best snowman, but one just the same. In Fellowship Hall, where the 6 p.m. reception for William Johnson was to be held, poinsettias with large gold bows lined the entranceway. A sign leaned on a large easel near the door, proclaiming: "Welcome, Pastor Johnson."

The ladies of the church chattered loudly, their laughter festive. The smells of fried chicken, sliced honey ham and hot biscuits filled the large room. The dessert table weighed heavy with pies, Nancy Lewis's fruitcake taking center stage, Mary Ann Haddock hovering over it, knife in hand.

"Nancy, you want me to slice your fruitcake?" Mary Ann asked. "Everybody will be here in just a few minutes."

Nancy said, "Might as well. But slice it thin. We don't want to run out."

Another lady sprinkled powdered sugar across the 8-layer chocolate cake Elizabeth Lindquist had baked despite her broken arm. The poor woman had slipped on an icy sidewalk in front of Patton's Drugs, more horrified when her dress flew up above her knees than by her injury.

Henry Patton himself came running out of his store, but he had trouble lifting the big woman. He called Haskell Drake from the hardware next door and together they slid her along the snow and ice to Dr. Casteel's office, only a few buildings away. Henry became angry when a carload of high school kids blew their horn and laughed at the sight. Said he'd call their mother's for sure. He did, and some empty Christmas stockings flapped in the crisp air, indeed a rarity in Ivy Log.

At precisely 6 p.m., the winter sun already set, Paula Jennings entered Fellowship Hall, the overhead florescent lights adding a purple cast to her red hair. Her green jacket was festive, as were the gold bell earrings that jingled when she walked. The gaudy Santa Claus pin she wore on her lapel flashed off and on in bursts of red and green lights, thanks to the Chinese who had shipped millions of them to American stores.

The welcoming reception for William Johnson was a charade, since he would be gone the day after Christmas. Paula would save face by telling some outlandish story about him skipping town and leaving the church without a preacher. And she'd play her part well. But for now she would hold the microphone close to her lips and welcome him with pretentious sincerity, knowing full well he was a doomed man, doomed even though he had a doctorate in theology from the prestigious Harvard Divinity School. She would have it her way, bask in the limelight, and then yank him from the warm parsonage and its four-poster bed and send him out into the harsh, cold December winter.

She entered the room, gliding to the microphone. The hiring committee members gathered behind her, unsmiling, their eyes everywhere but on the new pastor. They had been wheedled again, their backbone stripped from them as though a great beast had ripped them apart and devoured their integrity and principles. Who were they? They were sheep, slaves of Paula Jennings. Granted, they had withheld their votes at the committee meeting, delaying the formal decision to release William Johnson, but they knew it was just a matter of time before Paula mastered them, one and all.

William Johnson arrived at the entranceway, Wiley Hanson and Pyune Murphy at his side. Frank and Adela followed, their faces shining, their wedding day fast approaching.

Looking elegant as well as beautiful, Pyune wore a red silk skirt, tea length, and an ivory blouse tucked in at her small waist. She had delivered her lemon pudding cake earlier in the day, its top sprinkled with confectioner's sugar, a bright red cherry in the middle. Additionally, her pies lined up in a row across the dessert table.

Most everyone in Ivy Log had turned out to meet the new preacher. William H. Johnson was big news for this small town and its inhabitants, who fed off each other's lives as well as that of its preacher.

Reverend Johnson hesitated at the doorway and looked out across the room just as everyone had turned to look at him, his cashmere coat, his black skin. A rumbling murmur began at the back of the room and inched forward, past Vallie Thomas, Elizabeth Lindquist with her broken arm, and Mary Ann Haddock with powdered sugar on her dress, and finally to the edge of the crowd, where for no apparent reason the "Welcome Pastor Johnson" sign fell off the easel. It was not impossible for the devil to roam the room and flick the sign to the floor and whisper mocking words, words that could undermine this joyful occasion.

Henry Patton ran forward, flustered. "Oh, my goodness." He returned the poster to the easel and then stuck out his hand. "Here," he said, "let me welcome you. So glad to have you." He pumped William Johnson's hand.

From the podium, Paula, her mouth at the microphone, said, "Testing, testing." Her voice shrieked over the PA system, a grating sound that rattled the windows and shook the meringue on Marilyn Kilpatrick's perfect lemon pie. Doyce rushed over, turned down the volume, looked up at Paula, nodded for her to go ahead.

"Ladies and gentlemen," she crooned, "thank you for attending our new pastor's reception. The weather has been awful, but it looks like we have a nice crowd." She paused and looked around the room. A woman of steel, she felt herself gripping the microphone as though it were the neck of William Johnson. There would be no regrets as her heart remained hardened like the ice in Ivy Log Creek. "There are a few announcements to make before we get started with the program."

She looked across the room to Frank and Adela. "Just a reminder that Frank and Adela's wedding is coming up. Christmas Eve at two o'clock. Hope y'all have the time clearly marked on your calendar." She turned to Mary Ann. "Will you take care of any wedding gifts and be sure the bride and groom get them after the ceremony?" Mary Ann nodded dutifully.

"Pastor Johnson, can you come up here, please?" The hiring committee moved aside and waited for him to walk through the crowd. Paula watched him carefully, her eyes narrowing slightly. He had a lot of nerve sleeping in the parsonage, in Pastor Cobb's bed of all things. She would call the shots from now on, guaranteeing that the Christmas morning sermon would be his last act in this little town.

The pastor arrived at the podium alongside Paula. He was a magnificent specimen of an educated, intelligent man. Tall, trim, graying at the temples with eyes that conveyed trust, people could tell him anything and know they would not be admonished or judged. William Johnson would simply say, "Let us pray together." His gaze roamed the faces of the parishioners, his eyes seeming to say the same phrase.

Paula clasped the microphone tightly, her red lipstick shining like Vallie Thomas' nose when she drank too much cough syrup. "For those of you who have not met William Johnson, I would like to formally introduce him now." She paused and nodded graciously at William, her chin dropping in mock humility as everyone in the congregation applauded.

"Mr. Johnson, a graduate of the Harvard School of Divinity," she paused dramatically, "a devout Christian and, I might add, a pianist with a voice like an angel, arrived from Atlanta yesterday." She paused and fleetingly wondered if she had worn too much blush for the overhead lights. "I'm hoping each of you will welcome him with . . . with open arms."

She walked a few steps forward, toward the crowd, leaving the man in her shadow. "Pastor Johnson's previous church had a membership of over three-thousand, so you can imagine his . . . his coming to our little town, our little church and . . . and fitting . . . in."

Paula turned slightly and saw William Johnson out of the corner of her eye. He was still black.

"For those of you who haven't met Pastor Johnson, I'd like to introduce him now." She handed him the microphone and stepped back, as if disassociating herself from the man who had been utterly perfect until he walked through the doorway of The Boardinghouse and exposed his dark skin.

The minister took the microphone. "Thank you, Ms. Jennings," he said softly. He gazed slowly around the room, past the dessert table, to the fresh blue-spruce Christmas tree wrapped in shimmering gold garland, to the bald head of Wiley Hanson, to the beautiful, flawless face of Pyune Murphy, and finally to the room's high ceiling, on which angels perched themselves, their heavenly harps nearby.

Then, as if a maestro's baton had appeared, the room quieted and the reverend's eyes lifted toward heaven and his lovely baritone voice began, "But the Master of the sea heard my despairing cry and from the waters lifted me, now safe am I. Love lifted me, love lifted me, when nothing else could help, love lifted me."

~~~ ~~~

Chapter 30

The sound of "amens" traveled around the room, a "praise God" or two ending the last chorus of the old hymn "Love Lifted Me." The disciple Peter was quickly judged for sinking in the waves, yet eleven other disciples never stepped out of the boat. William not only stepped out of the boat, he believed love would lift him into the hearts of Ivy Log.

~~~ ~~~

Chapter 31

In a shadowed corner in Fellowship Hall, out of the spotlight, Paula nibbled on Penny Capps's Christmas cookies and watched as William Johnson clasped hands, patted backs and placed his arm around the shoulders of the citizens of Ivy Log. The parishioners reveled in his warmth, laughed merrily and made him promise he would eat their cake, their casserole, their pie, and come to dinner on Christmas Sunday.

"Pyune said you had a cat?" asked Vallie.

"Named Delilah."

"Oh, my. You know, Pastor Johnson, they say people who love cats make very good friends."

"Are you married, Pastor Johnson?" asked Nancy Lewis.

"A widower, ma'am," he answered, a shadow crossing his face.

"Pastor Johnson, let's sing some Christmas carols," yelled Henry Patton.

William sat at the Ellington Victorian upright and played and sang "Jingle Bells" with such enthusiasm that old sourpuss Emory Hysell sallied up behind him and sang along, his toothless gums flapping, "Jingle bells, jingle bells."

Across the room, Wiley Hanson meandered to Paula's side, a cup of Christmas punch in one hand and a piece of fruitcake in the other. "Looks like everybody's havin' a good ol' time." He chomped down on his cake and delighted in the candied cherries and pecans. Crumbs fell into his beard when he tapped his foot to "Winter Wonderland."

Paula, her words sour, spoke quietly into the festive air, "Of course, they're having a good time; it's the holidays." She paused and looked around the room at all the smiling faces. "But," she said, her voice lifting slightly, almost happy, "by sundown, Christmas day, he'll be gone." She laughed out loud and turned to Wiley. 'You'll Be Gone By Sundown' would make a good name for a country song, wouldn't it?" She popped a cookie into her mouth. "How sad."

Wiley, a deliberate man, a man who above all else prized integrity in an individual, slowly drank the last of his punch. His bald head glistened in the bright overhead lights and reflected the shimmering gold of the nearby Christmas tree. He loved the sunrise and always looked across the mountains in the evening for the last glimpse of a sunset. But, now, as he turned back to Paula, his eyes were hard. "You can't feel good about this. Give the man a chance."

Impervious to his comment, she brushed a cookie crumb from the front of her jacket and looked at Wiley with wide eyes. "Whatever do you mean? The man doesn't deserve a chance. He misrepresented himself. He's an imposter as far as I'm concerned." She nodded a greeting at someone across the room. Then, cold, harsh words, measured and full of contempt, came out of her mouth: "We didn't hire a black preacher - that's all there is to it."

~~~ ~~~

Chapter 32

Frank and Adela sat across the table from Pyune. They held hands as they chatted with Pyune.

"Can't wait to begin your wedding cake, Adela." Pyune smiled at Frank. "They'll be a groom's cake too."

"I know they'll both be perfect," said Adela.

Adela looked to her right at a woman whom she did not recognize. She leaned slightly toward Pyune. "Do you know the woman in the red jacket, sitting near the Christmas tree?"

Pyune glanced across the room. "I know her name — she's Anne Smith — but I really don't know her. Lives in Blairsville. Married a doctor named Schuyler and moved to California years and years ago. When he died awhile back, she returned to Blairsville."

"She's beautiful."

"Yes, she is. My mama knew her mama back in the day. Mama kept house for her for a while."

"Wonder why she's here tonight?"

"Now you got me thinkin' the same thing," Pyune said.

"She seems a little lost. I think I'll go talk to her." Adela excused herself, placed a cookie from the dessert table onto her plate, refilled her punch cup and found Anne sitting in a chair.

"Hello, my name is Adela Harper. I don't believe I know you."

Anne was a tiny woman, just over five feet tall. Large blue eyes opened wide and looked up at Adela.

"I'm Anne Schuyler, formerly a Smith, originally from Micanopy, Florida." She smoothed her hair. "My grandfather was the mayor there for many years. Perhaps you've heard of him. He also ran moonshine over at Payne's Prairie for as long as I can remember."

Adela laughed. "It sounds to me like the Smith's were interesting people."

Anne rolled her eyes. "Yes, they were. But they never went to jail as far as I know." She paused. "Course, if they did, they never told me."

The women laughed together while Adela sat in a chair beside Anne. "I'm wondering . . . curious if you know our new pastor."

Anne shook her head. "No, I have not had the pleasure of meeting him." Anne's gaze wandered to the dessert table. "I wonder if you could get me another piece of that wonderful fruitcake. My arthritis is giving me a fit — this cold weather, you know." She frowned. "A lot of folks don't like fruitcake. But I simply adore it, don't you? Why all those nuts and candied fruits are just marvelous. Have you ever put orange peelings in your fruitcake?"

"Orange peelings? Why, no, but I am sure it adds a nice flavor. Let me go get you a piece of cake."

Adela left her chair and was able to get the last piece of fruitcake for Anne. Behind her, Pyune asked, "You make a new friend?"

"Sure did. She's a delight. Easy to talk to."

Pyune turned around and looked at Anne Schuyler. "You reckon she's an angel just passing by? She sure looks like one. Look at that sweet face."

Adela smiled and carried the fruitcake to Anne, saying, "See that lady over there by the punch bowl? The one in the gold blouse?"

Ann craned her neck. "The tall, thin woman?"

"Yes. She made the fruitcake. Has pecan trees, and that's why there are so many nuts in the cake."

"All I can say is *yum*."

Adela shifted in her chair. "Anne, did you know Pastor Cobb?"

"Oh, yes!" she said, turning to face Adela. "Pastor Cobb and

I were lovers."

~~~

"So who is the lady in red?" asked Frank as Adela returned to stand beside him.

Adela hesitated, glanced across the room at the woman in red, and softly replied, "Oh, she's just an old friend of Pastor Cobb's."

From across the room, Wiley wandered past the dessert table, picked up a few cookies dusted with powdered sugar and filled with walnuts. He ate one while he eased up behind Frank and Adela.

"Got my guns all cleaned and polished, Frank. Let's say you and I head out early one morning before the big day and shoot us a rabbit or two." He grinned at Adela. "Be your last chance as a single man."

Frank chuckled and pulled Adela close. "I'd still have to ask permission from this beautiful woman."

~~~ ~~~

Chapter 33

The lights in Fellowship Hall dimmed as William Johnson's fingers moved across the piano keys and Pyune's fine soprano voice began "Silent Night.

It was a *holy night*, a blending of hearts, thought the pastor as he studied the faces of those who had come to welcome him to The Church of Ivy Log.

Paula had said she wanted to see him after the reception. He suspected more conversation regarding his tenure, and specifically his *lack of full disclosure* as she had put it, which entitled the committee, at her behest, to rethink his employment with The Church of Ivy Log.

Despite Paula's stand regarding his color, and even the illegalities involved, he found himself caring about the woman —an odd feeling when someone is so very antagonistic. Yet, she was obviously unhappy, had built a stone fence around her heart, had not experienced the joy of unconditional acceptance. She had not learned to love freely and without judgment, which was the greatest gift of all.

He had turned the other cheek, the Christian thing to do. Still, he wondered at the fairness of it all. Paula had not considered him as a person, but rather viewed his color as if his blackness had something to do with what was inside him. He smiled. What if he disliked her for her red hair? A silly thought, but another instance of how an opinion would be based solely on appearance. He felt the beginnings of anger but swallowed it. It could be so different. Yet, it wasn't. Paula was seeing to that.

He saw her across the room, alone, unsmiling, her gaze wandering aimlessly. Even her Santa Claus pin had stopped blinking its erratic red and green flashes. He wanted to reach out, but she'd have none of that. He would pray for her later. That's all he could do. But for now he would sing, " . . . sleep in heavenly peace . . . sleep in heavenly peace."

~~~ ~~~

Chapter 34

The dessert table was empty, platters and plates with crumbs only, a dab of icing here and there, a lonely candied cherry on the bare fruitcake plate. The lights on the Christmas tree were unplugged, the blue spruce forgotten in a dark corner. Nearby, the ladies of the church gathered together and in only minutes returned Fellowship Hall to its usual orderliness, with the floors swept, dishes washed and counters wiped. Church ladies were the queens of cleanliness, and those in this congregation were exemplary.

A calling of "Good nights" resonated at the entryway, along with hugs and the shaking of hands and the slapping of backs; and, of course, the wishes of a Merry Christmas, as the townsfolk headed out into the cold and then to their warm homes.

Pastor Johnson shook the last hand, waved to Elizabeth Lindquist and Karen Perkins, and called to Wiley, who talked with Frank and Adela about the suit he planned to wear as best man.

The reverend came up to them and asked Wiley, "Any chance you can bring some more firewood?"

"You can count on me, Pastor Johnson." Wiley waved and walked toward The Boardinghouse, where a thin tendril of chimney smoke snaked above the rooftop.

From Fellowship Hall, in an eerie quiet, William Johnson walked down the long, darkened hallway that led to the church office. At the end of the hallway, a beam of light tunneled its way from a half-closed doorway, from where he knew behind the door Paula waited.

~~~

The church office was small. A desk, a few bookcases lining the wall, and a copy machine on a table near the window. Paula felt the cold air seep through the window behind her and shivered as she heard the preacher's soft footsteps. She sat upright in the chair and folded her hands on the desk and felt herself prepare for what she thought was a divine act: Fire the preacher. Of course, how could he be fired when he was never really hired? A mistake, that's all it was. A misunderstanding that could not have been foreseen by anyone. Why should she languish over a business decision that would be made by the entire hiring committee, not just her?

And another thing, why would a black pastor want to minister in a church that had a long history and tradition of a white leader? It was quite clear to her that she and the hiring committee were doing the best thing for everyone concerned. William Johnson would return to Atlanta and find a more appropriate church. It wasn't at all that complicated.

~~~

"Hello, Ms. Jennings." He noticed her flinch at the sound of his voice. "What a lovely reception. And what a nice bunch of folks."

She ignored his comment. "Have a seat, Pastor Johnson." Her eyes swept the room, the desk, but not his face.

He sat across from her and leaned back. He found himself smiling a knowing smile. A smile that said, "We are all God's children." He waited.

Paula cleared her throat. "The hiring committee and I met earlier today and discussed your employment application." She was all business, picking up a pen and tapping it on the edge of the document, which rested on the desk. "Although we've delayed a formal vote, we're afraid you do not meet our expectations for the pastor of The Church of Ivy Log."

William said nothing. His eyes rested on hers. And he

waited. A long silence followed.

Paula picked up William's application. Her fingers fidgeted around the edges while her eyes darted to its contents. "Of course, if you like, you may perform the nuptials for Frank and Adela and deliver the Christmas-morning sermon. After that . . . ." She hesitated and turned the document over. "Any questions?"

William's gaze fell on the piece of paper, then to the woman across from him. He felt the beating of his heart, slow and steady. His words came out smooth and soft, like a soothing balm to her obvious anxiety. "No questions, but I would like to pray with you."

"Pray?" She fiddled with the pen, clicking it open and shut. "I don't think that is necessary. There's no — "

"Prayer might not always be necessary, but it sure is nice." He bowed his head and leaned forward in his chair.

"Dear Heavenly Father, I come to You with a heavy heart and ask that You calm my troubles, lift me up in Your grace. I come boldly before You seeking Your divine guidance and direction concerning my life. It is my desire to do Your will. I ask You for Your wisdom regarding my future. I ask You to help me be strong and of good courage as you lead me. In Jesus' name. Amen."

Paula's hands flew in the air as she wrapped her scarf around her neck. "Amen, as well . . . and unless an avalanche blocks the road leading out of Ivy Log, I'm certain that *He* will guide you right back to Atlanta." She looked at William Johnson with a lopsided sneer. "Shall I help you pack?"

In the long moment that followed, a winter wind blew fiercely, accompanied by a shrill whistle as it whipped around the corner of the church. A sound like the ripping away of the rooftop rumbled across the church, followed by a loud boom. The pastor and Paula jumped from their chairs, with him sprinting down the hallway and Paula following as best she could in her 4-inch heels.

Outside the church, Wiley, flustered and waving his red wool hat as though announcing the end of a race, zipped back and forth on the snow-covered sidewalk. "Pastor Johnson, come quick! The steeple done been blowed off the church and fell on your car. It smashed it all to smithereens!"

The grin on the minister's face stretched wide. A soft chuckle began in his chest and moved up to his throat, ending in a howling laugh that could be heard all the way to Atlanta.

~~~ ~~~

Chapter 35

At midnight, Pyune made coffee and scavenged for leftovers in The Boardinghouse kitchen. Wiley, diligent in his fire-keeping duties, placed an oak log along the back of the deep fireplace. "That ought to hold us for a while," he said, wiping his hands on his pants. "Whoever would a thought we'd burn so much wood this winter?"

At the table by the bay window, Pyune poured coffee for William. He shook his head and ran his hand over his head. "Oh, my. Can you believe it? The church steeple sitting right on top of my car."

"All I got to say is thank goodness you weren't in it when it happened," said Wiley as he pulled out a chair. "Yep. I'd say that was truly a miracle." He chuckled softly and looked from Pyune to the pastor. "Course, I'm confused just a little bit. Coulda been the devil at work."

"The devil?" Pyune sliced a piece of leftover cranberry bread into three pieces and everybody took one.

Wiley grinned. "Course, depends on how you look at it. Could be the hand of God. I'm a thinkin' — "

The door burst open, and with a rush of cold air Paula stomped across the dining room, her coat wet with snow, her hair wind-tangled. She dropped a glove as she tried to grab her scarf when it fell to the floor. Stumbling, and out of breath, she swung her arm wide and pointed to the pastor and then to the doorway. "Don't you be getting comfortable, Mr. Johnson. Car or no car, I'll find you transportation back to Atlanta!"

She whirled around like a tornado and was out the door and into the night, leaving both her scarf and glove where they lay.

~~~ ~~~

Chapter 36

It was 1 a.m. when Wiley drove his truck to Paula's house and parked along the street. The truck idling, he sat and wondered for the hundredth time why Paula had a hold on him. Perhaps it was their history, long and passionate, that forever bound them together. Maybe it was that city-girl thing again, that longing for more than his life in the mountains could give him. And, now, as he knocked on her door, he had to try one more time to understand the woman she was, and if they could ever find common ground.

The door opened. "Hey, Wiley," she said softly into the cold night air. "Thought you'd come by."

She seemed calm, not the woman who had exploded into The Boardinghouse and pointed an accusing finger at William Johnson. She had brushed her hair and pulled on a nightgown. Her makeup had been removed and her freckles had marched to the forefront of her skin like soft pink soldiers.

"I'd like to come in and talk about some things. May I?" His face was shadowed, his eyes dark and brooding.

"Always, Wiley." She stepped back. "You're always welcome here."

He felt vulnerable when she looked at him. Helpless, as though nothing he said would matter, his words drifting past her to that hidden place where she painted them with her own colors.

When he came inside and the door closed, she put her arms around him and he smelled her perfume. She kissed him and he felt the warmth of her body and the softness of her hair as it brushed his face.

"Paula," he began, gently unleashing her arms. "Let's sit down a minute." He led her to the couch, but she didn't sit with him; instead, she picked the chair covered in fabric from the Atlanta rummage sale.

He searched for words from his heart, not the ones he had learned in the academics of Georgia Tech. "This thing about the new pastor — I'm not so sure you're handling it just right." He leaned back so she would think about his words for a few fleeting moments without always holding a sword in her hand. He would be wrong.

"Wiley Hanson, don't you go preaching to me about this. You don't know a thing about it."

Wiley took his time. "There's a lot of things I don't know, but I do know about right and wrong. You can't take a good man and treat him like you been doin'. You and the hiring committee. I'm not blaming it all on you. But, here's the thing: William Johnson is a man of God. In the short while I've spent with him, it's clear to me he'll do a good job for The Church of Ivy Log and for this town." He paused and took a deep breath. "Can't you just give him a chance to prove himself?"

Paula fiddled with the tie on her nightgown, finally tying it into a small bow. Her fingers then drummed on the arm of the chair, her face twisted in thought. "The decision has already been made. He's going back to Atlanta."

Wiley nodded thoughtfully. "Okay. It looks like you aren't going to change your mind." He rose from the couch and walked to the door, slipping on his gloves as he made his way.

"Can't you stay the night?" she asked as she followed right behind him.

"No, I won't be staying," he said, not even turning to her as he opened the door and left.

~~~ ~~~

Chapter 37

Like a grieving widow, Paula watched Wiley pull away from the curb, the truck's red taillights bright against the snow. Her gaze followed him until he turned the corner and headed toward the mountains.

The mountains. He had taken her there years ago, showed her his favorite fishing creek and hiked to a peak so high they could see the tall buildings in Atlanta. They made love in his log cabin. Afterwards, as Wiley slept, she saw a mouse run across the fireplace stone, only to be caught by a large rat snake that lay in wait on the mantle. She lay on the musty mattress and studied the spider webs on the bare rafters, heard the grunting of wild hogs near the creek and felt the dampness that crept up from the bare wood floors. It was then that she decided she could not be a mountain girl, could not adapt to the unrefined life that the mountains would require of her.

She told Wiley she loved him and wanted to get married. He said he loved her, too, but could not leave a place so high he heard the angels sing. He told her if they married she'd have to live in the towering peaks of the Appalachians, where bears roamed and running water came from a cistern a quarter mile above the cabin. *Rainwater?* she had asked him. He'd replied, *Yes, rainwater. I drink it and bathe in it.*

She thought about that for a long time. And she couldn't wear her New York coat in the woods or crack walnuts with her painted nails. Her life would be everything she hated — she'd be common.

When she told him she could never live in the mountains, away from the luxuries she enjoyed, he was thoughtful before he replied. She remembered his words as if they were spoken only yesterday: *Paula, I would die if I left these mountains, and what good would a dead husband be to you?* That pretty much settled it for them. They continued their passionate trysts in her upstairs guest bedroom with the magnolia wallpaper. When they lay on the four-poster bed, panting and satisfied, Wiley said the same thing he always said: *Well, I reckon I better get on up the mountain.*

The last glimmer of the truck's taillights disappeared as Paula unplugged the Christmas lights and walked up the staircase to the empty guestroom, where she'd often go to muse over past trysts with Wiley that occurred in that very setting.

~~~

As she lay alone, she admitted Wiley's discussion with her had been hurtful; yet, the decision to sever The Church of Ivy Log's affiliation with William Johnson was carved in stone. And their personal relationship had no bearing on church matters.

In the lonely dark of the guest room, Paula shivered, a startling revelation chilling her bones. Wiley had rejected her. And, with such finality. It was as though he'd ended whatever it was they had. He'd left her cold and untouched in her empty house, never to make love to her again. He had become disillusioned with her. He no longer desired her.

Her breath became shallow. Was it her dismissal of the new preacher that had caused his discontent? Or, had it begun with Pyune Murphy and that damn lemon pudding cake recipe?

~~~ ~~~

Chapter 38

William Johnson pulled a heavy quilt across the four-poster bed. "Delilah, you know the church won't like you sleeping in the parsonage's bed." He ran his hand across the back of his old cat, her meow expressing her pleasure. She did what all cats do when they're rubbed, she purred and asked for more.

"Okay, I won't tell anybody if you won't. Come on up here." He patted the bed. Delilah jumped and found her favorite spot alongside his back. She burrowed in and continued purring.

His bible was as worn as any used book could be, its pages ratted and curled on the edges. He opened the cover and read the inscription he'd never tired of, no matter how many hundreds of times he'd read it: *To my darling husband. Ephesians 5:33. All my love, Clara.* He rubbed the words with his fingertips, always mentally tracing the flair of her handwriting whenever he did this. Strong but feminine.

He closed his eyes, his hands holding the bible, and found himself not talking to God but to Clara. *You won't believe what happened today. The church steeple fell right smack dab in the middle of my car. And, guess what else? I'm marooned in a community where the wrath of a redhead has pushed and pulled me up and down every street in this entire town.*

He then found himself laughing out loud. He roared, held his stomach and kicked his legs in the air, causing Delilah to jump off the bed. Had he cracked? Gone cuckoo? Pushed himself over the edge? His car had a 2-ton church steeple on top of it, he had no job, and the liveliest redhead since Bruce Spring-steen's "Redheaded Woman" had told him to "get outta town." Bruce had said "It takes a redheaded woman to get a dirty job done," and Paula Jennings had proved it to be true. She had fired him, threatened him, belittled him and banished him back to Atlanta. He hadn't been this happy in a very long time.

His happiness, however, was fleeting. Alas, his quest to embrace a small town and its citizens as his family seemed to fall along the wayside. His vision had been simple: a small-town church where he could minister the word of God in small doses to people who were real, had faces he recognized, and with whom he was involved on a daily basis. His previous church had no such intimacy. The masses had one face. He had preached at a microphone, high on a podium, where his words spread across the throng and landed on thousands. But he longed for his words to fall on one, and he wanted to know that one's name. *Hey, Bob. How is your family? Oh? Which hospital? I'll be there. Hey, Jack. What? Your brother died? Let us pray.* He wanted to reach out and really touch someone. Such a cliché. *Reach out and touch someone?*

He was just a 12-year-old when he ran away from home and found the streets of Atlanta and the poor black communities, places where the struggles were worse than his own.

Then, he found Clara. Or she found him. Only to lose her so soon. Perhaps that was it. She had provided his core amongst the throngs of people. She had been *one*, one whose face he could see, whose cheek he could touch. That was all he wanted now. To feel that closeness again, something he did not find in the masses who came to hear him preach. So simple yet so complicated. And all because of his color.

He lay in the quiet dark of the parsonage bedroom and deliberated between an all-out thrust against the prejudices that loomed before him or a quiet, submissive acceptance. It would be difficult either way.

~~~ ~~~

Chapter 39

Paula sat in the middle of her bed. This was the second time she had read all the letters. Sixty-three of them, all signed by "O" – whoever "O" was - had to be read still again, beginning with the oldest date. Some of the letters were only a few lines, some a short paragraph; some pages and pages. All of them were filled with adorations for the bald, scrawny preacher. Paula had learned a lot about the preacher Aldelpheus Cobb through the letters he had received from the mysterious woman in Blairsville.

More than that, she had learned about the woman who called herself "O." Her letters had been heartfelt, filled with glorious reminisces of times gone by. Her youth. Her youth with Aldelpheus Cobb. She had referred to him as *my hand-some chap*. She had written him poems and asked if he remembered them. She had cited a few lines by Yates in one of her later letters.

Their favorite song had been "Among My Souvenirs," a song with lilting lyrics that echoed a deep, hurtful memory of love lost.

Paula leaned back on a pillow and closed her eyes. Love lost and then love found. "O's" letters lamented the choices she and Aldelpheus – or Al as she called him – had made. Love lost.

Love lost? Had she and Wiley lost their love? She looked down at the box of letters. There was only one remaining. Throughout the 63 letters, "O" had expressed love, devotion, concern, commitment and trust to Aldelpheus Cobb. Paula wondered if she had expressed all of those things to Wiley - and him to her? She leaned back, her fingers resting on the last letter.

She reread the last letter. *My darling Al, your question to me was a surprise. I jumped with joy, giggled and then, in a fit of uncontrolled laughter, slumped to the floor and lay there, holding your letter. What have you done to me? I will give you my answer Sunday. All my love forever, "O."*

Sunday? Paula looked at the date on the letter. Three days before Aldelpheus Cobb died.

~~~ ~~~

Chapter 40

The sun rose with such brilliance that most everyone in Ivy Log left their homes, dragging sleds, ice skates, or cutting sprigs from the 100-year-old holly tree across the street from Drake's Hardware. The Siberian white breath that had ravaged the town for over a week, closed roads, toppled trees and piled snowdrifts higher than Doyce Conley's prized Holstein cow, had moved north along the east coast and was heading toward Baltimore, then Boston, sure to hit both cities and parts in-between with a vengeance. Unfortunately, the weatherman said to be on the lookout for another front, due the next day.

But this day loomed sunny for Adela's wedding shower. The temperatures remained in the teens, but the wind had ceased and not one snowflake fell.

Earlier, Pyune had taken the last of the pies out of the ovens and poured her second cup of coffee. She was restless, her thoughts rambling. Thoughts mostly of Wiley. She remembered his words from two nights ago: *Somehow, some way, I feel as though I have . . . come home. And, there you are. Waiting for me.*

They had held each other in the center of the mammoth kitchen, among the pots and bowls and dozens of spices and knives and sugars and spoons and the smells of cinnamon and rosemary. He told her he smelled the sweetness of candied cherries on her skin.

Each had walked the same distance to the center of the kitchen. It had been a mutual decision to touch, to breathe quietly, and say nothing. When he let her go, she stepped back and looked at him. He had returned her gaze, a look that said *This is good — this is very good.*

Wiley. Wiley, who adored her, who had taken her to the smokehouse for years, who had called her his friend and once, when she had let him come up the stairs into her little alcove of a home, had said he loved her. What kind of love was it? Honky-tonk love? He had honored her in every way except, of course, the way any woman would want to be honored. Their love, honky-tonk or not, was hidden, secret to most everyone. Folks had their suspicions, but she and Wiley were so well-liked they had survived the small-town gossip.

Hidden to most everyone except Paula and her contemptuous nature. Nothing escaped the eyes of Ivy Log's most diligent snoop. Or, whatever one would want to call her. Paula hid behind her grand façade of perfection, her fashionable clothes, her upstanding membership in the church, her lovely soprano that sang "Whispering Hope" as if her voice was piped directly from heaven. Underneath it all, she was as cunning as the devil could make her. And Paula had a personal investment in Wiley Hanson and any shenanigans he had going on with Pyune Murphy.

The knock at the back door of The Boardinghouse was not Wiley's knock. This knock was gentle, hesitant. Pyune looked out the window and saw William hopping back and forth on the stoop, a parsonage quilt wrapped around him, Delilah in his arms and the look of a lonely orphan smeared across his face.

When she opened the door, he jumped. "Oh, my. Thank goodness you're . . . home." He stepped in, his feet lifting high into a few prancing steps. He pulled the quilt tighter around him. He stuttered. "N-never been so cold. Walked from the parsonage. Coat in the car. Underneath the steeple." His teeth chattered. "G-got some hot coffee?"

She had hot coffee. She had leftover cornbread. She had apple butter. She had cold ham. She had day-old bread pudding. They sat like an old married couple, elbows propped on the table, Delilah sneaking up the back stairway, William unshaven, Pyune in her furry bedroom slippers.

"Got Frank and Adela's wedding vows all worked out?" she

asked him.

"Oh, yeah. Stayed up last night late and wrote them out. Talked with Frank and Adela at length about what they wanted." He looked up from his plate. "They're good together."

Pyune nodded. "They belong together. She was a widow for most of her life. Him too. Military man. Secret stuff all over the world. Came back to Ivy Log to die." She grinned. "Only Adela wouldn't let him. She told me they fought like cats and dogs. They were neighbors at the lake. Feuding neighbors."

"She's a beautiful woman."

"Ivy Log's most beautiful widow. Course, that will change when she marries Frank. Then she'll be the town's most beautiful bride." She laughed at her own joke.

"She have children?"

"Yes, a daughter and a granddaughter. You'll meet them at the wedding. Close family."

"What about Frank?"

"Has a son stationed in Afghanistan. Don't believe he'll make the wedding, though."

Pyune, her slim brown fingers wrapped around her coffee cup, narrowed her eyes at William. "The steeple on top of your car?"

William looked surprised. "There's a steeple on top of my car?" He laughed and brushed some crumbs away from the edge of the table. His hands were masculine, hands that had opened the Holy Bible an uncountable number of times and turned its pages late into the night.

She studied his face as he concentrated on the cornbread crumbs, sweeping them up as though they were gold dust. It was a perfect face, well-balanced, no feature standing out more than the other, all culminating into a handsomeness that was pleasing to the eye yet awash with humility.

"Ah, yes, the steeple," he said, wrinkling his brow. "Some insurance policies state if your claim was caused by an act of God, you cannot collect. Can you imagine? An act of God?" Laughter rumbled in his chest, came up slowly and spilled into the room. But, his next words were solemn, as near a whisper as one could get. "If ever there was an act of God, Pyune, it was that steeple falling on my car at that very moment."

"Might be," she said, having to think about what he'd just

said.

He looked up to the high ceiling of the kitchen, perhaps through the clapboard and directly into heaven, and he said quietly. "I don't plan to go anywhere. An act of God has told me to stay."

It was then that Pyune understood what William Johnson had said, and she gave him her warmest smile.

~~~ ~~~

Chapter 41

I n the driveway of the parsonage, William Johnson's car, with
the steeple on top of it, had become quite a spectacle. A crowd
gathered and discussed solutions to the problem. Doyce Conley
said it would take a crane to remove it, and the closest one he
knew of that was large enough to do the job was 100 miles away,
in either Chattanooga or Atlanta.

"Why couldn't we get Tom Keeling's horses to pull it off that
car?" asked Henry Patton. "Or, we could get a big ol' Deere and
just push the car and the steeple off the side of the mountain."
Idea after idea swept the small town as though it was a contest
and whoever came up with the accepted solution won a prize.
And for William Johnson? He just sat back and smiled.

Inside Fellowship Hall, preparations for Adela's bridal
shower were underway as the church ladies hurried about doing
what busy women do.

"Anybody seen Wiley?" Pyune asked, straightening the white
linen tablecloths that seemed to be everywhere, while the other
women arranged flowers in tall vases and filled dessert trays, nut
dishes, and punch bowls.

"Haven't seen hide nor hair of him," replied Elizabeth
Lindquist, who despite her broken arm poured mints into the
small dishes on each table. "He was supposed to bring some
cedar boughs for decoration. Promised he'd be here by 10
o'clock."

"He didn't deliver my firewood either," said Pyune. She
looked out the window, hoping to catch a glimpse of Wiley's

battered blue truck. But there was no sign of him.

Wiley had strutted around for days, proud and honored to be Frank's best man. The renowned Frank Carberry, richer than a sheik, had picked him —a mountain man — to stand beside him at his wedding. Can you imagine that? Wiley in a suit? Pyune wondered if he'd trim his beard. She made a mental note to inspect him carefully before the ceremony, now just a few days away.

Pyune left the main hall to search the kitchen for matches. As she looked through cabinet drawers, she hummed and wiggled her firm body in a little jive-dancing move.

Paula leaned against the frame of the doorway, arms folded, watching Pyune. "Well, well, well. Aren't we happy this morning?" A grin molded her face but her eyes were cold, the grin gradually fading as she stared at Pyune.

Holding a box of matches, Pyune turned around. Her eyes found Paula's, settled on the woman's smug face, then moved lower but did not find a hint of humility in the heart sitting underneath the coat with the fur collar. "Lots of reasons to be happy. Frank and Adela's wedding. Christmas."

"Oh, I don't know, I can think of another reason." Paula sauntered around the kitchen, straightened a wall calendar, wiped her finger across the counter, then opened the refrigerator door and peered inside.

"Yep," she said, without turning around. "If you won that twenty-five thousand dollars, that would be a reason to be happy." She whirled around to face Pyune. "Of course, that's not going to happen. You see, I've decided to call contest headquarters on Monday morning and tell them the lemon pudding cake recipe was stolen from me. Been my family recipe from years and years ago. And I can prove it."

Just as Pyune was about to tell Paula how misguided she was, and in no uncertain terms, the kitchen door flew open with such force that it slammed into the wall behind it, knocking a calendar free and sending it sailing across the floor.

Doyce Conley, his face pale, yelled, "You ain't gonna believe this! Wiley and his truck done gone off the side of the mountain!"

~~~ ~~~

Part 2

Chapter 42

Doyce, a high-pitched whine now in his voice, waved a map in front of both of the stunned women. "See here." With shaking fingers, he pointed to a spot on a rough map of Brasstown Bald. "I drawed it out."

Trembling, Pyune watched Doyce make an imaginary circle in an area close to the Bald. Paula, frozen in place, her eyes wide and questioning, looked on from across the kitchen.

Calvin Anderson and Harley Bradley were next to plough through the doorway. Calvin said, "Doyce, let us take a look at that map. Everybody's ready to go."

Pyune leaned over Doyce's shoulder as the three men solemnly studied the map.

Doyce said, "From what Obed told me, he saw tire tracks about here." He pointed to a spot, a pained expression on his face. "It's one a them switchbacks off Aricaquah Trail; a logging road near Wolfpen Ridge."

Harley knew the area well, born and raised only two miles away. "Dang. That's a mighty sheer drop off."

Doyce took a deep breath. "Worst on the peak." He lowered his voice. "This don't look none too good. Can't get any equipment up there, that's for sure."

"All we got is rope," Harley said, downcast all around.

"And some strong men," said Pastor Johnson as he came up behind everyone.

"Preacher, you better start doing some good praying, 'cause this peak is over 4,500 feet up," Doyce said.

The new preacher had no stake in the small town nor its residents; but, as he faced the men, he seemed bigger than any of them — stronger and definitely determined to participate in Wiley's rescue. He said, "I'll do more than pray."

The three locals looked at each other. Harley said, "No disrespect, but this ain't no job for a city man. These here mountains are rough. You'll get yourself kilt or hurt, for sure." He raised his voice. "We don't want nobody on the mountain who's . . . who's inexperienced."

Doyce folded the map. "That's right, preacher. This ain't no easy game."

William studied the three rough men, men who had been born and bred in the mountains, probably had Cherokee blood in them, had hunted the mountain's brown bear, had fished its streams and been on the peaks when the clouds hid the tops of the yellow birch.

"Well, now, gentlemen, it seems to me you are missing out on some God-given talent here," the preacher said.

Harley said, "We're wasting time here, preacher. We gotta go."

"Wait a minute," Calvin said, "What are you talking about, God-given talent?"

William raised his eyebrows. He reached into his pocket and pulled out a key ring. "Ah, here it is." He grinned and twirled around the keys until he reached a small silver token.

Calvin leaned over and read out loud: "Member Atlanta Climbing Club."

"Well, I'll be danged," said Doyce.

The kitchen door opened and Adela Harper looked from one face to another, then in a fear-filled voice, whimpered, "Frank is with Wiley."

~~~ ~~~

Chapter 43

Adela walked slowly into the room, as if her entry signaled the lights dimming on the town Christmas tree, the star on top going dark, and the promise of Christmas cheer vanishing. "I must do something. What can I do?" She held up her hands. "You men, please tell me what to do."

Pyune stepped forward and pulled Adela to her. "It's okay. Things are gonna be okay." She squeezed her tight. "Honey, Frank is just fine."

"Are you *sure* Frank is with Wiley?" Doyce asked.

Adela nodded. "They decided late last night to go up to the summit at first light. You know, one last outing for Frank as a free man, as Wiley put it. All they were going to do was hike a mile or so to the top, along an old logging road off Jack's Knob Trail."

From a dark corner in the kitchen, Paula asked, "How do we know this happened — and where?"

"Phone call from Obed Ledford," said Doyce. "He was trailin' his huntin' dogs and saw skid marks on a switchback around Jack's Knob Trail. Had his binoculars with him. Saw the tail end of Wiley's truck about two-hundred feet down. Looks like it tumbled end to end for a ways. Didn't see any sign of movement or hear anything. Called me first, then I called Calvin and Harley."

"Any rescue crews coming in?" Paula asked Doyce, sounding more peeved than concerned.

"How can they? Roads are closed." Doyce glanced around

the room. "We're it."

"We're wastin' precious minutes here," Harley said. Let's go. We got just four hours or so of daylight left."

"May I come?" asked Adela.

Doyce hesitated. "This ain't gonna be easy."

The pastor moved forward and reached out his hand to her. "She needs to be there with us."

"I'll go with you too," Pyune said as she opened a cupboard door and pulled out a several large carafes with lids, the same type she used at The Boardinghouse. "At least we can take some hot coffee with us."

Pastor Johnson, who was taller than any of the men, moved into the middle of the group. "Doyce, since I don't have a drivable vehicle, is it okay if I ride with you?"

"Sure enough, preacher." Doyce paused a moment and looked him up and down. "You wearing those clothes and shoes?"

"It'll take me just two minutes to change." He ran out of the room, his plaid scarf flying in the air.

Paula eased up behind Pyune as she was filling the church's large coffeemaker. "Now Pyune, it doesn't seem . . . appropriate for you to go on this rescue mission."

"Appropriate?"

The ease in which Paula had glided up next to Pyune was indeed stealthlike, startling the woman. Paula leaned forward, her breath on Pyune's face. "Tell me, what is your interest in this? Shouldn't you be back over at the restaurant? Cooking?"

Pyune smelled Paula's perfume as her words crept into her head and lingered. All she had ever learned, all she had ever felt about the woman, seemed to rise to the surface and form into a white-hot anger. But just as Pyune was about to verbally lay into Paula, Adela called out. "Pyune, tell me what you need."

Never taking her eyes off Paula, she called out, "Please get some Styrofoam cups from the cupboard." And to Paula, she asked, "Shouldn't you be in the church, on your knees, asking God to forgive you?"

"Forgive me for what?"

Pyune gave her a knowing smile. "Just about everything, I imagine."

The kitchen door opened and Harley stepped in. "Come on, Adela and Pyune. Y'all can ride with me."

~~~ ~~~

Chapter 44

On the old logging road off Jack's Knob Trail, Obed Ledford waited for Doyce Conley and the rest of the men who would traverse the mountain road and begin the seemingly impossible task of dropping 200 feet down to an ominous expanse of rock that jutted out at an elevation 4,000 feet above sea level. An accumulation of snow had smothered the earth at least 3-feet deep, leaving the bare trees poking up like orphan scarecrows without clothes. The Moundbuilders, or Cherokees as they were known, had named the mountain Etowah.

Obed remembered the last time there had been a fall off the mountain; a hunter, 35 years earlier. Only a bone or two had been recovered some years later, quiet speculation as to what had happened. Now, as he looked up into the fading light of the bitterly cold day, he wondered what they would find when they reached Wiley's truck. Large snowflakes had fallen since noon and obscured all but the tailgate of the crumbled truck. The temperature was falling; presently 29 degrees. By nightfall, it would be closer to 18 degrees. He shuddered, looked down the road and noted the time: 4 p.m.

When Obed heard the rumbling motor of an approaching vehicle, he laid on the horn of his truck, scrambled out from behind the wheel, fired his shotgun, waited. Mountain men were a different breed. Calm and confident, they were not ruffled by too much. But, Obed shuddered as he peered over the edge of the drop off and now saw only a few square inches of Wiley's blue truck, the rest buried under even more snow — and most likely devoid of any living, breathing thing.

~~~ ~~~

Chapter 45

It was silent in Harley's truck, Adela squeezed in-between the big man and Pyune, the trio staring through the windshield as the wipers struggled to fight through the heavy snow that pelted the glass. Adela seemed in a trance, her face solemn and fixed, her eyes on the sky and the fading daylight.

Her Frank. Her love. Her friend. The man who had come into her life like a thundering storm, an unrelenting force that had whipped her relentlessly . . . until.

In the beginning, he had rebuffed her, had made it clear her presence in the tiny lake cottage next to his towering three-story mansion was unwelcome, an incursion that festered and fed his intense disdain . . . of this woman. He cursed her, threatened her, admonished her for who she was; the grand-daughter of the Cherokee woman who had wooed his grandfather into the mountains, never to be seen again.

But nothing ever remains the same. Frank had sat on the porch of his house and looked across the fence where Adela trimmed her roses, cleaned fish from the lake and washed her hair in rainwater. Day after day, drinking his Pappy Van Winkle whiskey, he simmered. At the end of summer, his drunken stupors became less frequent and he eased over to the fence and called out to her, "Mrs. Harper, if I bring you some fish, will you fry them?"

She had looked up, startled, her auburn hair piled on top of her head, a yellow ribbon tied around it, the ends lifting in the breeze. He had thought her beautiful. Her rum-dark eyes watched him for a long moment. He rested his hand on the untouchable fence, the physical boundary that had enabled the emotional division between them, the symbol of the feud that had lasted longer than 30 years. "Fry them for whom? You?"

"For us," he replied softly. "Me. You. I'd like hushpuppies too. Got a recipe?" Almost flippant, as if this was a common occurrence, he casually rested his bare foot on the bottom of the fence rail.

She stared at him, at his rumpled pants, his bare feet, his disheveled beard. "It's my grandmother's recipe."

"I didn't ask you whose recipe. I asked you if you had one."

She stepped off the terrace, closer to the fence, closer to the man who had been a recluse who shunned her, the man who had despised her, and all because her Indian grandmother had loved his grandfather. "What makes you think I'd want to fry fish for you?"

The retired major general, administrator of thousands of soldiers, fighter of wars, killer of enemies, was bemused by her question. He faltered, felt himself weak, unsure. He saw the breeze pick up the hem of her skirt and reveal her slim brown legs, saw the top of her breasts as she leaned down and pushed her skirt into place. Why did he want her to fry fish for him? He knew how to fry fish, even knew how to make hushpuppies; but, something had changed.

Perhaps throughout the long days of summer, almost moment by moment, he had melded into a softer man, a lessening of the hardness around his heart. Had felt himself emerge as a man who succumbed to the softness of a woman, the sweetness of Adela Queen Harper. Just over the fence, in the little cottage, where he could hear her humming, where, when the breeze came from the west, he could smell her perfume.

"Will you fry some fish for us?" he asked again, capturing her eyes and holding them.

"And just why should I do that?" she asked, turning up her nose.

"Because it would be the beginning of something good," he said, almost in a whisper but heard by the widow.

He lifted his leg and stepped over the fence, stepped over the 30 years of feuding, stepped over the clashing between them — and stepped into something called love.

~~~

"Adela! You're crying." Pyune picked up Adela's hand. "Honey, it's okay."

The windshield wipers froze to the glass, a grinding of the motor as the truck crawled higher up the mountain and crunched the snow that covered the narrow road. Pyune hardly breathed. She leaned forward and prayed Harley saw the sheer drop off to their right. Her feet were getting cold and she longed for the fireplace at The Boardinghouse, where she could prop her feet on the hearth and watch the flames. Wiley. Sweet Wiley had built a fire the day before, and she had watched him carefully lay out the wood; but first the kindling underneath the dry oak.

How many fires had he built for her over the years, how many logs had he cut and loaded in his truck and brought to her? What would she do without him? She turned cold inside and imagined him hurt, lying on the side of a mountain, the snow covering him. *You can't leave me, Wiley.*

No one in Ivy Log knew that Wiley had financed her purchase of The Boardinghouse. He had come to her after Nettie Moxley had died and the restaurant came up for sale.

"Say, Pyune, I been thinking about something." He had shuffled around in the kitchen of The Boardinghouse, pulling open drawers looking for a spoon for his coffee, found one and then began looking for the sugar.

Pyune sat on a stool peeling potatoes. "Uh, huh," she said, hardly paying attention. She finally looked up. "Sugar's in the cabinet to your right. Second shelf. Where it's always been."

"Did you hear me?" He pulled down the sugar bowl, almost spilled it, and removed the top.

"I heard you. Thinkin' 'bout what?" She continued peeling the potatoes, the sharp paring knife twirling around them like a spinning top.

"I think this place would be a mighty fine business for you. Especially since you're the best cook in all the Appalachians." He sat down at last, content with his coffee.

"I can't argue with that. But, you're missing one important thing, Wiley Hanson. You got to have money to own a place like this. I mean, there ain't no fairy godmothers out there."

He slurped his coffee, swiped his beard and cleared his throat. "I ain't saying I'm no fairy godmother, but I sure as heck could buy this place if I wanted to."

The paring knife stopped, as did Pyune's hand, as did the potato. She simply stared at Wiley.

His gaze roamed the kitchen, the ceiling, the floor, the rows and rows of spices, finally resting on her black pearl eyes. "I'm thinking I'd like to buy this place for you." He swiveled around on his stool and laughed. "You feed me all the time as it is. And I practically live here in the winter."

Wiley paid cash for the two-story, 100-year-old house. Upgraded the kitchen equipment, the dining room, the upstairs that served as her home. He also made love to her. Had found her in the smokehouse one day, hanging up country hams, and considered that he might be in love with her. She, for her part, wondered about the mountain man, this college-educated soul who gave up his professorship, returned to the high peaks of the Appalachians, lived the life he was born to live. An existence ruled by simplicity, unhurried and uninfluenced by the rigors of the outside world.

Adela's shrieks pulled Pyune from her reverie. "Pyune! Look! There's Obed Ledford. There!" Adela pointed ahead to Obed's truck, the men soon gathering around it. Doyce and Calvin began pacing about in the falling snow, their heads covered by stocking caps, their bodies layered with clothing and down-filled outercoats, their feet comfortably ensconced in heavily insulated winter boots. Merle Betts, Wiley's cousin, followed their steps, glancing nervously down the mountain.

The pastor, wrapped in a long gray half-coat, walked to the edge of the ridge, his eyes searching the mountainside, his mind calculating. He saw sheared trees where the truck had skimmed them, limbs lying mangled from the path of the vehicle when it tumbled down the drop-off. At what he estimated was 200 feet down the ridge, he saw an odd shape, something that didn't belong there. It was the truck, wedged between two trees, its bed protruding in the air. He pulled out a pair of binoculars, and in the fading light surveyed the entire area. There was no evidence of movement, nothing that would indicate any kind of disturbance other than the slicing of the limbs by the falling truck. He estimated the truck had hit with a force equivalent to a head-on collision. Surviving the crash would be a miracle.

From the edge of the ridge, he studied the rocks and the trees. The sheared off trees would provide good anchoring for ropes, if necessary. The drop-off was not completely vertical and offered a fairly manageable grade that ended farther than he could see. He excelled at rappelling but had no rings or equipment other than rope, and his belay devices would have to be the rocks. Ropes and rocks, together with a strong body, would be all he'd have to work with.

He squatted at the side of the mountain and plotted his route, encouraged that perhaps rope would be all he needed. When he turned around, he saw the men staring at him. They would have to follow his lead and depend on his expertise to make it down the mountain and not get killed in the process.

~~~ ~~~

Chapter 46

The pastor stepped away from the mountain edge and returned to the somber men. "Anybody got any ideas about medical treatment?" He averted their eyes. "In case we need any?"

Doyce said, "We got Dr. Castell here with us. He's too old to go down the mountain, but we got a couple of folks who know CPR."

"Anybody thought about calling the ranger station?" Calvin asked, pulling out his phone.

Harley spit. "Ranger station? Place been closed since the beginnin' a December. Nobody's gonna man that shack this time a year. 'fraid we're on our own."

"Obed, what time did you find these skid marks?" The pastor asked, reaching over and extended his hand. "Don't believe we've met."

Obed hesitated a moment. "Obed Ledford. And you?"

Doyce stepped up. "That's our new preacher, Reverend William Johnson. Knows a thing or two about mountain climbing."

Obed nodded at the pastor. "I'd say 'round 2 o'clock. I was up on the mountain lookin' for my dogs. Finally heard them barking something fierce. It was my dogs who found him. Then those dang rascals ran off, and I ain't seen 'em since."

"Look like it just happened?" Pastor Johnson asked.

"Oh, no. Those tire tracks done snowed over a bit. I'd say they was about an hour or two old when I got here."

"Look here," Harley said. "Just chattin' about all this ain't gettin' the job done. Let's go!" He pulled his collar tight around his neck and glanced at the sky.

The plan was clear to the preacher. Assemble all their meager equipment and descend the mountain. Eight men and only one an experienced climber. Not much of a plan. He paused. He wasn't the man in charge. He looked skyward and closed his eyes. They were going to need all the help they could get.

"Everyone grab your ropes and let me take a look at them," the pastor said in a tone he hoped didn't sound too commanding.

The sound of rushing boots broke the pristine quiet of Jack's Knob Trail. Tailgates slammed, chains rattled and ropes whizzed across truck beds as anxious men readied themselves — for what they didn't know — only that they were attempting to rescue one of their own. These men had known Wiley his entire lifetime. They would get to him, one way or the other.

That other fellow, Frank Carberry, well, they didn't consider him a mountain man. But if he was with Wiley, he was worth going down the mountain for, as well.

The pastor scattered the pile of ropes. Most were in good shape and the right size, but he kicked aside several that did not meet the standards required for serious climbing. He squatted, took off a glove, ran his fingers over one of the ropes. "Everybody familiar with tying knots." He looked up. "Strong knots? Knots that will hold?"

Harley said, "Preacher, you ain't working with no sissies here. We all learned to tie knots before we could walk."

Pastor Johnson nodded and listened to a bit of grumbling in the background. "Didn't mean to hurt anybody's feelings or question anyone's abilities, but many lives will depend on how well each of us can tie a knot." He lifted a rope so everyone could see it. "Here's the strongest knot a mountain climber will ever need." A few flicks of his wrist, followed by a tug, and a knot appeared in the rope. "This knot will hold a 250-pound man."

"That leaves out one of us." Calvin looked over at a man he identified as Joe Thomas. "How much you weigh now?"

Joe grinned, his chest ballooning under his clothing and

thick jacket. "'bout three hundred, I reckon. Maybe a tad more."

The Pastor said, "We'll leave you here at the top. You can get a fire started." It wasn't the rope strength William was worried about. Climbers needed to be agile; a 300-pound man was generally not agile.

The men grabbed their ropes and followed William Johnson to the edge of the rocks. He hesitated. "All of you stay put for the moment. I'll be going down by myself to start — see what we have at the bottom."

He began to descend, one end of his rope tied securely around a large bolder, the other end tied around his waist. Alongside him, another man had lowered himself over the edge and matched his every move. The pastor grinned at him. "Now don't you go and make me look bad. You look like you're twenty years younger than me."

"Name's Merle. Wiley's my cousin. I'd go to the ends of the earth for him."

"Of course you would." Pastor Johnson caught his breath. "Speaking of the end, are you a praying man?"

"Don't worry about me, preacher, I'm a prayin' man, for sure." He smiled. "'specially now."

~~~

Thrashing through the snow, Joe lumbered his 300-plus-pound frame through the trees and rummaged around for old limbs to build a fire on the ridge top. He made preparations for Wiley and Frank to be placed in the back of Doyce's pick-up. Dr. Casteel had fashioned it into a makeshift aid station, since in addition to its double-cab, the truck had an extended bed that was covered.

The doctor had supervised everything carefully, knowing full well that two body bags might be all they needed. He had laid them out on the snow where Adela and Pyune couldn't see them. And when he'd walked to the edge of the ridge and peered down the mountain, he was fairly certain he would need to use them.

He observed the preacher and Merle methodically descending a few feet at a time, now halfway to Wiley's truck. Steady and determined, they worked silently. Soon, it was difficult to see them at all, the gray of day becoming darker, the shadows longer — hope fading right along with the daylight.

~~~

Farther down the logging road, in the quiet of Harley's truck, Adela and Pyune waited. They sat quietly, occasionally letting their thoughts become words that rambled with the "what-ifs" that loomed before them. Like waiting for boats to appear on the ocean horizon, they watched the edge of the cliff, watched through the falling snow, watched through the gloom that settled itself upon them and turned them colder than the frigid weather outside ever could.

Soft laughter caught in Pyune's throat. "'member that first day of school, first grade? Wiley come down from the mountain carrying his lunch in a small burlap bag his mama had sewed together? With red thread? Had embroidered Wiley's name on the side? Spelled it *Wyllie*?"

"I do remember. Everybody called him Willie for half the school year, no matter how many times Miss Proctor corrected them. Mercy, the kids called me Adelaide instead of Adela."

Pyune laughed again. "Nothing as bad as what they called me. Can you imagine? They turned Pyune into picayune."

"Well, that was Miss Proctor's fault. She thought it was picayune on the first day of school. I do recall, she wrote it on the blackboard."

"I can still see it up there in chalk. When I told her it was not spelled right, she said to go home and ask my mama how it was spelled. I told her quite forcefully that I had been writing and spelling my name since I was three years old." Pyune sighed. "And how would my mama know? She couldn't read nor write."

"Well, how did you learn to spell and write your name?"

Pyune shook her head. "I'm having a hard time understanding that myself." She turned to Adela. "You know that lemon pudding cake recipe? The one Paula claims is hers?"

"Oh, yes. Everyone in Ivy Log knows about that. It's disgraceful, if you ask me."

"I've got a letter from my granny saying she was going to give me that recipe. Just don't know where the recipe is. Don't know who wrote that letter for her, either."

From behind them, headlights glared into the cab of Harley's truck. "Wonder who that is?"

They both turned and saw the red torch of Paula Jennings's hair. Illuminated like a flaming comet, it swept toward them and stopped at the truck's window. Pyune looked through the glass into Paula's face, and as she had done so many times in the past, braced herself. Paula, perfectly groomed as though for an afternoon tea, tapped on the glass and through it said, "You can stay here in the truck, Pyune. I'll take care of things from here on out."

Pyune, her face close to Paula's, separated by only the thin window glass, gathered what little patience she had for the redhead. "I'm here for Wiley, 'case he needs me."

Paula blinked a few times, snow flakes on her lashes. "Pyune, honey, I took your advice to heart. I've been at the church praying to God for two hours, and He told me to come here and wait — because Wiley would be needing me."

"You don't say." Pyune looked across the clearing, to the fire that Joe had blazing high into the darkening sky. When she turned back to Paula, her voice was strong, confident, and clear. "I do believe we have the same God, and that same God done told me it would be my name that Wiley would be calling when he comes up from the bottom of that mountain. That's Pyune: P – Y – U – N – E."

~~~ ~~~

Chapter 47

The mountainside was slick, its crevices filled with snow, ice covering the rocks that jutted outward and caught the wet air. Thirty feet from the truck, the pastor stopped to catch his breath. He looked down at the calm whiteness that covered the vehicle and the surrounding area. It was serene, the quietness almost holy. The truck rested, cocoonlike, as though it were meant to be there; perhaps meant to shelter a living thing, much like the artificial reefs in the ocean. He could imagine a raccoon sneaking inside and concealing itself in the glove box, under a seat or under the hood. He pressed onward.

Now less than 20 feet away, he called out, "Wiley. Frank." Nothing. The only movement, the subtle drifting of wet snowflakes that found the surface of the truck with such silence that William thought it heavenly; the snow, however, encasing the truck as if it were a tomb.

There was no bottom to reach, no real ground to claim that lay beyond the truck. The angle of the ledge at the point of impact was less than what they'd come down, but not much. They could stand, but barely. The truck sat wedged between two large birch trees and several jutting rocks — the only things that kept it and its passengers from continuing to race down a path into nothingness.

Balancing on the slight grade, they kept their ropes attached to their waists and each grasped a small tree nearby for added support as they made it the last few feet to the truck. "Did you bring a flashlight?" the pastor asked Merle, with both men panting hard.

"Yeah." Merle reached in his small backpack and handed it to the pastor, who turned it on. The snow had blown in drifts across the doors and windows. The windshield had exploded on impact and left a gaping hole. He went to the driver's side, brushed the snow from the edge of the open area, and shined the flashlight inside. Sitting calmly in the driver's set, his nose bloody, a gash across his forehead, Wiley stared into the light. A slight smile creased his pale face, and that was all Pastor Johnson needed to know. Wiley Hanson was alive!

"Take a gander," the reverend said to Merle. "Wiley's looking mighty good over here." But when he moved the light to the passenger side, the sudden euphoria ended. The seat was empty.

~~~ ~~~

Chapter 48

Merle walked up as far as he could without assistance and yelled to the men at the top that Wiley was alive, and they were still looking for Frank. In the meantime, the pastor set about to figure out a way to extricate Wiley. A tree sat squarely against the driver's door. The passenger-side door was also wedged against the trunk of a large tree. The two trees were like a harness, the truck lodged securely in place, its door immovable.

"You see any sign of Frank?" the pastor asked Merle as soon as he returned.

"Gimme the flashlight for a minute," Merle said.

The pastor passed it to him, and he shined the light around the immediate area and then to the end of the cliff, which wasn't ten feet away. Its beam reflected off a countless number of tiny shards of glass scattered across the snow, which for whatever reason fresh downfall hadn't covered. A detached fender lay crumpled a few feet from the truck. A short while later, Merle hollered, "No sign of Frank. No footprints, no nothin'."

He moved the beam to the front of the truck, through the hole where the windshield had been, to see Wiley watching him. Merle grinned. "Hey, cousin. Reckon you'd like to get outta this here truck and back up the mountain?"

Wiley nodded. "That'd be mighty nice of you . . . whoever you are."

The pastor said, "I'm going to crawl through the front and

see what we have here. Just be sure to hold that flashlight on me so I can see what I'm doing."

The truck's front end was two feet off the ground, as if it belonged there. The pastor placed his boot on the jagged metal of the truck frame and hoisted himself up, grabbing the edge of the rooftop and pulling himself halfway inside the cab.

"Well, Wiley, my friend, looks like you're in quite a pickle here."

"Who are you?" Wiley squinted and licked his lips as he looked into the black face. The blood from the gash on his fore-head had run across his cheek and into his beard. His right eye was swollen shut. Blood smeared his nostrils.

"It's me, William Johnson, the pastor." He reached his hand behind him. "Merle, hand me that flashlight."

The preacher shined the beam on his hand and asked, "How many fingers am I holding up?" He held out four fingers, inches away from Wiley.

"I ain't seein' nothin'." Wiley coughed and grimaced.

"What's your name?" He placed his hand on Wiley's shoulder.

Wiley gave a half-hearted grin. "Well, you called me Wiley, so I reckon my name is Wiley."

"Wiley what? And where do you live?"

"Just Wiley. And I live with the bears."

The pastor leaned back and looked around the cab. They would have to pull Wiley through the hole in the windshield and carry him up the mountain. Harness him somehow.

"Wiley, where's Frank?"

Wiley wrinkled his brow. "Frank?"

"Yes, Frank. You two went up the mountain. To Brasstown Bald."

Wiley closed his one good eye, opened it, stared out the broken windshield, said, "Heck if I know."

~~~ ~~~

Chapter 49

The jet-black night came quickly. One moment there was a dull light on the horizon to the west of them; then, as though a blackout shade had been pulled, all light disappeared and a winter darkness fell across the mountainside. The temperature plummeted along with it. Bitter cold grabbed and held onto everything it touched: the trees, the rocks, the humans working on the mountainside to save Wiley Hanson and Frank Carberry.

The pastor gently nudged Wiley. "Your cousin Merle and I are going to get you out of this truck and haul you up the mountain."

"Who's Merle?" Wiley turned his head and looked over Pastor Johnson's shoulder. "That ugly feller over there?"

Merle leaned into the cab. "You call me ugly one more time, I'll leave you on the side of this mountain for good."

Wiley grinned and mumbled softly through swollen lips, "Will y'all please get me off this mountain? I'm gettin' really cold."

The steering wheel seemed undamaged, Wiley's chest held away from it by his seat belt. Because of Wiley's long legs, the seat had already been extended to its fullest, allowing the precious room necessary to maneuver him free of the cab.

The pastor said, "Wiley, I'm going to place my arms around you and pull you over a bit. Think you can put your arms around my neck?"

"I'll try." Wiley closed his eye again.

"Okay. Hold on tight." The pastor placed his hands on Wiley's back and pulled him forward. "Go ahead and put your arms around my neck."

His eye still closed, Wiley did as he was told. "I'm holding on as tight as I can." And, he was, clasping his hands together and squeezing.

"Here we go." Pastor Johnson pulled Wiley's body onto the passenger side of the cab and reached down to move his legs.

Wiley hollered, a dying pig kind of scream, adding a somber, "Take it easy."

"Sorry. We're almost out of here." The pastor backed out of the cab and onto the slanted hood of the truck, holding onto the window frame.

Merle leaned in. "You doing all right, cousin?" No answer from Wiley. "Wiley! You okay?" He reached out his hand and took Wiley's and squeezed it.

Wiley opened his eye. "Yep, doing just fine 'cept I can't feel a dang thing in my legs."

~~~ ~~~

Chapter 50

O n the edge of the mountain, Doyce Conley watched the sweeping beam of the powerful flashlight from 200 feet below. Behind him, the flames of the fire captured big wet snowflakes and sizzled them into nothing, while anxious men waited nearby and talked in quiet voices about the treacherous switchbacks on the mountain and the sudden drop-offs into empty space.

Down below, William Johnson looked up toward the fringe of firelight shining above the ridge. "Doyce, can you hear me?" he yelled.

"I hear you, preacher."

"Can somebody throw us another rope?"

"Is 50 feet enough?"

"That should do it."

Doyce ran to his truck and pulled out his rope. From the edge of the drop-off, he threw the coiled rope as far as he could. With the men standing next to him and shining their lights below, he watched nervously as Merle made it up the ledge to where the rope had caught on a rock.

"What's going on?" Doyce hollered down.

"Got to make a harness to haul Wiley up to the top." Merle reached for the rope, and after a couple of swipes was able to grab it. "Just stand by and be ready."

"What about Frank?"

"We ain't found Frank yet."

Merle half-slid down the grade until he reached the truck.

"Here you go, preacher," he said as he brushed the snow off his britches.

Pastor Johnson backed off the truck hood. He noticed Wiley watching him. "You sit tight. Going to make a harness to carry you up this mountain. Shouldn't take but a few minutes. Merle will stay with you."

He lowered himself to the ground and took the rope from Merle. "Keep him talking. It's important to keep him awake."

Merle nodded and pulled himself up to the hood of the truck and leaned into the cab. "Hey, cousin, you remember that time you shot granny's dog thinkin' it was a pig?"

Wiley Hanson's character was washed with a worn patina that heralded his stature as a man. He lay in the broken cab of his faithful blue truck, his body bleeding and in pain; yet, he felt he was a blessed man, a man who had discovered the secrets of life in his beloved mountains. If his days on Earth were to end here on the snowy mountainside, he would accept it. His heart unable to go on, he would fade away into the mountain mist and go to that place where rabbits danced and the clouds met the mountaintops and revealed the mysteries hidden there. He'd see it all, feel it all, floating above and grinning like a fool.

"Wiley!" Merle touched the mountain man's shoulder. "Wiley, what are you mumbling about?"

Wiley kept his eye closed and licked his lips. "Yeah, I do remember shootin' granny's dog. Felt real bad about that too. Poor ol' granny loved that dog."

"You ever tell her it was you who kilt it?"

Wiley opened his eyes. "No, cousin, I told her it was you who done it."

The pastor uncoiled the rope and looped it together into a suitable harness. Then he tied off sections secure enough to pull Wiley up the mountain. He prayed the climb would be smooth and his injured friend would survive it. But, first, they had to get him out of the truck.

He laid the harness out on a smooth area near the truck. "Ready?" he asked Merle.

Merle backed out of the cab. "I'm smaller than you. How about I climb into the cab as far as I can and maneuver Wiley up to the hood?"

"That's a good idea." The pastor pulled himself up to the hood of the truck and wiped as much snow away as he could while Merle crawled farther inside the cab.

"Okay, cousin. I'm gonna slide you this way and lean you forward so the preacher can pull you out of the cab. Ready?"

Wiley didn't answer.

"Hey, Wiley. Come on, let's get out of here." He patted him gently on the cheek.

Wiley didn't move.

Merle leaned next to Wiley's ear. "Wiley, can you hear me?"

Wiley opened his eyes. "Of course I can hear you. I was just thinkin'. I feel real bad 'cause I told granny you killed her dog. So, if I don't make it through all this, and I get to heaven, I'll be sure to tell her the truth."

~~~ ~~~

Chapter 51

Cold had gripped the mountainside, not in a whisper but in a loud, howling breath that hunted down and devoured every morsel of warmth from everything it touched. The pastor braced himself on the hood of the truck and waited for Merle to lift Wiley from the cab to the hood. He felt himself shivering and looked up toward the ridge. A rim of firelight gleamed orange on the ridge top, a beacon that drew them to warmth and safety. But getting Wiley to the top would not be easy.

Wiley moaned. "Here you go, Wiley." Pastor Johnson reached out and placed his hands under Wiley's arms and gently pulled him forward. "You're doing great, my friend." He slid off the hood and to the ground and clasped Wiley to his chest and held him there until Merle crawled out of the cab.

"Got him," the pastor said while Merle gently moved Wiley's legs. Working quickly, they adjusted the ropes around his body and created a sling for his arms and legs to fit through, much the same as a baby's swing.

The two men grabbed the harness from each side, Wiley hanging like a rag doll between them. "You okay?" Merle asked.

Wiley grunted. "Hell, no, I ain't okay. You got my love spuds all tangled in the rope."

"Well, I'll be danged if I'm rearranging them," said Merle.

Wiley hollered, mad, and ready to fight. "All I'm asking you to do is loosen this getup a little."

"We can do that," the pastor said and adjusted the rope that made the diaper-like harness looser at the bottom. "That better?"

"A whole heap better." He looked at his rescuers. "In case ya'll don't know it, them love spuds is quite important."

~~~

Rock by rock, tree by tree, the pastor and Merle, with Wiley between them, ascended the mountain, the fire at the top becoming brighter, and the men who leaned over the edge reaching out with cold hands and yelling encouragement: "That's it. Keep a comin'. Keep a comin'."

Doyce angled himself down the grade several yards, as did Harley, both being secured by ropes that Joe Thomas held in his paw-like hands.

Dr. Casteel hovered nearby, a full syringe of pain killer waiting. He'd treated many mountain injuries, as well as attended many mountain deaths. He'd heard Wiley's loud complaining as they neared the top: "For Pete's sake, Merle, I'm not a sack of potatoes. Take it easy." But to the doctor these were sweet words; Wiley was alive.

The men who were gathered at the top laughed heartily. Doyce said, "You tell him, Wiley. You get up here, boy. Dr. Casteel wants to take a good look at you."

Only a few yards away, Wiley looked up at his shivering welcoming committee. "I don't want no shot, Doc. Just give me a little nip of Johnny Walker and I'll be just fine."

Dr. Casteel chuckled. "All in good time. All in good time.

The moment they reached the top, a dozen outreached hands laid Wiley on a thick blanket just spread out on the ground. Dr. Casteel slipped a needle into Wiley's arm and began a quick check of his injuries.

"This gash needs stitches." He ran his hands down Wiley's arms, across his chest, down his legs. "Where's all your pain, Wiley."

"My pain? I don't have a lick of pain now that them two ruffians over there have done let me loose."

Dr. Casteel looked up at the pastor and Merle and smiled. "What did he complain about when you found him?"

Pastor Johnson said, "He was a little disoriented at first, but he seemed to come around."

"What else?" Dr. Casteel looked into Wiley's eyes with his

special light, carefully pulling up the lid on the one swollen shut."

"Said his legs felt funny," Merle said.

"Hmmmm." Dr. Casteel reached into his bag and pulled out a small instrument. "Pull off one of his boots."

"Oh, sure, doc. Freezing out and you want me barefooted?" Wiley rolled his good eye.

"Wiley, you're the worst patient I've ever treated." Dr. Casteel laughed and jabbed a large needle into the bottom of Wiley's foot.

"Holy shit!" Wiley hollered. "What the hell are you a doin', pokin' me like that?"

Dr. Casteel looked up at everyone and smiled. "Wiley's going to be fine. Let's load him up and get him down the mountain to Blairsville. He'll just need some X-rays and a few stitches."

~~~

Farther down the logging road, Adela and Pyune continued sitting in Harley's truck and watched the ridgeline. Their vigil had been constant, their eyes ever-watching as they waited.

"They've got them. Let's go." Pyune opened the truck door, Adela right behind her, hurrying through the snow. Behind them, a screeching Paula pushed her way forward. "I'm coming, Wiley." She shoved Pyune aside and passed her at a dead run, her witchy red hair flying, her legs pumping like a threshing machine.

Pyune watched Paula's behind bounce along as she ploughed through the deep snow, calling out, "Wileeeeee. Wileeeeee." Pyune looked up at Adela. "If we're lucky, she'll run right past Wiley and over the edge of the mountain." Adela reached out and pulled Pyune to her feet.

At the campsite, Wiley had been loaded into the back of Doyce's truck. Wiley's blood pressure and heart rate were normal — he was a mountain man.

"Wileeeeee." Paula rushed up to the side of the truck. "Oh, dear Lord, Wiley. I'm so glad to see you." Paula reached inside and caressed Wiley's cheek. "I've been praying for you."

Wiley half-smiled. "Hey, Paula, you seen Pyune?"

~~~ ~~~

Chapter 52

Adela felt the fear long before she reached the makeshift campsite. It grabbed her like a vise and held on and squeezed until she could hardly breathe. *Frank. Where was Frank?* She saw Doyce and Harley. Saw the preacher and Merle. Saw Dr. Casteel and Joe Thomas. When she reached the edge of the camp, silence smothered her. She saw their faces, their lack of eye contact. "Tell me," she said, looking at everyone. "Pastor Johnson, you can tell me. It's okay." She felt her throat tighten and pushed down the scream that waited there.

He walked slowly to her. "Adela, we're not sure about Frank." He glanced at Wiley. "He wasn't in the truck with Wiley. We looked all around the area but didn't see a thing. Wiley's having trouble remembering everything."

"What do you mean, he wasn't in the truck?" Her gaze fell on Wiley.

The pastor reached out and touched her shoulder. "The windshield popped out, so it's possible Frank went through it. But we searched around the truck and couldn't find anything. He might have been tossed into the woods and wandered off. We just don't know. What I can tell you, there was no blood on the ground, so that's a good sign. We'll wait until daylight and then go back down and find him."

"Wait until daylight! We can't wait — it's supposed to get into the low 'teens' tonight! He'll freeze to death!" She quieted down as Doyce's truck carrying Wiley lumbered down the road. She followed it with her eyes until the taillights could no longer be seen. Adela spun to face the preacher. "Wild animals will find him before we do."

"Adela, please believe me, we'll find Frank. But it's too dangerous for us to go searching at night. We just don't have the manpower or equipment. I promise we'll be here at first light and go back down the mountain."

"Then it will be too late, preacher."

~~~ ~~~

Chapter 53

The ride down the mountain was treacherous and slow. Wiley slept, leaning on Pyune's shoulder. He mumbled, whimpered, and jerked his body until Pyune reached over and smoothed his face.

She whispered to him, "After we get back from the hospital, I'm gonna make you a lemon pudding cake. Just for you. I'll give you a big ol' spoon and you can eat it all by yourself. You won't have to share it with nobody."

She looked at his sleeping face. "You know you have to be mighty special for me to make that cake any day but Tuesday." She pulled him closer, the warmth from her body next to him like one of her grandma's quilts. *Her Wiley. Yes, he was her Wiley.*

At the Union County Hospital, the emergency room staff was small but efficient. The physician on duty, Dr. Christoph Meyer, ordered X-rays and prodded and poked and then chatted with Dr. Casteel about deer hunting while he stitched up Wiley's forehead. A two-inch gash near his hairline required sixteen tight stitches. Wiley murmured sleepily to the doctor to do a good job as he was due to pose in Playgirl magazine at any moment and didn't want any scars. Then he fell back to sleep, his eyelids, even the bad one, fluttering.

In the darkroom, numerous X-rays hung from clips. "What's that film look like?" Dr. Casteel said over Dr. Meyer's shoulder.

"Amazing," Dr. Meyer said. "Not one thing broken. And you

say his truck went over the mountain and landed about sev-
enty-five yards away?"

"That's right. I think the truck was slowed along the way as
it grazed a few trees. Landed between two of them and wedged
itself there." He sighed. "Coulda ended up a lot worse."

"Look here." Dr. Meyer pointed to Wiley's chest. "Old frac-
tures here. Three ribs broken at one time."

Dr. Casteel chuckled. "Oh, yes, I remember those breaks.
Wiley came to me some years back. Said he fell out of a tree.
Wasn't much I could do but tape him up good. I asked how he
fell, and he said he actually jumped out of the tree. Said he
climbed up the tree to wait for a deer. When he got good and
settled on a branch, he looked up and a bear was sitting at the
top, watching him. That's when he jumped."

Each doctor shook his head and laughed. "I can't find one
thing that alarms me with his CAT scan either," said Dr.
Meyer. "He'll be sore for a while, but that's about it. Twenty-
four hours of observation would be good, though. Let's go tell
him the good news."

~~~

Wiley slept in his bed in the hospital, Pyune by his side,
holding his hand and not once letting go. The blood from his
wounds had been cleaned away and he looked rather angelic as
he breathed softly, a soft putter at the end of each breath. In a
short while, without opening his eyes, he asked. "What time is
it?"

"Around midnight."

"I got to go." He sat up, grimacing a little, and swung his
legs over the edge of the bed. "Get my clothes for me."

"What? You know very well the doctor will not release you."

"I'm ready to go. Are Doyce and Harley in the waiting
room?"

"I believe so, but you're not going anywhere."

"Heck if that's so. Help me put my socks on."

Pyune didn't move. "I'm not helping you do nothing. Not
until Dr. Meyer says it's okay."

"We'll see about that. Now, help me with my clothes."

Pyune poked her head out the door. At the nurse's station,
Dr. Meyer and Dr. Casteel were huddled over coffee and

donuts. She ran up to them. "Dr. Meyer, Wiley wants to leave."

Dr. Meyer walked with Pyune to Wiley's room. He grinned at her and said, "So he wants to leave? That's no surprise. I don't have a problem with that as long as he takes it easy for a day or two. He's one tough bird."

Pyune leaned through the doorway. "You hear that, Wiley."

"I heard it. Now, help me with my dang socks. See you, Dr. Meyer." And the mountain man was whole once more as he slipped on his socks, his jeans, his plaid wool shirt with the torn pocket, his down-filled jacket, and his favorite wool hat that had been chewed on by his old hunting dog. He rejoiced as he thanked both doctors, and especially Dr. Casteel. Then he walked down the long hospital corridor to the waiting room where he found his good friends Doyce and Harley. They would understand his need to go home.

~~~

The ride back to Ivy Log was quiet except for Doyce's gentle humming and half-singing every verse of "Do Lord," his voice a deep rumble, the notes soothing. *I've got a home in glory land that outshines the sun . . . .* Wiley was going home. But, where was home?

"I reckon I want to go to The Boardinghouse, if that's all right with y'all," Wiley said out of the blue, tapping his fingers as Doyce was now singing "Do Lord" in full voice.

Doyce grinned and looked into the rear passenger section of his truck, in which Wiley was leaned way over and resting his head on Pyune's lap. Doyce asked Pyune, "You got any pie left over?"

"Uh, huh. And cake. Might have some cold biscuits too. Ham also."

"I say let's all go to The Boardinghouse," said Doyce.

From the back seat, Wiley came upright in one motion. "Hold it!"

"What's wrong?" Pyune asked, placing both hands on his arms.

"Frank? Where's Frank?"

~~~ ~~~

Chapter 54

Doyce found Wiley's face in the rearview mirror and stared into the swollen eyes. "That's what we all want to know."

Wiley jerked his shoulders a couple of times and said, "I . . . I can't remember. Seems like we went up to the summit of The Bald. Then . . . ."

It was to be a bachelor party — just Wiley and Frank. One last hike as a single man, Wiley had said. They'd go up to Brasstown Bald despite the snow, despite the cold. They'd look out from the summit and listen to the song of the birch trees and take in the breathtaking view of the valley below.

Wiley closed his eyes and saw Frank standing in the falling snow, looking back down the mountain. "We'd better head back. Adela's gonna be worrying about me." He turned away and started back down the trail.

"Hold up, Frank. Let's scratch the date on this rock. It'll just take a minute."

Frank waited as Wiley leaned his rifle on a rock, pulled his pocketknife and scratched out "*12/17/13 Frank Carberry was a free man.*" Wiley said when finished, "Ah, that'll be there forever. Let's go."

The men left the summit and trudged down the trail to Wiley's truck. They'd be eating Pyune's hot grits at The Boardinghouse in less than an hour.

~~~

Doyce's truck rounded the last curve on the ridge. Ivy Log lay below them, the lights of the towering Christmas spruce piercing the midnight sky. Main Street sat deserted except for Vallie Thomas's big yellow cat, Heathrow, who sat statuelike on the brick ledge of Drake's Hardware. Like a port in a storm, The Boardinghouse chimney rose high, smoke drifting from the stack and mixing with the falling snow.

The truck crawled along Main Street, every store window lighted with Christmas displays. The town-square's Christmas music played "Little Drummer Boy," the notes lifting above the rooftops.

"Hey!" Doyce said and pointed. "Looks like somebody's beat us to them biscuits." Lights shone in the restaurant windows and outside on Main Street, where Dr. Casteel's car was parked against the curb, along with several others.

"Looks like most everybody in town's here," Wiley said.

The Boardinghouse had indeed become the gathering place for those who had been on top of the mountain and participated in Wiley's rescue. Together, everyone would make plans to go back up the mountain to search for Frank Carberry.

Doyce pulled around back and parked his truck next to Calvin's. He said to Wiley, "Let me get one of the boys and we'll help you inside."

"I reckon I can manage by myself." He reached out and took Pyune's hand. He saw concern in her face. "I'm fine. I got the full feelin' back in my legs. Just let me drink something hot. Eat a little bit." He hung his head for a moment but righted himself. "We gotta find Frank."

~~~

The Boardinghouse kitchen hummed with the sound of frying bacon and the low voices of men who stood around drinking coffee and warming their bodies. The pastor moved a frying pan over the fire, a fork in his hand and a dishtowel tucked in his pocket. "Thank goodness you're here, Pyune. Joe and Merle were starving and — "

"You 'bout to burn this bacon, preacher." Pyune took the fork from his hand and turned down the burner. She swatted at him. "Now you get out of my kitchen and let me do the cooking."

"I started a pot of water for the grits. What else can I do?"

"Oh, you've done enough," she said, dumping grits into the

pot of water.

"Come sit down, preacher," Doyce said. "Just leave everything to Pyune."

"Dr. Casteel," Pyune called over her shoulder. "Please take a look at Wiley just one more time."

Dr. Casteel leaned over the battered man who had survived a fall down the mountain. "Wiley, you are a sight, that's for sure." He moved closer and studied his face. "You'll have some swelling in that eye for a few days. It'll turn black and blue for sure."

"Don't worry about me," Wiley said, his Roy Rogers and Trigger cup in his hand as he wobbled his way to a seat amidst his friends Doyce, Calvin, Harley, Joe and cousin Merle. "Would somebody please find me some coffee? I done fell off a mountain and I'm plum pitiful."

A moment later he held out the cup while Merle poured the coffee. Wiley noticed his hand shaking, and he felt a slight buzz in his head. Surviving the fall down the mountain had been a miracle. Now he wanted a miracle for his friend, Frank Carberry, who lay either dead or injured somewhere down the mountain. Wiley had every intention of returning to the mountaintop in a few hours and looking for him.

He sipped his coffee and wondered how he'd get away from Pyune and Dr. Casteel, both of whom were watching him and his puffy, closed right eye. *Hell, ain't they ever seen a black eye before?*

He cleared his throat. "Listen here, fellas, as soon as it's daylight, we gotta get back up that mountain. I got a mind to go now, but we couldn't do much good in the dark." He looked at his watch. "It's one-thirty, so we got some time to do some planning and maybe get a little sleep."

Calvin said, "That's right. You reckon we ought to call in a rescue team from somewhere?" Calvin looked at each of the men. "There's no telling what we're up against. If it keeps snowing, that's gonna hinder us for sure."

"I don't care if the blizzard of the century hits," said Wiley, now swigging his coffee. "I'm going up the mountain. I was thinking of gettin' Obed to bring his dogs. Those are good tracking dogs from what I hear."

Harley, ever the pessimist, said, "Obed said they done run

away. And how they gonna track in this weather, anyways?" He shook his head. "Let's be smart about this. The weather is stacked up against us. And that dang drop off ain't no picnic. The preacher and Merle will swear to that."

Pastor Johnson said, "I will vouch for that. But, we have to go, and as I've thought about it more, I think we need to get some food in us and head back right away. Frank's likely injured, and if not he's certainly freezing." He paused and looked around the room. "I'm not so sure he can survive until morning."

"Don't see how he could," Doyce said, sighing loudly. "Even if his injuries ain't life-threatenin', no man's tough enough for those temperatures. What is it out there? Eighteen, nineteen degrees?" He blew hot steam away from his coffee cup. "Why, I bet ol' Frank don't even have matches to start a fire."

"Course not," Wiley said, his mind beginning to drift off. A memory of something tugged at him, but he couldn't quite pull it up. "Frank ain't no mountain man — that's why we got to get out there real quick, like the preacher says. Maybe we should go back up the mountain now. Build a big fire just in case he's near enough to see it."

"That's not a bad idea," said the pastor. "Why don't we head back up there and do just that." He looked around at the many faces, and to a man what he saw projected the same urgency. The men began nodding and mumbling their agreement.

"I'm ready," said Wiley loudly as soon as he wolfed down what Pyune had placed in front of him.

"Heck if that's so," said Pyune from across the kitchen. "You having trouble remembering what Dr. Meyer said?"

Wiley squinted at Pyune with his one good eye. "If you'll feed me just a little more hot grits, I believe I'll be like new."

"Don't change the subject. You aren't going back up the mountain."

Don't tangle with Pyune. She'd lock me in a closet before she'd let me go back up the mountain.

From the end of the counter, Harley, his face grim, shook his head. "We're just fooling ourselves, folks. They's no way Frank's gonna come out of this alive. We can go, but we'll be huntin' a dead man."

No one moved. The quiet of the room simmered and brewed doubt along with it. Harley was right — it had taken courage to speak the hurtful words, to admit that no amount of hope would allow a man to survive a night of subfreezing temperatures during a brutal Appalachian storm. Heck, they might not even be able to make it back up the mountain.

Wiley caught Pyune's eye. "Know where Adela is? We need to be with her."

"She's over at the parsonage, resting for a while. Said she'd be back here in an hour or so."

"What do you think about Frank surviving a night on that mountain?" Wiley asked Dr. Casteel. "Is it possible?"

Dr. Washington Casteel was a man of few words, but when he spoke one could count on truth and simplicity. He had been Ivy Log's resident doctor going on four decades, delivering babies, setting broken arms and holding the hand of countless folks who said goodbye to the mountains one final time. He was among lifelong friends, folks he could never replace or lie to. His words were soft but clear: "A miracle is possible."

"Amen," said the Reverend William Johnson. He grinned at the men who brooded and perhaps thought about miracles. "Why, old Frank could walk through that door at any moment."

As though pushed by the winds of a devil of a storm, the back kitchen door flew open and Frank Carberry burst into the room, his face red from cold, his eyes with fire in them. He glared at Wiley.

"Wiley Hanson, I been looking everywhere for you. Where the hell you been?"

~~~ ~~~

Chapter 55

Wiley, his eyes wide and his mouth hanging open, rose from his chair and gawked at Frank. "Well I'll be danged. Now I remember."

Frank growled his way across the room. "It's a little late for that, isn't it? I spent most all night waiting on you to find your rifle. That's the last I saw of you." He paused, his head swiveling around the room at all the questioning faces. "What's going on?" He saw the bandage on Wiley's forehead and his swollen eye. "You been in an accident or something?"

"Lot's happened since I saw you last," Wiley said. "Come sit down and warm your bones."

"Where have you been?" Dr. Casteel asked Frank as he thrust a cup into his waiting hand and then filled it with coffee.

Frank took a deep drink and a deeper breath. "I've been at Tom Keeling's half the night waiting on Wiley. He dropped me off to visit with Tom while he went back up the mountain to get his rifle. About dark, Tom and I decided he got stuck on the mountain and went up looking for him. Couldn't find him anywhere."

Someone laughed and Frank glared in the direction of where the noise had come from. He continued, "We decided we'd better come into town and alert someone, but we couldn't find a soul. We were headed back up the mountain when we saw all the cars parked over here. Frank pulled out a chair. "Would somebody please tell me what's going on?"

"It's like this, Frank," said Wiley, "I feel real bad that I forgot I dropped you at Tom's, and I don't even remember leaving my rifle up at the Bald or going back for it." He shifted in his chair. "I don't even remember going over the side of the mountain."

"The side of the mountain?" Frank leaned forward. "You went off the side of the mountain? Where?"

"Don't know exactly were, only that I did. But, I'm okay. I was knocked unconscious for a while and couldn't remember a dang thing when the preacher and Merle found me." He grinned a little at Frank. "Worst thing is, I forgot about you."

Doyce said, "He went off somewheres around Jack's Knob Trail."

"Ah, heck. Tom and I looked everywhere but there." He gave Wiley the once over. You look pretty beat up, you okay?"

"Oh, yeah. I'm fine. The fellas took me over to Blairsville and the doctor patched me up. Nothing serious."

He caught the preacher's eye. "It was the preacher and my cousin Merle who went down the mountain to get me." He paused and shook his head. "My old blue truck's done smashed all to heck."

Pyune came over and put her hand on Frank's arm. "Adela is over at the parsonage resting. She went up there with the men. She's a wreck, so you need to quit all this talkin' and go to her. She'll be real glad to see you."

"Oh, my God. Did Adela think I went over the side of the mountain with Wiley?"

"'fraid so, Frank. Like I said, she'll be glad to see you."

~~~ ~~~

Chapter 56

M iracles are as constant as sunrises and as prevailing as stars in the universe, although sometimes hidden like a green tree frog in a honeysuckle vine. Had Frank been in Wiley's truck when it careened down the mountain, perhaps Ivy Log's new preacher would be presiding over his funeral and Ivy Log grieving over its loss. The subject of miracles was fixed in Pastor Johnson's mind, and one day soon he would preach about it.

~~~

Frank left the warmth of The Boardinghouse and walked under a snowy sky to the parsonage, his hands stuffed in his pockets, a dry wool hat pulled over his head and ears. As always, the glow of a lamp filled the front window as well as the lighted Star of Bethlehem. Delilah set on the sill like a sculpture, watching Frank step onto the portico. Frank eased the door open.

"Adela?"

Stretched out on the couch with a blanket and pillow, Adela murmured, "Frank?"

"It's me, Adela. Let's go home."

The blanket flew from the couch, along with the pillow, Adela flying into Frank's arms. He held her, felt her tremble, wiped away her rapidly flowing tears. "It's okay, my love. Everything's all right. I'll explain what happened. Heck, it's all Wiley's fault."

~~~ ~~~

Chapter 57

Dellwood Avenue lay undisturbed, its houses dark underneath winter-white rooftops. Occasionally, smoke coughed from a chimney and hovered in the wet air. In the two-story brick house with the gabled roof, Paula sat in the dark and waited for daylight. Her fingers were intertwined tightly in her lap while her foot tapped endlessly on the carpet. She peered at the hands of her grandfather clock, as though its laboring movements were paramount to her very existence. Her thoughts came fast and furious, like jackrabbits on the run from the wide scatter of shotgun pellets.

If it weren't for Pyune, Wiley Hanson would be in her upstairs guest room right now, making love to her, perhaps telling her he loved her. Pyune had snared him. Had taken him to the smokehouse behind The Boardinghouse and put a spell on him. But her biscuits and lemon pudding cake were nothing compared to Paula's lithe body and sensual charm, a combination the mountain man couldn't resist.

Paula leaned forward in her chair and placed her face in her hands, her thoughts streaming with hatred for Pyune Murphy. Then, as if someone had entered the room and spoken to her, she lifted her head. *What? No, I can't do that. No, I won't do that. That's impossible.*

She dragged herself up the stairs to her bed. And when sleep finally came, fitful though it was, her dreams were of Wiley.

~~~ ~~~

Chapter 58

Six weary men left The Boardinghouse in the wee hours of Sunday morning. Before they left, they helped Pyune clean the kitchen, even washing greens for Sunday's dinner and leaving twice the money for the generous helpings of grits, bacon, coffee and pie. Their faces were tired but happy. Wiley Hanson had been rescued off the mountain to hunt bear again, to fish its streams, and to talk to the mountain when he'd had too much of Johnny Walker's company.

And their friend, Frank Carberry — as if he were a mirage — had appeared in The Boardinghouse kitchen, providing them all with enormous relief as well as a good laugh. Every man would have risked his life to go back up the mountain to find him, there was no doubt about that — and Frank knew it well. But, now, everyone could rest.

Pyune took off her apron and hung it on a hook by the stove. He smiled at her. "Tired, ain't you?"

"Yes. But I'm happy."

"Me too," he said. He reached out his hand. "Come here." His one good eye twinkled, the other closed and swollen, already a soft yellow and blue to match his plaid shirt.

Pyune walked to the table where Wiley sat. She noticed a little blood on the bandage covering his stitched forehead. "My goodness, I might need to change that bandage."

He pulled her into his lap and laid his head on her shoulder. "What would you have done if I had died on that mountain?"

Pyune placed her arms around his neck. "I don't know." She tried to keep it from happening, but her eyes became glassy. "I just know it would have been the saddest day of my life."

"That right?"

She nodded.

"I never want to leave you, Pyune."

She leaned back and looked at him. "We've been together a long time, haven't we?" She ran her fingers along his cheek, caught them in his beard and rested them there. "You ready for bed?"

He blinked. "Here?"

"Of course, here." She laughed. "How else am I going to keep an eye on you?"

~~~

They crawled under her heavy quilts, with Pyune careful of Wiley's battered body and bandaged head. Her feet were ice cold and he yelped when she touched him. "Would you go get some socks on? I fell down a mountain and you're tryin' to freeze me to death."

She left and came back to bed. "That better?" she asked, rubbing his thigh with her foot, a wool sock on it.

He laughed and had to gently push her inquisitive toes away. The sound of the old creaking house soon lulled him into a peaceful place. "Pyune, you know something I never did ask you?"

"What?" she murmured.

"Do you got a middle name? All I know is Pyune."

"Uh, huh."

"Well, what is it?"

She giggled. "Eversweet."

"Eversweet?"

"Uh, huh."

"Pyune Eversweet Murphy. Now, ain't that somethin'."

"Uh, huh."

They went to sleep, her back to him, his arm around her, holding her like he'd never let her go.

~~~ ~~~

Chapter 59

The march to the parsonage from her house on Dellwood took Paula only seven minutes. On Main Street, she passed Patton Drugs and Drake's Hardware, without looking through the windows. No matter, it was Sunday and stores were closed. She rounded the corner at Church Street and shuddered when she saw the fallen steeple resting on William Johnson's crushed car, both covered with fresh snow. She had made a phone call to the insurance company and told them of the freak wind that blew the steeple off the rooftop. She didn't mention where it landed. A claims adjuster would arrive from Atlanta in a couple of days.

Earlier, she had called Doyce to find out about Wiley and Frank. He gave her all the details. She listened patiently, said "thank you" and hung up.

She stepped onto the porch and bristled when she spotted the black cat in the parsonage window. She hated cats, especially black ones. She planned to ask the pastor to keep the cat outside. Of course, cat or no cat, he'd be gone the day after Christmas.

Before she could knock, the door opened and a smiling William Johnson spread his arms wide. "Good morning, Ms. Jennings. What a delight to see you."

She brushed him aside. This was business; all business. "I'm here to discuss . . . the situation. Do you have a few moments?"

"Of course. Come in and sit down."

"Don't get too cozy here, Mr. Johnson. This is your temporary home, you know."

"How well I know, Ms. Jennings." He cocked his head. "What is it you would like to discuss?"

Paula sat in a chair near the fireplace and noticed a small fire. The wood that burned was probably delivered by Wiley. Wiley had yet to deliver wood to her, which she had requested weeks ago. She turned back to the pastor, her expression one of disdain.

"Mr. Johnson, I want to reiterate my position regarding your employment." Her lips turned up in scorn, not an inkling of kindness in her eyes. "Or, shall I say my position regarding your *unemployment*." She wanted to laugh out loud.

She shifted in her chair. "It is with the utmost generosity that the Church of Ivy log is allowing you to stay in the parsonage as its interim pastor until the day after Christmas, at which time, you will exit the premises. Are we clear on that?"

"Perfectly clear." The pastor seemed to stall a moment in his thoughts. "Is that a unanimous decision of the church board, Ms. Jennings?"

Paula jerked. Nervous, she reached up and patted her hair. She lied, saying, "By all means."

"I see." He leaned back and crossed his legs and waited.

"Since our church budget is small, we will be unable to provide compensation for the sermon on Christmas morning. Since we are not asking you to pay for staying in the parsonage, perhaps you'll consider our courtesy in this regard compensation enough."

The pastor uncrossed his legs and waited.

Paula picked at a thread on her jacket, looked around the room and then back at him. "About your car. A claims adjuster is due next week to assess the damage to the church as well as your vehicle."

He held her gaze and watched her clasp her hands together and open her eyes wide.

"Any questions?" she asked.

He chuckled. "Seems like you have thought of everything, Ms. Jennings."

"My efficiency is well known," she said, picking at the repellent thread again. "As is my faith in God's will." Her mouth was set in a prim line — the same mouth that opened wide on Sunday mornings and sang "Standing on the Promises" as if divinely inspired.

"I can see that your faith is quite strong." He held up a finger. "One thing though. I'd like to meet with the entire church board. Would you set that up for me, please? Or, if you'd like, I'll ask the board's secretary to do so." He paused. "At everyone's convenience, of course."

"A . . . a board meeting?"

"That's right. There are six members, including you, correct?"

She nodded. "I see no reason to schedule a board meeting, Mr. Johnson. Let's just call it a day." A smirk filled her face, extending her cheeks into pockets of contempt, leaving her eyes narrowed and cautious. "Or, for that matter, why don't you contact the Harvard Divinity School — I'm sure they can answer your questions."

"Since you mention it, I must tell you I've done just that. They're sending someone over next week to mediate on my behalf." He grinned. "I believe you know the person."

"Oh?" Paula found herself glued to her seat.

"His name is Sam Cobb."

~~~ ~~~

Chapter 60

The line of folks gathered at The Boardinghouse for Sunday lunch reached out the doors and onto the porch, where the crowd waited anxiously for news about Wiley's daring rescue. Folks were mesmerized by Merle and Joe's account of the truck flying off the mountain, across the tops of trees and rocks and coming to rest between two tall birch trees, hanging there like a butchered pig.

By the time Joe and Merle finished their story, the truck had been travelling at least 100-miles-an-hour when it sailed off the mountain and landed a half-mile away. But, not before shearing off a dozen tall trees and grazing the boulders at such a high rate of speed that sparks glinted off the rocks and could have started a fire had the ground not been covered in snow. Their story had no end to it, and it grew into a tale that would wander through the mountains for decades. Pecos Bill had nothing on Wiley Hanson — or the men who'd rescued him.

"Why, that truck was in a hundred pieces by the time it reached the bottom," Joe said, hunching his mammoth shoulders and squeezing his thumb and forefinger together. "There weren't but a little, biddy piece of truck left, and guess who was sitting inside jus' waiting for somebody to find him 'fore the coyotes did?" He looked around the table before he leaned forward and whispered, "Wiley Hanson."

A hush rushed from the crowd as they listened wide-eyed and breathless and waited for more.

"Yes, siree," said Merle. "There was our Wiley, all squashed inside that truck, bleedin', his blood beginning to freeze and then — "

"That's right," interrupted Joe. "Frostbite was a settin' in, for sure. And the worst part was, he didn't know nobody. Didn't know where he was. Didn't remember a dang thing about Frank." Joe made a worried face. "Hope Wiley's brain ain't been damaged none."

"Aw, heck no," said Merle. "By the time we got him to the hospital, he was fine as grandma's buttermilk clabber."

From the kitchen, Wiley eased into the room. He saw Merle and Joe, their hands waving in the air as they described the "great flight" off the mountain. Henry Patton sat nearby and laughed at the endless exaggerations. Dr. Casteel sat across from Joe, who was squeezed in between Haskel Drake and James Stephens. He looked for Doyce and Harley, but they were oddly absent.

Across the room, at Paula Jennings's table, the pastor sat with Pyune, his familiar plaid scarf hanging from the back of his chair.

"Hey, everybody," Wiley called out, stepping a few more feet into the room. The room quieted, even Merle and Joe stopped their bottomless chatter and looked up at Wiley.

Wiley's gaze roamed the room and landed on William Johnson. "In case y'all didn't know it, it was that man over there who shimmied down that mountain and found me and then hauled me back up." He pointed to the pastor. "Weren't for him and my cousin Merle, you'd be planning my funeral right about now.

The crowd murmured and folks smiled at the pastor as Wiley waited for everyone to quiet down. What Wiley said next didn't have the slightest bit of hillbilly twang to it, as there were no truncated words or "y'alls." Instead, he could have been speaking to his doctoral committee at Georgia Tech.

"William Johnson came to Ivy Log a stranger, but that didn't stop him from putting his life on the line for me. And, I'd like all of you to know how very grateful I am for him — and for his unfailing love of his fellow man." He cleared his throat. "He's got a lot more to do in this town. He's going to marry Frank and Adela on Saturday, then preach on Christmas morning."

The minister saw it coming, held his breath. Pyune felt it, too, and squirmed in her chair.

Wiley reached up and wiped his swollen eye. "There are some people around here who'd like to see William Johnson head back to Atlanta. I want all of you to know that I'm not one of them."

The pastor eased up from his chair and glanced over the crowd and then to Wiley. "Thank you for your kind words. I can't adequately tell you how much I appreciate them. But I'm positive you'd have done the same if it had been me on the side of that mountain."

Just as Wiley was about to walk up and shake the reverend's hand and pat his back until it was sore, the doors to The Boardinghouse opened and Paula Jennings rushed inside. Behind her, all five members of the church board lingered, each one staring aimlessly around the room. Paula, the fur collar of her coat framing her face, looked across the crowd. "Hello, everyone. I'm here to make an announcement."

~~~ ~~~

Chapter 61

The fake mole above Paula's left eyebrow had smeared, leaving a shadow the shape of Lucifer's pitchfork. She moved farther into the room, stopping only after she was certain she had everyone's attention.

A cryptic smile spread across her face, like Mona Lisa's. She said, "Since most of you are longtime members of the Church of Ivy Log, I thought The Boardinghouse would be a good place to let everyone know a new interim pastor has been chosen."

She reached into her handbag and with a flourish pulled out a small white bible. She held it to her chest, close to her heart, and said, "As president of the church board, I called a meeting a few hours ago to discuss and vote on the replacement of Pastor Cobb." She paused and looked heavenward. "God rest his soul."

In her next breath, as if announcing the Second Coming, she raised her voice and proclaimed, "It is my honor and privilege to serve as your new interim pastor."

~~~ ~~~

Chapter 62

Pyune's prediction had come true. Paula Jennings would indeed preach at The Church of Ivy Log, would slam her fist on the pulpit and declare that the devil was hovering in the church rafters, just waiting to pounce on some weak soul. She'd pound her bible and tell everyone they were going straight to hell, then she'd prance down to The Boardinghouse for Sunday dinner and talk about how fat Vallie Thomas's legs were in her too short dress.

From Paula's table by the bay window, the pastor caught Doyce looking at him and the sadness in the farmer's face. Calvin slumped beside Doyce and fiddled with the cap he held in his hands. Wanda Osborne and Dale Cochrane flicked from one thing to another, never settling on anything for more than a second. William Johnson looked back at Doyce, whose rigid body seemed otherworldly. Harley had the appearance of a man who'd been embalmed.

Paula wandered toward her table by the bay window, touching shoulders as she walked, nodding as she passed Wiley, finally ending her parade by what had always been *her* table.

"I hope I'm not intruding on anything important," she said. "May I sit down?"

Pyune placed her hands in her apron pockets. "I was just leaving. Got a cake in the oven."

The pastor pulled out a chair for Paula. "Coffee?"

"No thanks. I've been up since daylight and have had too

many cups as it is."

He said nothing as he refilled his cup and looked out the window at Main Street. He noticed it had stopped snowing, a reprieve after a week of an arctic system that seemed everlasting. If he tilted his head forward, he could see the lighted Christmas tree in the town square. Someone had straightened the crooked star. Probably Doyce. When he turned back to Paula, she was looking at him. Waiting.

"So the church board had a meeting without me," he said matter-of-factly.

Paula's eyes were steady, a slight glint in them, the same kind of glint a predator might have before a kill. She nodded, the fingers of her right hand playing with an earring. There was no light in her eyes. A Siberian cold had crept into them, making them darker than a witch's brew.

"It is my feeling, Mr. Johnson, that you are having a hard time recognizing God's will. He did not intend for you to pastor The Church of Ivy Log. God's will is quite clear to me."

There was a slight wobble in the universe above Ivy Log, a sort of reckoning that seemed to shift the balance of power. It seemed good versus evil was at play. The players were ordinary folks who, as a small town sometimes dictates, found pleasure in stirring up things. Paula Jennings was a master in her quest for control.

William watched the red fingernails tap the table for a moment, then found the redhead's dark eyes. "Ms. Jennings, it is amazing to me, the insight you have into God's will."

She leaned back casually, her arm draped over a chair back. "It comes from prayer, Mr. Johnson. Fervent prayer."

He chuckled, a soft rumbling from his throat.

"What's so funny?" she asked.

"Oh, just thinking." He carefully folded his napkin and placed it next to his plate. "It's almost like that red telephone in Washington. You know, the one that goes directly from the President to Russia." He cocked his head and squinted his eyes. "It looks like you have one of those red telephones hooked up straight to heaven."

He saw her body stiffen. "Your sarcasm does not become you, Mr. Johnson."

If anyone had been watching William Johnson, they would

have seen his jawline harden, a coldness entering his eyes. He caught himself and took a deep breath, let it out and looked across the table at Paula.

"It was a rhetorical statement, Ms. Jennings."

"I get it, Mr. Johnson. You're questioning my motivations."

He paused, choosing the right words. "You talk about the will of God. I believe it's God's will that I should be the pastor of The Church of Ivy Log. He stood and put on his coat, wrapped his scarf around his neck and patted Paula on the shoulder. "Don't forget to set up that board meeting. And I'd like to address the entire board before Sam Cobb's arrival."

~~~ ~~~

Chapter 63

*W*ho the hell does he think he is? Paula stormed out of The Boardinghouse and got in her Lincoln and drove around town as if it was under her inspection. Only when satisfied all was right did she round the corner at Dellwood Avenue. When she parked her car, she saw Wiley standing on her front porch. She slowed her walk to her door and stared at him as he leaned on a post.

"This is a surprise," she said as she pulled out her house key.

"I hope you have time for a little chat," he said.

"A little chat? There was a time you wanted more than a chat." She pushed open the door and he followed her inside.

"Things don't always stay the same." He sat on her couch and watched her turn on the lamps, plug in the Christmas tree lights and take off her coat. She sat across from him and took off her gloves.

"At least you didn't die on the mountain."

He laughed. "No. Looks like I'll be around for a while."

She studied his face for a moment. "You've obviously had excellent care. I'm sure Pyune saw to that."

He let a few seconds go by while he reached over and took a piece of hard candy out of a dish shaped like a snowman. "Pyune has always been a part of my life. Always will be."

"Why, of course. That old smokehouse will be there as long as you need it."

The mountain man, whose intellect far surpassed the

woman who sat across from him, eased forward on the couch and placed his hands on his knees. "Your pettiness is unbecoming, Paula. It's my hope you will outgrow your need to hurt Pyune. She is a fine woman."

Paula threw her head back and laughed, a throaty laugh. "Oh, please, Wiley. We're talking about a *cook* at The Boardinghouse. A black woman. An uneducated black woman, no less. And, she runs to the smokehouse anytime you want. Of course, she's *a fine woman*." She became instantly brittle. "Much finer than *me*, it seems."

Wiley saw a thin line of perspiration on Paula's upper lip, the reddening of her cheeks and the anger that sparked from her eyes. He said, "I've lost the will to please you. I've decided I don't want to endure your pretense and hypocrisy any longer." He paused as he noticed the glistening of tears. "It's been a slow melting away of what we had at one time. There is no more of it left. And it has nothing to do with Pyune. Nothing at all."

Paula merely stared at him and let a tear roll down her cheek. The infallible Paula Jennings could shed a tear, could feel pain. But, it was short-lived.

She said, "You walked through the cold to tell me that? To question my integrity?" Her words were clipped and came through lips that seemed carved out of granite. "My dear man, you have deluded yourself. I am certain as long as Pyune keeps you well fed and accompanies you to the smokehouse anytime you want, there will be a *relationship*. Love? You didn't mention *love*." Paula raised her head and grinned. "Can you imagine being *in love* with Pyune? That's the most ridiculous thing I've ever heard."

Wiley left the couch and looked down at Paula. "What do you know about love?" He started for the door but turned around. "By the way, I had a conversation with Doyce and Harley. They told me about the spur-of-the-moment board meeting. Doyce even said you threatened to call in the demand note for the sixty thousand on his new tractor if he didn't vote the way you wanted." Even from across the room, he saw her flinch. "Where was the integrity in that?"

The door closed, a click of the lock and then quiet. Paula sat still in her chair and stared at the angel on top of the

Christmas tree. The room was cold, the temperature outside dropping. Afternoon came with Paula sitting in the same spot, the dreariness of another winter day pushing its way across the mountains.

~~~

It was true. Paula had taken Doyce aside and looked at his big farmer hands and hound-dog face and his denim overalls as he eased into the office chair across from her as she sat at the desk in the small office in the church. She'd said, "Thank you for coming on such short notice. Bet you've been up for hours."

Doyle didn't like being alone with Paula. "That's right. Had a fire going at daylight." He rambled on. "I'm about out of fire-wood. Looks like Wiley might be laid up for a while, so I might have to go out and cut me down a tree or two."

Paula didn't give a lick about Doyce's or anybody else's running out of firewood in the dead of winter. *Enough chitchat.* "I've been doing a lot of praying about The Church of Ivy Log and its lack of formal leadership since the passing of Pastor Cobb. By the grace of God, I've been called to embrace the church with my leadership and guidance." She took a long moment to let that sink in and so Doyce had ample time to notice her open bible, a silk bookmark the color of her lipstick stretched between the thin pages.

Doyce said nothing. He was too big to cross his legs, but he shifted around in his chair as best he could.

"Of course, a motion would have to be made, nominating me to the position of interim pastor." She gave him her most innocent face. "And seconded, of course."

Though Doyce was a simple man, he understood Paula's intent. She expected the unanimous ratification of her nomina-tion. Doyce felt his heart pick up speed and a ringing in his ears. What if he said no? He already had the answer to that question. He glanced past Paula and looked out the window that faced the mountains. The peaks were as white as an angel's dress and reached toward the heavens like a caravan of camels, one after the other, until they disappeared into the mist.

"I'm thinking that preacher from Atlanta would do a good

job," he forced his mouth to utter.

Her head came up and her eyes narrowed. "You forget. God's will is at work here. It's my leadership He wants at the Church of Ivy Log. Not that . . . that . . . Mr. Johnson."

"I see." Doyce looked more closely at the bible again and saw it was opened to I Corinthians, from which he remembered the missive of the Apostle Paul alluding to the role of women in the church — that they must remain silent. He studied Paula for a moment, saw the fierceness in her features, her eyes streaming with an intensity that poured across and settled on him like a river of lava. The apostle had obviously not contemplated women properly, and certainly not one like Paula Jennings.

Doyce said, "I'm not so sure the Board will approve your position as the temporary pastor of the church. You know your scriptures very well, the workings of the church and everything, but you have no seminary education. Mr. Johnson is a graduate of the Harvard Divinity School and you said yourself — "

"I know what I said." She stood and towered over him as he remained seated. "You lack the understanding of the situation here. I have been divinely led. I must govern this church, as it's the will of God. Why is that so difficult for you to understand?" Irritation now sprinkled over her like drops from a fast-moving shower. "I expect you to nominate me — and everyone on the board to vote in my favor. Is that clear?"

"I'm not so sure everybody — "

"Looks like that note on the money you borrowed from me to finance your new tractor is a demand note." She yanked a blue folder from her purse, pulled out a copy of loan paperwork, waved it in his face. "I can call this in anytime, can't I?"

Doyce furrowed his brow. "I told you it'd take me two crops to make enough to pay you back. You said I could have two years on that note."

"Don't you remember, when the bank turned you down, how happy you were that I lent you that money? Tractors are important to you farmers — that's why I was so glad to help you out."

Doyce sunk deeper in his chair as he heard the other members of the board arriving for the meeting. A sudden, deep cold filled the room, so frigid his lungs burned as he gasped for air. He saw nothing but black empty space, but he heard laughter, heinous sounds that could have easily been the Devil's.

~~~ ~~~

Chapter 64

Wiley's question - *What do you know about love?* – settled in Paula's mind. She knew plenty. Her love affair with Pastor Cobb's son had taken her young heart and made it sing. Now, after 30 years, he was returning to Ivy Log.

She closed her eyes and tried to visualize the tall, handsome boy of her youth. Aldelpheus Cobb's son had been wild, as wild as she. But, that was so long ago. She'd heard he was a bigwig at Harvard, a professor who excelled in his teachings of the New Testament. She also knew he had left Ivy Log in the middle of a hot summer night, a rebellious young man who defied his father's decree that he go to seminary school. He had also left a 17-year-old sweetheart, who even 30 years later had not forgotten the pain of abandonment.

Aldelpheus Cobb and his son had been estranged all those years and now the prodigal son was returning — returning a little too late to talk about the bible with his father. But, perhaps not too late to align with Paula and her newfound position as pastor of The Church of Ivy Log.

~~~

She turned on the lamp at her reading chair and reached down for the box of Pastor Cobb's love letters. She pulled out #62 and reread it. At last, a letter that contained some clues that would lead her to the woman who wrote them.

So sorry I left in such a hurry. But, I look forward to seeing you Saturday. There is construction on Meadowbrook so turn left at Mayfield Court and then right on Meadow-

brook to avoid the congestion. If I'm not there when you arrive, I'll be next door at Doreen's — #1235. Can't wait to see you.

In the morning, she'd drive to Blairsville with the letters and knock on the mystery woman's door. She'd hand over the box and at the same time see exactly who wrote them. Mystery solved.

From there, she'd return home and call contest headquarters and tell them Pyune Murphy's lemon pudding cake recipe was a stolen recipe. She looked at the information again: *Bakers' World Magazine for its 50ᵗʰ year anniversary will award $25,000 to the winner of its Dessert of the Century Contest.* There was a picture of the skyline of New York City, a woman in the foreground dressed in an apron. In her hands, she held a large ceramic bowl and a spoon. On the side of the bowl, in bright red letters: *$25,000.*

Paula leaned back in her chair and wondered what she would wear for her first meeting with Sam Cobb in more than 30 years.

~~~ ~~~

Chapter 65

S am Cobb's memories of Ivy Log ran deep. His three-decade absence had not muted his mind's-eye vision of the quaint mountain town and its inhabitants. After all, it was home.

When he was 17, he struggled with the God thing, had questioned his father late into the night, had challenged the bible as though an author with a flair for the dramatic had written it. *Parting the sea? Really?*

In the middle of one cold, star-filled night, he decided to settle things once and for all — he would hike up to Brasstown Bald and talk with God himself.

In passing through his mother's kitchen, he saw the remnants of cold biscuits on the stove and stuffed a few in his pocket. Nearby, a leftover pork chop, fried to a crisp because his mama was afraid of unclean pork, lay under a piece of aluminum foil. He wrapped it carefully and placed it with the biscuits. When he reached the back door, he hesitated. Should he take his bible?

No. He knew exactly what he wanted to tell God.

When he eased the door shut, he looked up and saw Galileo's Milky Way streaming across the universe as if in a powerful proclamation that spoke only to him. The myriad of stars seemed to blink a riveting message: *How could you question God when all you have to do is look at the beauty of the universe? Stay home, son,* the white-hot stars said.

He lingered on the porch steps and breathed the mountain air. He slowly let go of the screened door. It was between him and God, not between him and Galileo and the Milky Way.

~~~

Brasstown Bald lay 27 miles southeast of Ivy Log, a trip his little pick-up made with no problem. On Jack's Knob Trail, he began the 3-mile climb with an energy only 17-year-old kids had.

He passed Rabbit Run, then the gap where last summer he had seen a black bear with two cubs cross a stream, the mother turning and looking at him as though debating whether or not to charge. He had debated running up a tree. But why? Bears climb trees. He ran in the opposite direction. He must have made the right decision.

When he reached the logging trail that carried him up a steep incline, he could feel the air thinning, turning colder. He stopped for breath and looked down into a small valley and thought about eating his mama's biscuits. He decided against it when he heard the call of a wolf. Instead, he sat on a rock, retied his shoelaces and kept going.

In a half-mile he reached the summit and found a boulder larger than his pick-up truck. He crawled up on it and looked toward the heavens. *Here I am, God. Let's have a talk.* He told God he wasn't ready for seminary. He waited for God's reply. And waited.

He tried again. *Just because my father is a preacher doesn't mean I have to be one.*

God did not reply.

My father cannot make me go to seminary.

God did not reply.

The bible does not have all the answers.

God did not reply.

The winds swept from the mountaintop to the valley below, the moon glinting off the open pastures and the tin roofs of houses and other buildings.

Here's what I think, God. I need to figure things out on my own. I won't forget you — I'll be back up here again and we'll finish this conversation.

~~~

And here he was. Returning to Ivy Log. He packed a small

bag, his laptop and his bible, the latter not the one his father had given him when he was a 10-year-old. That one had remained in Ivy Log at the parsonage, in his tiny bedroom at the rear of the house. He knew the inscription by heart. *To my loving son on his 10ᵗʰ birthday. May God bless you and keep you. I look forward to the day your mother and I can sit in the congregation of a church and see you in the pulpit preaching God's word. Love, Dad*

It never happened. His exodus from Ivy Log had closed too many doors, and now that his father was dead they could never be reopened.

At 5:30 in the morning, the traffic on I-85 was light, a cold mist on his windshield. He tuned his radio to an oldies station and Willie Nelson's "Always On My Mind" pulled him once more into his Ivy Log memories. He remembered exactly when he heard the song for the first time. Willie's music had crooned across the waters of Lake Nottley one hot summer night as he and Paula Jennings made love for the first time.

~~~ ~~~

Chapter 66

The chatter at The Boardinghouse had jumped from Wiley's flight off the mountain to Paula Jennings's meteoric rise to even more prominence as the new interim pastor of The Church of Ivy Log. It was all discussed over Pyune's special holiday breakfast of Christmas grits, which would be served every morning throughout the holidays.

Pyune had kept her promise to Wiley and made him his own special pan of the dessert on Monday, and it waited on the stove in the fragrant kitchen of The Boardinghouse until he arrived.

"Pyune, honey, I feel so loved," Wiley said. "You done made a lemon pudding cake for me — and it's not even Tuesday."

"Told you I would." She took the biggest spoon she could find from a drawer and set the oversized utensil on the counter. He winced as he pulled up his legs. His black eye remained swollen and now painted with numerous colors ranging from pink to green, adding a certain quality to his existing incomparable character.

Pyune laughed and placed the entire cake and a cup of coffee on the counter. "Just enjoy. I made the coffee with love too."

"You always do." He grinned.

They were quiet for a moment, Pyune stirring a steaming pot of greens, pans of hot cornbread nearby. She hummed and occasionally tapped her foot.

"What are you so happy about?" he asked, digging into his

first piece of cake.

"Oh, I got a call last night. My cousin Alease and her husband, Ted, are coming by for a quick visit. They're on their way to New York for the holidays."

"Alease? Oh, yeah. Alease. You two spent a lot of time together growing up, didn't you?"

"Sure did. She's about five years older. Her mama and my mama were sisters. She met Ted, married him, and they went to south Georgia. They're innkeepers in Folkston. She does about the same thing I do — cooks and runs the inn."

"Hope I can meet her and her husband."

"You'll get your chance. They'll be here tomorrow afternoon. When we talked, I told her about Paula claiming the lemon pudding cake recipe wasn't our family recipe. Alease sure didn't like hearing that. Paula better stay clear of her if she starts in about the recipe being hers."

Wiley watched her between licking his spoon. "You hear about Sam Cobb coming back?"

She nodded and began peeling sweet potatoes. "Now, that's gonna be a sight. Remember when he left town in the middle of the night and his mama and daddy blamed it all on Paula?"

"On Paula? Why they'd do that?"

"You mean to tell me you done forgot about all that mess?"

"I reckon so."

"You probably was off to college when it went on."

"Don't keep me in suspense. The least you can do is fill me in after all these years."

Pyune reached into the drawer and found a regular spoon and sat across from Wiley. "Mind sharing of a piece of that pie with me?"

Wiley looked stricken. "I thought this was all mine."

"It is, but I'm tasting it to make sure it's perfect"

He pulled it away. "Well, I'm telling you it's perfect."

She looked at him and raised her eyebrows. He pushed it back.

"So Paula was blamed for Sam Cobb leaving Ivy Log?"

"Yes, she was. Pastor Cobb made it quite clear at the time that the redhead was to blame."

"I don't understand. If the pastor blamed Paula, why did he keep her in the folds of the church?"

"Who knows? Pyune pushed the cake pan closer to Wiley and got up from her stool.

The kitchen filled with the fragrance of vanilla as Pyune whipped sweet potatoes. She made sure a dash of nutmeg made it into a large bowl where beaters fluffed the potatoes like amber clouds. Then she ran the beaters around the edge of the bowl until the mounds peaked high and waited for a layer of marshmallows.

"Did Sam ever marry?" Wiley asked.

"Heck if I know."

"Wouldn't it be something if sparks flew when Paula and Sam get together?"

Pyune looked at Wiley like he'd just stepped off a space-ship. "Oh, honey, sparks will fly, but they won't be the kind you're thinkin' about."

~~~ ~~~

Chapter 67

Paula pulled out of her driveway on Mulberry and passed The Boardinghouse, smoke lofting through the chimney and racing east. Without slowing down, she drove past Patton Drugs and Drake's Hardware and the row of Christmas trees that had been discounted to $20 — no matter the size — the holiday now just a few days away.

She headed southeast on Highway 129 toward Blairsville and slid in a CD of Christmas music. By the time she was a mile down the road, she was singing "Away In The Manger" in perfect key. A thought occurred to her — as interim pastor of The Church of Ivy Log — she would sing a solo at least every other Sunday. She made a mental note to review her favorite hymns.

In the seat beside her, in a dark-green shoebox, the letters to Aldelpheus Cobb lay in a neat stack, one after the other, in chronological order. Aldelpheus Cobb's lover was in for quite a surprise — all of her love letters returned.

Paula slowed on the outskirts of Blairsville and drove through the center of town until she came to Kimsey Street, then right on Hood Street. She meandered east for a half-mile, lovely houses sitting in neat rows with Christmas decorations on lawns and rooftops.

The directions in "O's" 65th letter were clear. Turn right on Arrowhead Trail, with "O" living next door to #1235. Paula saw the house and pulled into the driveway, next to which a cedar tree was trimmed neatly into a conical shape. She felt a twitter in her chest. After all this time, she was to meet the enigmatic "O."

   She rang the bell only once before the door opened and a lovely woman, tiny and with snow-white hair pulled up into a sleek French twist, greeted her. "Well, hello, I've been expecting you."

~~~ ~~~

Chapter 68

The door opened so quickly Paula blinked several times before she found her voice. "Oh?"

"Well, yes. Al told me all about you."

"Al?"

The petite woman laughed. "Aldelpheus. Aldelpheus Cobb." She opened the door wider. "Won't you please come in?"

Paula stepped into the foyer and followed the woman through a small sitting room and into a large living room with two soft blue couches facing each other. On a low table between them, silk poinsettias lay like large red stars waiting for Christmas.

"Do find a comfortable seat, Ms. Jennings."

Grasping the box of letters, Paula sat on one of the couches. "How do you know who I am?"

Again, warm laughter. "As far as I know, there's only one redhead in Ivy Log."

Paula, used to having the upper hand, found herself foundering as she watched the woman who had not given her name, take a tissue out of her pocket and pat at her lips.

"You said you were expecting me?"

"Oh, yes. I saw you at William Johnson's reception and knew you were Paula Jennings from Al's description."

"I don't understand. Who are you?" Paula, one hand resting on the green box, leaned forward. "Have we met?"

"I can see your confusion, Ms. Jennings. No, we have not met. I did, however, as I mentioned, see you a week ago at the reception for William Johnson."

"You know William Johnson?"

"Not until a week ago."

"Then, why did you attend the reception?"

"Ah, good question." Her face became dreamlike, a drifting away of her mind as her crisp blue eyes traveled around the room. "But, let's start at the beginning. You asked who I was — I'm Anne Schuyler. Used to be a Smith from Micanopy, Florida. Met Dr. Schuyler, married him and moved to California." Anne laughed. "Can you imagine a southerner moving to California?" She jumped up. "I'm going to fix us some tea. The water's already hot. Come into the kitchen with me."

Paula's head was spinning as she followed Anne into the kitchen and sat on a stool and watched the woman's tiny hands place two elegant bone-China cups on the counter.

Paula couldn't wait any longer and got to the reason for her visit. "You wrote the letters?"

"What letters?"

Paula looked through the doorway to the blue couch and the green box of letters. "The letters I brought."

"You brought letters?" The tea water was steaming, and Anne poured it into the cups over cinnamon teabags.

"Yes. I'll get them." Paula left the counter and returned to the living room. The box seemed even more mysterious. The "O" signature did not correlate with the name Anne Schuyler. She picked up the letters and walked back to the kitchen.

Anne's eyes opened wide. "Oh, my. A box of letters. Do let me see them." She reached out her hands.

"Oh, my," she said, as her fingers flicked through them.

Paula watched as Anne replaced the top on the box. "So, you wrote those letters?" Paula's voice had sounded accusatory, but she was way past the point of caring how she came across.

Anne threw her hands to her cheeks. "Oh, no. These aren't my letters."

Paula, her irritation mounting, reached over and picked up the box. "Well, do you know who wrote them?"

"Why, I most certainly do." She added sugar to her tea and stirred gently, her blue eyes bluer than ever.

Paula waited, and after hearing nothing but Anne softly

sipping her tea, blurted, "I'd like to know who wrote them."

The words came from Anne Schuyler as though she'd rehearsed them a thousand times. "I'm sure you would, Ms. Jennings. But Al told me, shortly before he died — if ever you came snooping around — not to tell you a thing."

~~~ ~~~

Chapter 69

William Johnson sat at the neat desk in the study of the parsonage, his bible open to the Apostle Paul's letters to the Ephesians, his finger resting on the page at Chapter 4, Verse 1-3.

As a prisoner of the Lord, then, I urge you to live a worthy life of the calling you have received. Be completely humble and gentle; be patient, bearing with one another in love. Make every effort to keep the unity of spirit through the bond of peace.

He was certain he had received his calling. And, at the moment, he was working on being humble and patient. However, Paula Jennings had made that quest quite difficult. Had he not been so sure of God's will, he would have taken the fast track to Atlanta and never looked back. He often wondered why he had fought so hard. Was it a fear of rejection? Rejection because he was black? What was it that God wanted him to do in this place called Ivy Log? Perform a miracle of some kind? Teach a redhead a lesson?

The knock at the door startled him. He looked at his watch. Barely past 9 a.m. He left the study, Delilah right behind him. He opened the front door.

A nice-looking, middle-aged fellow stumbled backwards in the snow, doubling over in laughter. "Hey, my man. Looks like your car had a fight with the church steeple." He stood upright and now spoke in a deep voice. "And, brother, I do believe that thar steeple has won." He did a little soft-shoe and bowed deeply. "Sam Cobb at your service, kind sir."

The pastor shook his head. "I knew this was a mistake. What was I thinking?"

Sam stepped through the doorway. "What was you thinking? You was thinking, I sure would like to see ol' Sam."

He slapped his friend on the back. "I can't disagree with that." He closed the door against the frigid air and pointed Sam to a chair by the fireplace. "Sit down. Coffee?"

"Coffee's good. Black."

The pastor hesitated. "Did you say something about my color?" He looked down at his friend, who had propped his feet on the ottoman and leaned back into the soft, overstuffed chair.

Sam howled. Their banter with regard to William's color had begun many years ago at Harvard, culminating in a solid friendship between two men whose paths were much the same, both men teaching theology classes at the university and attending professional and social events together.

While the pastor made coffee, Sam looked around the small room, bare of his parent's personal things. Their lives had been austere, simple, except for his father's complex mind, which he fed with the myriad of books in his study. While his father read, his mother was the consummate homemaker and wife. She saw to it his father never wore mismatched socks or a tie that clashed with his jacket. He was never exposed to his parent's intimate life, assuming after their door closed at night they were like any other man and wife.

The pastor returned with a tray of coffee, a few breakfast bars and a banana.

"Here you go."

"Ah, Will, I love having you wait on me like this."

"I'm not waiting on you *like this*. You're on your own — just like old times."

Sam nodded. "We did have some old times together, didn't we? And, here we are, back together again — just like Butch and Sundance."

"Will settled in his chair and saw sadness in Sam's eyes. "Hard to come back here? This town? This house? These people?"

Sam shrugged. "I got over it a long time ago. Just wished I

hadn't missed mom and dad's funerals. Out of the country both times and didn't get word until it was too late." He drew a deep breath. "Of course, I didn't deem the funerals to be important in the first place. They were merely an afterthought when you think about it. The importance lay in their living and my relationship with them."

The pastor studied his friend's face. "In all those years, you never came back?"

"Only once." Sam looked at him and grinned. "Saw you in the kitchen with Pyune Murphy."

He wrinkled his brow. "So, that was you? I thought I saw your coattail flying across the snow that night. Said to myself, that couldn't be Sam Cobb. Or could it?"

"Oh, it was me all right. Cussed you all night while I waited in the bushes for you to go to sleep."

"Why didn't you just knock on the door? I would have let you in."

Sam's thoughts lingered a moment as he unwrapped the breakfast bar. "I know you would have. It . . . I was a little fragile. You know — coming back. Mom and Dad gone." He looked at William Johnson in silence. "It's . . . been a long time."

Delilah jumped into Sam's lap and stretched her paws across his chest. The pastor said, "I see Delilah remembers you."

"Oh, yeah. Delilah and I are good friends." Sam rubbed her back and the top of her head.

"Will crossed his legs and watched the fire. "Why'd you come back to the house that night?" he asked, softness in his words.

Sam didn't answer for a long time, staring into the fire and stroking Delilah. "My bible. The white one Dad gave me when I was ten years old. Wanted something he had given me. Couldn't find it. Looks like the church ladies stripped this place pretty good. I couldn't find anything but my father's reference books. Guess they'll stay with the parsonage."

"Maybe I can help you find it."

"We'll see." Sam closed his eyes and leaned his head on the back of the chair. "I never understood my father's estrangement from me. He was the most learned man I knew — miles above my own knowledge, leaps and bounds beyond my wisdom. It didn't make sense to me for the longest time." Sam opened his eyes and looked at the ceiling, perhaps to the heavens that soared beyond. "Then, one day, I figured it out." He looked at his college friend. "He forgot to love me."

The pastor laid a log on the dying fire and poked it until it flamed up, its embers cracking and popping like a man tap dancing. "Your father loved you, Sam."

"I'm sure he did. I just didn't know it. When I left home, I was certain he'd come after me, fold me in his arms and tell me he loved me. But, he never did. I called many times. Always talked with Mom. Seems Dad was never available."

Sam leaned forward and took off his jacket and placed it across the back of his chair. He picked up Delilah and returned her to his lap.

"Did he know you went to Harvard seminary?" "Will" asked.

"Not sure," Sam said. "Waiting until I was thirty to go to school was not his idea of the way to get an education. And, look where I am — almost a perfect copy of him academically." He looked up quickly. "Almost a perfect copy — except I sure as heck know how to love."

"That you do. And speaking of love, Pyune tells me you and Paula had a thing at one time."

Laugher rumbled from Sam's chest. "That we did." He shook his head slowly back and forth. "That redhead twisted me around her finger." He grinned. "And, at 17, I loved every minute of it."

"Nervous about seeing her again?"

The room became quiet, the crimson and orange flames now dancing in the fireplace like flamingos with hot feet. "I won't lie to you, there's a part of me that's curious about her. No doubt about it, she was a huge influence when I was a youth." His words became soft, his face brightened. "You never forget your first love."

The pastor nodded. "Your dad like Paula?"

"Are you kidding? Dad said it was Paula who filled my head with *unclean* thoughts and kept me from going to seminary."

"Did she?"

Sam deliberated for a few moments, rubbed his fingers

across his brow. "When I was 14, I knew I wasn't ready for the seminary. I tried to talk with Dad about it, but he wasn't interested in my thoughts. A few years later, when Paula and I started dating, she never said one thing about it to me. Heck, she was only 17. And she sure wasn't interested in my education. She only had one thing on her mind, and you can guess what that was. But I was no better." Sam left his seat by the fire, paced the room before coming back to the chair. "Will, let's forget about me and talk about this mess you're in. Are you or are you not the pastor of The Church of Ivy Log?"

~~~ ~~~

Chapter 70

Paula fumed all the way back to Ivy Log, her Lincoln traveled over the speed limits on roads cleared of snow but dangerous as she took the curves and hills with a blind fury.

On the seat beside her, the mysterious letters in the green box lay in abstruse silence. She'd burned the dang letters before she'd ever give them to Anne Schuyler. *If I ever came snooping.* How dare she intimate Paula was snooping?

She had the good sense to slow down as she drove into Ivy Log, noonday cars parked like a beaded necklace on the curb in front of The Boardinghouse. Doyce and Harley lumbered down the front steps, shoulders hunched, hats pulled over their ears. She didn't wave.

On Dellwood, she whipped her car into the drive, picked up the box of letters, mumbled to herself as she opened her front door. When she slung the box of letters onto the couch, the lid popped off and the intimate messages scattered across the room, the box tumbling after them. And, scrawled on the bottom of the box, a name she knew very well stared back at her.

~~~ ~~~

Chapter 71

Bakers' World Magazine's headquarters had operated out of Long Island, New York, for 50 years, with a sister office in Chicago. Its name was familiar not only to most every professional baker in the U.S. but to a large contingent across the globe, as well. However, it was the "little people," as the publisher referred to the hordes of ordinary women anxiously awaiting each month's copy, who were the backbone of the incredibly popular magazine.

The annual recipe contest was the periodical's most effective branding medium, its $25,000 grand prize a sure way to pique the interest of every woman who baked or even thought about toasting a slice of bread.

Late into the night, women from around the world pulled out their special recipes and dreamed that the resulting concoction would win the grand prize. These ladies visualized dollar signs on the batter-smeared pieces of paper that contained their grandmother's or mother's cherished recipes — with all the closely guarded ingredients. Pyune Murphy considered her grandmother's recipe for lemon pudding cake worthy of the $25,000 prize. But it was pride, not money, that had motivated her to enter the contest and share the recipe.

Trouble was, Paula Jennings possessed none of the same altruism. So, when she picked up the telephone to call Bakers' World, she set her jaw in a hard line, her lips so curled they were almost hidden.

When the lively voice at Bakers' World answered, "Good

morning, Bakers' World Magazine. This is your personal baking assistant. How may I help you?" Paula stuck out her tongue as if gagging.

She said, "I have a complaint and I want to talk with someone who has the authority to — "

"One moment, please"

Paula heard a click, then music. From "Chocolat." She could see Johnny Depp playing the guitar, his seductive eyes —

"This is Sharon Clark. How may I help you?"

Paula grasped the telephone closer. "My name is Paula Jennings, and I'm calling to warn you of fraud."

"Fraud? What do you mean?" The woman's voice was definitely interested. Paula found herself smiling, a feeling of satisfaction washing over her.

"It's about the twenty-five thousand dollar dessert-recipe contest. One of your five finalists is Pyune Murphy. Pyune Murphy of Ivy Log, Georgia. That recipe she entered is a stolen recipe." Paula waited, a smug look on her face that resembled Teddy Roosevelt's when he reached the top of San Juan Hill.

"I appreciate your call, Ms. Jennings. But, the fraud has already been reported."

~~~ ~~~

Chapter 72

The fraud has already been reported? Paula was stunned. "What did you say?"

"You heard me, Ms. Jennings. Bakers' World Magazine is well aware of the fraud. We were notified last week that we would be receiving a phone call from you."

"What . . . I . . . who called you?"

"I'm not at liberty to discuss any details. Good day, Ms. Jennings."

Good day, Ms. Jennings? She listened to the emptiness at the other end of the line until two words entered her thoughts. *Pyune Murphy.*

~~~ ~~~

Chapter 73

A t The Boardinghouse, Wiley laid new logs on top of the fire and stepped back and replaced the screen. "That ought to do it for a while." He watched the fire flame up for a moment, then meandered to Frank and Adela's table, a slight limp that no one noticed because of his aurora borealis eye, the colors continuing to intensify.

"Frank, if you've forgiven me, I'd like to sit for a while." A smile played at the corners of Wiley's mouth.

"Pull out a chair." Frank stared at Wiley's eye and the bandage on his forehead. "Just don't ask me to go up to Brasstown Bald anytime soon."

Wiley grinned. "Close call, huh?"

"For you, not me. I was safe and sound at Tom Keeling's."

Adela peered at Wiley's eye. "It's looking worse than yesterday."

"Doc said it would be a while before it looked normal. But I'm handsome no matter how you look at it, ain't I?"

Adela laughed. "I'm just relieved you're well enough to still be best man at the wedding."

Wiley nodded and looked at Frank. "I'll be there. Right on time."

Pyune brought Wiley a cup of coffee. "Nice and hot," she said.

He nodded his appreciation, took a sip and said to Frank. "If I'd never come back from that mountain alive, who'd you have asked to be your best man?"

Frank leaned to the side and folded his arms. "I'm afraid no one could have replaced you. I think Adela and I would have canceled the wedding and mourned your passing for the rest of our lives."

Wiley's eyes opened wide and he gave Adela a quizzical look. "That so?"

"That's so," she said, giving him no idea if she and Frank had been serious until the two of them burst out laughing.

~~~

The doors to The Boardinghouse opened and Paula, her red hair askew, stepped into the dining room, pulling the door shut with a loud bang. Her gloves came off with great ceremony, as did her scarf. She walked to her table, her eyes straight ahead. The noise in the dining room quieted as heads turned to the stone-faced woman who sat at the table in front of the bay window.

Wiley, across the room, murmured, "I'm a thinking Paula's mad about somethin' or other." He couldn't help but let a slight grin slide across his face

Behind him, Pyune came through the kitchen doorway and called across the room, "Iced tea, Paula?"

Paula stared at her through narrowed eyes. "That would be nice." Her words fell into the room like chips of ice that even Wiley's now roaring fire couldn't melt.

Pyune came to Paula's table; a menu tucked under her arm, a set of tableware in her hand, the iced tea in another. She said nothing as she placed everything in front of Paula.

Paula leaned back and watched in silence, an eyebrow raised as though she were the inspector general of table settings. When Pyune finished, Paula reached out and took Pyune's wrist.

"My dear," she began, her voice smoother than Kentucky's best bourbon, "it seems we need to discuss that recipe."

Pyune looked at Paula's fingers wrapped around her wrist, saw the gaudy rings, the red polish, and then moved her eyes to Paula's face. It appeared as though her eyes had no pupils, only a solid dark circle around each that seemed otherworldly.

"You may remove your hand from me," Pyune said, the words so low they could have been a growl — an utterance that signaled imminent danger if her request was not obeyed.

Paula hesitated only a moment. "But, of course." She patted the table in front of the chair to her right. "Got a few minutes to sit with me?"

Reluctantly, Pyune sat down. "Make it quick."

"Certainly. I'm sure you have things on the stove or in the oven that need your attention. Being a cook must be quite stressful."

Pyune waited silently, her breathing slow and steady. "You want to get to the point?"

Paula fiddled with her rings. "I had a very interesting conversation this morning with that recipe-contest company. You know . . . Bakers' World Magazine." She waited for a reaction from Pyune. When she didn't get one, she continued, "I felt it my responsibility to inform the magazine of possible fraud concerning the recipe for my lemon pudding cake."

Pyune's stoic eyes stared back at Paula's. She noticed an odd glint begin to appear. "Okay."

"But it seems like you headed me off at the pass. Bakers' World was quite aware of possible fraud. Said someone had already contacted them and said to expect a call from me." Paula slapped the table and grinned at Pyune, a toothy grin showing lipstick smeared on her teeth. "Who would do such a thing?"

"Beats me. Want to order lunch?"

Hot breath left Paula's mouth along with the words, "You're telling me you know nothing of this?"

"Not a thing. You ordering lunch or just want tea?"

Paula stood so fast her menu fell to the floor. She leaned close to Pyune. "You're lying to me, Pyune Murphy."

The gentle woman felt the fire coming from Paula's mouth as if real flames were generating it. She bent down, picked up the menu, stood up and walked toward the kitchen.

Paula called out. "I haven't placed my lunch order."

Pyune turned around. "Lunchtime's over. Just missed it. 'bout two minutes ago."

~~~ ~~~

Chapter 74

A light snow fell across Ivy Log and then swept eastward toward the higher elevations, marching through the peaks as though a conquering legion of miniature white soldiers.

William and Sam reminisced over old times, their struggles with their studies while at Harvard, their romances, and finally their views of the world.

"The way I see it, Will, is that women are born to make a man happy. It's what they do best. Why can't they be satisfied doing just that? You know, having babies and keeping her man happy."

The pastor had never seen Sam drink hard liquor before, but there he was, a big glass of bourbon in his hand — a sipping whiskey he was told was warm and smooth. Sam had of course offered some to William Johnson, and of course William Johnson had refused.

For some reason, as Sam got inebriated, the pastor found himself remembering Clara. His marriage to her had been idyllic. Her death had forced him to reevaluate his life, something he was still doing. For now, however, the thoughts faded. He kept the fire going the entire afternoon. Delilah, disloyal to her master, kept going from one lap to the other until settling in Sam's.

"So, the board meeting's not until Thursday?" Sam asked.

"That's right, only time everyone could get together. I expect they're all dreading a confrontation with Paula."

Sam slapped his knee. "There doesn't have to be a . . . con-

frontation. I'm here to mediate. After that, we'll call for a . . .
." He seemed to lose his train of thought. Sam searched the
air with his eyes, as if this would help him remember what
he was wanting to say. He stroked his chin. "We'll call for a
vote and that will be it." He finished the drink in the water
glass the pastor had provided and poured another from the
bottle he'd brought along in his briefcase.

"Why are you drinking so much?" the pastor asked him.

Sam stopped and looked at his buddy Will. "How much is
so much?" He got up and teetered sideways, placing his
hand on a doorframe to steady himself.

"You know what I mean. I've never seen you like this."

"I've never *been* like this before."

"Like what?

"Drinking."

"Why is now different?"

"Are you kidding? I'm meeting Paula at 7 o'clock
tonight."

Both men collapsed in laughter.

The pastor rubbed his eyes. "Perhaps prayer would be
appropriate at a time like this instead of bourbon." He held
his friend's eyes with his and saw the discontent, the sadness
that had settled within them.

Sam nodded, then drank some of the whiskey he'd just
poured. "Prayer is a good thing, I won't deny that. Right
now, though, I feel I must brace myself for an encounter
with a gal who, as a teenager, had me so confused I fled this
little town for fear of the consequences." The handsome professor paused and seemed to gather himself. "At least that's
what I told myself at the time. In retrospect, it was the fear
of the seminary that was the real culprit." He again sat in the
chair across from the pastor.

William Johnson saw his friend as a 17-year-old: skinny,
hardly shaving, crawling out of the parsonage window and
taking off for parts unknown, unaware it would be 30 years
before he'd return. "Is that a regret? Leaving the redhead, I
mean?"

Sam took a deep breath and stared into the fire. "Ah,
such a good question. But I can't answer it. What did I know
at 17, when everything was based on lust? My hormones

were churning like the rapids on the Chattooga River." He leaned forward, narrowed his eyes. "And now that I'm back, I have no idea how I'll handle this go-round with Paula Jennings."

~~~ ~~~

Chapter 75

She could have been beautiful, but it seemed as though a bitterness ran through her, a poison had tarnished the edges, roughing up the exterior of the person who was never as soft as she was attractive. Sometimes, it was though a cleansing was needed to wash her soul. Perhaps, late some night, the angels would come and stand over her bed while she slept and discuss the possible resurrection of whatever good was left in her.

Paula's path, however, had been crafted by the hurt she'd inflicted on others, the scars manifesting themselves in the whims of her personality. The angels would give her a slim chance of reformation.

Sam's phone call had come to her late at night, as if she were an afterthought. Thirty years had passed — *oh, let me call Paula and see how she's doing.*

His voice was deeper, smoother. A 48-year-old man who was calling an old girlfriend. What could she expect? He was a stranger. If he had called her honey or sweetie, she surely would have hung up. But, he hadn't. He simply said, "Paula, this is Sam Cobb."

At first, she said nothing. Then, "Hello," with no warmth. He was a stranger.

"Have I caught you at a bad time?"

"No," she said, not adding anything else.

A long silence followed. She could hear his breathing but could not visualize his face. Thirty years was a long time.

"I . . . I wanted you to know I will be in Ivy Log in a few

days."

She said nothing.

"I'll be there to mediate on behalf of the university for William Johnson."

"I heard."

She heard him sigh, could imagine his thoughts racing.

"Paula. Thirty years. That's a long time."

"And?"

Another sigh. She would give him nothing.

"And," he said, exasperation evident, his voice rising, "plain and simple, I'd like to see you."

Ah, the *male* in Sam Cobb had surfaced. The man/woman thing – *I'd like to see you.*

She felt her power, relished in it.

"When?"

"Monday evening? Seven o'clock?"

"Where?" she asked.

"Dinner out. Not The Boardinghouse." *Of course, not The Boardinghouse. Everyone in Ivy Log would be there.*

"Blairsville?"

"Blairsville's fine. Any place special?"

"Jim's Smokin' Que will work. It's on 129."

"Sounds good. I'll pick you up at your house at seven."

She hung up without saying goodbye. Calm, her heart beating at a steady pace, she had learned long ago that she could not live in the periphery of anything — she had to be in the main arena. She would have dinner with Sam Cobb, but nothing more.

~~~ ~~~

Chapter 76

Sam passed the house on Dellwood Avenue three times before he finally pulled onto the driveway. He sat a moment and watched Rudolph's blinking nose in the yard next door. Christmas lights twirled around the lamppost and illuminated the snow in red and green. Lights in an upstairs window, Paula's old bedroom, flicked off and he visualized her coming down the stairs, just as she had so many years ago.

He looked at his watch. Exactly 7 p.m. The car door swung open and he walked along the sidewalk, up the steps, to the front door. The doorbell glowed with a little yellow light. He pushed it once. He laughed when he saw his hand shaking.

The door opened, and a tall slender woman with red hair looked at him with large green eyes — eyes greener than St. Patrick's Day beer. He couldn't see them, but he knew they were there — freckles she'd covered with pale fine powder. He could imagine her as a pin-up girl. The only thing missing was a sweetness and perhaps a little cleavage.

"Hello, Paula."

She reached out her hand. "Sam."

He watched her face, ignoring her hand. He wanted to see a flicker of the girl he remembered.

Finally, she dropped her hand. "Come in while I get my coat."

She began to turn away when he reached out and took her arm. "Come here, Paula."

He held her close in the December night. No words. Just

breathing and the faint sounds of music floating from the town square, the fragrance of perfume mixing with the evergreen of the Christmas tree and the peppermint candy canes that hung on the branches.

Sam felt a lump in his throat and fought back tears. He had come home, and Paula Jennings was part of his homecoming.

She didn't respond to him, and he gently pulled away. "Forgive me. Your beauty startled me." His voice caught. "You're . . . you're just like I remembered."

Paula stepped back and looked at him, her eyes level with his, unwavering. "No, Sam, I've changed quite a bit." She turned from him and took her coat from the hall closet.

From the doorway, he waited as she settled the coat on her shoulders and slipped on her gloves. She gave him a smile he judged to be obligatory and announced, "I'm ready?"

Sam drove through Ivy Log, past the store windows bright with lights, the red wagon in the window at Drake's Hardware waiting for some little boy who had been very, very good. He picked up speed when he reached hwy 129 and headed for Blairsville. Beside him, Paula seemed engrossed by the snowflakes in the headlights, her mind apparently a million miles away. She said nothing.

He reached over and took her hand. "Can we talk about some things?" he asked.

She turned toward him but removed her hand from his. "Anything you'd like."

Sam cleared his throat. This wasn't the university classroom and he wasn't going to teach a lesson on the New Testament. He was simply going to reach out to someone who had once been in his life, who had been important to him. "Is there anything you'd like to say to me?" he asked.

"Not really," she said, so fast it startled him.

He reached over and picked up her hand again. His grasp was gentle. "I don't know where your thoughts are right now. But, I'd like to know." He paused, reflective. "Here we both are, with an opportunity to explore each other. We have a history and there's no reason we can't . . . ." He started to stammer but caught himself. "Damn it, Paula, get off your high horse and let's talk."

She snatched her hand away. "I've got nothing to say to

you."

"What? Have you held a grudge for thirty years? Been angry for thirty years? We were children, for gosh sakes. Go a little easy on me."

But she said nothing and they rode in silence. As the miles went by, he wondered where she had gone, the lanky girl with the light freckles on her face who danced under a summer moon in Ivy Log's town square until she heard her mama call her home. Who said you could never go home again? He was beginning to believe it.

"I'm lost," he said quietly.

She turned and stared at him. "What do you mean, lost?"

He slowed the car as a possum ran alongside the road on top of the mounds of snow. "Oh, I'd guess you'd call it a midlife crisis. Mom and Dad gone. No brothers or sisters. No wife. No children. Lost."

"You have your work."

He laughed cynically. "That doesn't do it for me like it used to. Somehow, I missed some of the important things along the way."

Paula nodded. "It's not too late." Her tone had sounded oddly not soft or not hard, but not in the middle either.

"Maybe not. But had I not agreed to do this mediation thing, I would have come back anyway. I'd been thinking about it for some time."

"What did you expect to find? The place is the same, the people are the same. Nothing has changed in the least."

"There's nothing wrong with sameness."

The snow swirled in front of them, heavier, the wipers struggling. Paula leaned forward to peer out the windshield. She said, "Guess it depends on what you want, what it takes to make you happy. Everybody's different."

"I won't disagree with that. I just have this kind of longing, a feeling of discontent that wakes me up at night. It's like I'm not in the right place — doing what I should be doing. Even now. Maybe I should be in Ivy Log, maybe not."

He reached over for the third time and took her hand. She didn't pull away this time.

He said, "I know it's been thirty years, and whatever our friendship means to us at this point, I don't know. But whatever it is, I don't want to lose it, and . . . I'm not basing anything I feel on memories from the past. I just want to do whatever I can to mend any hurts I caused you." His words were heartfelt, and he was relieved at finally having the opportunity to say them to her.

She pulled back her hand still again, and the cold of the most bitter winter night in the Appalachians could not match the brutality of Paula's next words, which came as hollow and unfeeling as if they were spoken by an executioner: "You've come to the wrong place to mend any hurts, Sam."

~~~ ~~~

Chapter 77

Jim's Smokin' Que was crowded, the aroma of its barbecue thick in the small dining room, where its earthy fragrance comforted the patrons as though a magical elixir. In the smoke room on the side of the building, ribs lay stacked in the stick smokers where they dripped fat that sizzled like bluegrass music when hitting the hot, wild-cherry wood.

Heads turned as Sam and Paula entered the restaurant. They were considered out-of-towners, perhaps even Yankees who had invaded the sacred halls of ribs and pulled pork.

At a back table, Sam pulled out a chair for Paula, away from the noisy front entrance. He helped her with her coat and waited while she removed her gloves and placed them in her handbag. He smelled her perfume, saw a row of gold bracelets on her arm, realized he was staring. Physically, she remained a lovely if not stunning woman.

He was a little numb from her hair-raising rebuke. Had she ever loved anyone, or was she even capable? It was sad. He hadn't seen an inkling of tenderness or the slightest warmth in a face that at one time might have graced the cover of Glamour Magazine.

They ordered barbecue sandwiches and fries and watched as the waitress placed three bottles of barbecue sauce on their table. Sam leaned back and simply took Paula in as best he could. He would say nothing more.

She stared back, unblinking.

So this is what a "cold war" means. He began to hum and

tap the table with his straw, totally absorbed in the beat of the Lucinda Williams song, "Greenville," which played on the speakers overhead.

He continued tapping the table, when she said, "Remember that plaid shirt of yours?"

He said nothing, nodding once and tapping to the beat.

"The navy blue and red one. Button missing on one sleeve.

He closed his eyes and sang the line, ". . . go back to Greenville," in a soft tenor.

"I sleep in it sometimes."

He opened his eyes and looked at her. "Flannel shirt with a frayed collar?"

She nodded.

"Why do you sleep in it?"

She held his gaze and he thought he saw her lips twitch. She shrugged.

"I stole one of your cheerleading pom-poms from the gym Homecoming night," he said, a flick of a smile at the corners of his mouth.

"I got in trouble because of that. We were supposed to turn those in at the end of every game." She made a face. "Do you sleep with it?"

He gave a slow chuckle, remembering. "No, I use it to flag cabs in New York."

"How do I know if you're telling the truth?"

"Can you tell me one time I ever lied to you?"

She became thoughtful, her gaze rambling around the restaurant and finally coming back to him. "Once."

"When?" He leaned forward, elbows on the table, giving her a courtroom stare.

She didn't answer.

He picked up the straw again.

"You said you were coming back," she said, her words almost inaudible.

Sam saw her green eyes shimmer and felt the slow thudding of his heart. "I know." His gaze fell to the labels on the bottles of barbecue sauce and he studied them intently while he struggled with the realization that he had truly loved Paula. His 17-year-old mind had adored her as only a young man's could. When he looked at her, he found her watching him, her eyes still wet with held-back tears. *Can heartache last 30 years?*

"I wanted to come back." He reached out and lined up the sauce bottles in a row and squared the salt and pepper shakers.

"Why didn't you?" Paula lifted her chin as though she already knew his answer.

His sigh was heavy, pulled from the ache he found in his heart, pain that had stayed and constantly reminded him of what could have been. When he finally answered, his words were held together only by his need to say them. "I believed, if I returned, I'd forever be in the clutches of my father, with no chance to be anything other than what he wanted me to be." He paused and leaned forward in his chair. "An age-old story, huh? At 17, I didn't have the maturity or experience to fight back any other way except to leave. So that's what I did."

Paula was now staring intently at Sam, ignoring the waitress who'd come by to place her drink in front of her.

Sam looked at her long and hard, equally engrossed. "If I had come back, it would have been for you — not him."

"What do you mean *for me*?" Her eyes were now holding his.

"Paula, I never stopped loving you."

~~~ ~~~

Chapter 78

They left Jim's Smokin' Que and rode in silence until they passed the Logan Turnpike Mill. Sleet caught in the beams of the headlights and Sam slowed the car as it rounded the curve from Blairsville.

"Never married?"

Paula shook her head. "No. You?"

"Nope. Came close once." He felt her watching him. He wanted to reach out and take her hand, but his being thrice refused made him wary. He imagined the two of them 17 again and her sitting with him in his old pickup truck, snuggled up to him and warm, his arm around her. "Seems like after I got out of the Navy, all I wanted to do was get my degree. Six years later, I was thirty-two. Then, forty-two. Now, look at me. An old man."

"Forty-seven is not old," she said, the hint of a laugh in her words.

They passed through Blairsville and turned west for a half mile until 129 took them toward Ivy Log. The music on WCNG played softly, "Have yourself a merry little Christmas . . . ."

He walked her to the door just like he would have after a Saturday-night date 30 years earlier. If she had asked him to come in, he wasn't sure he would — not that he didn't want to. But, she didn't make the offer; instead, leaving him alone under the porch light. He stood a moment in the cold quiet of the night, almost knocking on the door to ask her if she wanted to go to dinner again later in the week. However, he thought better of it. He didn't know why.

In the yard next door, Rudolph's nose was dark. Sam walked to his car, his thoughts on the plaid shirt, the pom-poms and the short skirt of her cheerleading outfit. He would have to write a book one day about redheads and their inimitable presence in the world.

He left Dellwood and drove down Main Street, past The Boardinghouse. Lights in the window and the unmistakable bald head of Wiley Hanson caused him to turn around and pull up to the curb. He eased out of his car and walked the few feet to the front window. He tapped on the glass and grinned at Wiley, who sat with of a bowl of chicken and dumplings, looking exceedingly happy. Next to him, Sam's friend Will held a spoonful of pumpkin pie in front of a pile of documents spread out across the table. Pyune unlocked the door, despite the "closed" sign that hung across the front.

"Sam Cobb. You rascal. Get in here." Pyune put her arms around him and squeezed.

"Ah, Pyune Murphy. The most wonderful girl in the world." He hugged her and half twirled her around.

She asked, "What can I get you? Coffee? Pie?"

"Oh, my. I'm totally full of barbecue from Jim's down in Blairsville."

"What? You drove to Blairsville when I could have fed you?" Pyune shook her finger at him.

Sam shrugged. "I'm not the smartest guy."

The pastor sat back and folded his arms across his chest. "Well, I see you survived the evening."

Sam took off his coat and eased into a chair. "Barely," he said and looked over at Wiley.

"Wiley, I'd give you a big bear hug but I understand you've got several bruised ribs and are generally in need of a new body."

"That might be true. But it's still good to see you, Sam."

Both men settled for shaking hands, and Sam said, "Ah, it's good to see you too. And good to be back to my old stomping grounds."

"Been a long time," Wiley said.

"Too long."

Sam looked over at the pastor. "What are you working on,

Will?"

He straightened the papers and laid down his pen. "Just finishing up the nuptials for Frank and Adela's wedding."

Pyune spoke up. "You're invited, by the way. Adela and Frank asked me to pass along the invitation. 2 o'clock Saturday."

Sam nodded. "Oh, my. The other most beautiful woman in Ivy Log's getting married. And, to that old cuss, Frank Carberry."

Wiley laughed. "Yep, that old cuss done become honorable. Adela saw to that."

"Heard you're going to be best man at the wedding."

"Planning on it." Wiley paused, his swollen eye now a lovely shade of dark green. "That is if I don't fly off another mountain in the meantime."

"Don't you even think that," said Pyune, picking up his empty bowl and taking it to the kitchen.

Behind the three men, the fire popped and the comfort of the warm room spread like a blanket on a cold winter's night. Wiley yawned. "I reckon it's quittin' time for me. Got to get up early and help Pyune in the kitchen." He reached out and shook Sam's hand again. "We'll catch up real good later. You staying over at the parsonage?"

"Yeah, I'll be there a few days. Might see you at breakfast."

Wiley nodded and looked over at the pastor. "Night, preacher."

"Good night, Wiley. Think Pyune would let us stay a few more minutes?"

"Gotta ask her. But I think she'll be in the kitchen a while longer."

They watched the mountain man walk away, a slight hitch to his gait.

Pastor Johnson grinned at Sam. "I don't see any missing limbs."

"I escaped by the hair of my chinny chin chin, even though she had her boxing gloves on when I picked her up. And she kept them on most of the night until she finally settled down a bit at the end."

"What now?"

"What now is the Thursday meeting. And I don't know

what to expect. It was clear to me that she wasn't going to dis-cuss your situation. I'll say this — she'll be quite a force to reckon with." He looked hard at his friend. "You ready?"

The pastor pushed his empty pie plate to the side. "You forget, I've already been subjected to a few of her mighty swats."

Sam stared into his empty coffee cup as the dining room lights went dimmer. When he looked at the pastor, he seemed tired, like a man needing rest from a long journey.

Sam took a deep breath. "I have to be completely candid with you, Will. It's quite possible you won't be staying in Ivy Log."

~~~ ~~~

Chapter 79

There was no sunlight to make a sunrise when morning eased over Ivy Log, the sky the color of granny's wash water. Wiley had been up for hours, peeled dozens of turnips, drank multiple cups of coffee from his Roy Rogers cup, and fed the *beaucoup* cats by the dwindling woodpile.

Three days after his miraculous rescue, he was almost back to being the ox his grandfather had remained all the way until his death at age 97. But Wiley had yet to return to his home in the mountains. Why would he when Pyune cared for him as though he were a baby, helpless and in need? He allowed her to dote over him. In his wisdom, he accepted her love with gratitude.

Their nights had been tender, with soft whispers that uncovered secrets and revealed truths that had long been hidden behind hurts and misunderstandings. His love for her had been there all along, but for all his intellect and common sense, neither faculty was acute enough for him to reconcile his feelings for what they meant. One day, he would have to drink his granddaddy's special moonshine to excess to help open the plugged channels of his heart and mind to the under-standing of real love.

After finishing his kitchen duties, Wiley trimmed his beard and laughed at his lizard eye as he looked at himself in the mirror. He dressed in the half-dark of early morning and waited at the kitchen back door for Doyce's truck.

Right on time, Doyce pulled up by the woodpile and tooted

the horn. Wiley eased out the kitchen door, scattering the cats, and pulled himself into the cab.

"Mornin', Wiley." Doyce put his truck in gear and they pulled out onto Main Street, then on 129 south to Blairsville.

"You okay this morning?" Wiley asked Doyce.

"A little nervous."

"No need to be. Everything's good."

"I know, I know. Just didn't sleep at all last night."

"Hope you're not going to be cranky all day." Wiley looked sideways at the man who had braved the mountain just three days earlier to rescue him.

Doyce laughed and rubbed his chin. "Not if I can help it. Course, if we stop at Jim's Smokin' Que for lunch, it would make me plum happy."

"What? And suffer the wrath of Pyune if she found out?"

Doyce slapped the steering wheel. "Lord, no. I sure don't want that." His heavy chin quivered.

"After we visit that lawyer fella, I want to buy me a new truck," said Wiley. "A red one."

"Four-wheel drive?"

"Yep. Maybe with a winch on it."

"How about one of those fancy electronic things that locate you if you fly off the side of a mountain?"

Wiley looked sideways at his friend and muttered, "Don't plan on doin' any more flying off these mountains."

~~~

In Blairsville's town square, the flurry of Christmas shoppers moved along the sidewalks as though in a frenzy. Doyce parked a block from Collins and Dyer, Attorneys at Law, which was as close as he could get to their offices.

Once inside, a pretty blond receptionist in a tight red sweater, whose southern twang was as pronounced as Wiley's, greeted them. "Y'all must be Mr. Conley and Mr. Hanson?"

"That's right," said Wiley.

"Y'all just come on in and have yourself a seat in Mr. Collins's office. He's in there working his crossword puzzle, mad as a hornet 'cause he cain't figure out a six-letter word for foolish. Ends in a "m"."

"That would be 'ulagam,'" said Wiley.

The pretty face hesitated. "Tell that to Mr. Collins — he'll want to hire you and fire me."

Wiley gave her sweater a glance and chuckled to himself and said under his breath, "Somehow, young lady, I think your job is safe no matter how much word help I might give your boss."

A booming voice came from a slight man whose thin hair was slicked to the side like frail rows of thread. "What'd you say the word was?"

"Ulagam."

"What about a five-letter word for a carpenter's tool — not level."

"Bevel," said Wiley.

Jesse Collins's face lit up and he motioned Wiley and Doyce into his office. "Ha! Two minutes and forty-three seconds. Can you believe it? That's certainly a world record." He pushed the newspaper with the puzzle aside and rocked forward out of his chair and shook hands. "Well, gentlemen. You're right on time. Have a seat."

He leaned back, his small frame almost lost in the large leather chair that was the color of an eggplant.

"Caity, how about bringing these fellas some coffee," he hollered through the open door. "Caity's my sister's girl. Sweetest thing in the world. Cain't spell though."

"Don't think she'll ever have to worry about it much," Wiley said, and all three men laughed.

The attorney opened a folder. "Okay, let's get right to it. As I understand it, Mr. Hanson, you've brought a cashier's check for sixty-thousand dollars, payable to Paula Jennings. That right?"

"That's right."

"And, that check is to satisfy the demand note Ms. Jennings holds for a loan to Mr. Conley, who's sittin' here. That right too?"

"That's right too."

"All right." He held up several papers. "These documents require your signature, Mr. Conley. Mr. Hanson can be a witness. Once you've signed everything, I'll deposit Mr. Hanson's check, and when it clears the bank I'll send a certified check to Ms. Jennings. She'll sign a paper stating the loan was satisfied.

I'll provide you with the original and keep a copy in your file. Then I got another document for you to sign for the loan from Mr. Hanson. Any questions?"

"Nope," said Doyce.

"Good. What's a seven-letter adjective for diamond?"

"Hardest," said Wiley.

~~~ ~~~

Chapter 80

Back at The Boardinghouse, the turnips Wiley had peeled simmered in a huge pot at the back of the stove. The remnants of several large pork loins lay in a bowl the size of a pig trough at Tom Keeling's farm. Wiley removed his coat and hat and directed Doyce to the front dining room while he removed the skins on a pile of baked sweet potatoes.

Pyune came through the door carrying two empty pie pans and an iced-tea pitcher. "Hey, handsome. Eye's lookin' better."

"I thought so too." Wiley grinned. "But I cain't get any more handsome than I am."

She laughed. "Got a call from my cousin Alease. Said she and Ted will be here around three this afternoon."

"They spending the night?"

"Nope. They'll stay a few hours, then head north."

"Why can't they stay longer?"

"Not sure. She just said it was important to see me. Wouldn't say why."

~~~

On Dellwood Avenue, Paula found herself rereading the 63 letters to Aldelpheus Cobb, not over the shock of discovering the familiar name scrawled on the bottom of the green box. Nothing made sense. The woman in Blairsville claimed she was not the author of the letters, yet they came from her address. That woman's name — Anne Schuyler — certainly didn't correlate with the enigmatic "O" signed at the close of each letter. Exasperated, Paula set the box aside.

The name on the bottom of the box — Osborne — would fit the "O" signature, but the woman who belonged to the name did not. Wanda Osborne had been a widow for years. Quiet and unassuming, her life in Ivy Log was always unpretentious and certainly not scandalous. She traveled infrequently, only to visit her sister in . . . Blairsville. Paula sat up. Wanda had a sister in Blairsville!

There was no one there to see the grin on Paula's face, but it spread like a morning sunrise after a long, dark night. She'd have to visit her dear friend Wanda as soon as possible — and especially before Thursday's board meeting.

~~~ ~~~

Chapter 81

Alease and Ted Kelly arrived at The Boardinghouse right on schedule. Pyune's cousin — tall, flamboyant, and outgoing — breezed into the kitchen wearing a fake fur that reached mid-calf. Ted, always her knight in shining armor as she explained him to Pyune, followed closely behind and carried a small bag covered in an animal print, a sack of wrapped presents, and a bottle of 100-percent pure cane syrup from the Southern Cross Farm and Sugar Mill in Hilliard, Florida.

"Oh, Pyune, dear cousin, come here and let me love on you," Alease squealed. She wrapped the petite Pyune in her arms, losing her in the folds of her coat. "My, my, it has been *too* long. If our mamas knew we had been apart this long, they would snatch us baldheaded." She rocked Pyune back and forth until Pyune gasped for breath.

"Hello, Ted," said Pyune, reaching from the smothering fur and hugging Ted. "You're looking well."

"Ted, my dear, bring me that bag of presents," called Alease. Alease kissed her husband when he placed the bag in front of her. "You're such a darling and I love you." She patted the chair beside her. "Come sit, Pyune. I have some wonderful things for you."

Pyune, five years younger than her cousin, dutifully sat beside Alease and waited while she pulled the gifts out, one by one. "You must open this one last," she said, placing a large envelope aside.

"Alease, you didn't have to do this," Pyune said, and

meaning it.

"I know, I know. But you're my favorite cousin."

"I'm your only cousin," Pyune said, laughing hard.

"Whatever," Alease said.

Pyune unwrapped a small square box covered in gold foil, its bow made of red velvet. "Oh, my, Alease. These are lovely."

"Hold them up and let me see them."

Pyune placed the necklace against her neck, the pearls like the color of a cream orchid against her warm skin. "I've never owned a string of pearls."

"Well, now you do. Go ahead. Open the next one."

Pyune looked at her cousin. "You're too good to me."

"I love you, cousin." Alease reached over and patted Pyune's cheek.

Pyune pulled the ribbon off a large box wrapped in green and red paper with bells and holly flowing in rows, one after the other. She removed the top and pulled out a white cashmere sweater with a dainty collar and tiny pearls lining the edges.

"Oh, my goodness, Alease. How beautiful."

"You're welcome," Alease said, adding her squeal.

Pyune leaned over and hugged her cousin. "How can I ever thank you enough."

"Just come see us in Folkston. You're welcome any time. And, of course, some of your wonderful chicken and dumplings would be nice." She reached behind her and placed the envelope in Pyune's hand. "This is the *real* gift," she said quietly.

Pyune opened the envelope and pulled out a page from an old calendar. *To my darling granddaughter, Pyune. Here is the family's lemon pudding cake recipe. I hope you will cherish it as much as I have. It was my grandmother's recipe so I suspect it's been in the family a long time. All my love. Granny Murphy*

Pyune looked at Alease. "I don't understand. Granny couldn't read or write."

"You're right — she couldn't. But she went to the Blairsville bank and had Mr. Dyer, the manager, write it out for her. That's what my mama said right before she died. Turn it over."

Pyune turned over the recipe and looked at a page torn out

of a Bank of Blairsville calendar that was dated December -
1974. "I was only ten years old. But, how did you get this?"

"Found it in a box my mama had. She had a bunch of
granny's things as well as your mama's."

"I never saw it before."

"Me, neither."

"You were the one who called Bakers' World Magazine,"
said Pyune, tearing up.

"Yes, I did. When you told me the story about that redheaded woman claiming it was her family's recipe, I started
going through every box of stuff my mama left in the attic.
Those boxes had been there ever since 1992, when she died.
Soon as I found the recipe, I knew you had all the proof of
ownership you needed. I even faxed a copy of both sides of that
paper to a lady at the magazine."

Pyune couldn't hold back her tears any longer. "I don't
know what to say."

"Don't say nothin'. Just hope you win."

~~~ ~~~

Chapter 82

Wiley slowly climbed the narrow stairs to the small rooms above The Boardinghouse kitchen. He was tired. Even peeling turnips had exhausted him and left him longing for Pyune's soft bed with its heavy quilts. He undressed, wincing when he pulled off his boots — the flight off the mountain reminding him he was bruised and battered. When he last looked at his eye, it was the shade of the wild grapes he picked as a kid. He had laughed at himself as he trimmed his beard earlier in the day. *You old cuss, you're a handsome fella.*

He pulled the covers up under his chin and waited for Pyune. His darling Pyune. He heard her in the kitchen below, a pot rattling, water running, and voices. *Paula.*

"Wiley here?" Paula's voice carried up the stairs, somewhat muffled but understood.

Pyune turned out the lights over the stoves. "It's late, Paula."

Paula looked around the kitchen, then leaned against the doorway into the dining room. "I think he's here — upstairs in your bed."

Pyune said nothing as she moved a basket of apples to the cutting table and removed her apron.

"Don't ignore me. Wiley's upstairs, and I know it."

"I'd like you to leave." Pyune walked to the door and opened it, the cold air rushing in as well as two cats.

Paula didn't budge. "You're nothing but a little ol' black cook, Pyune. Wiley will be done with you since he's got a new truck and can head back up the mountain. He's a mountain man, so don't get used to him warming your bed."

The sight of a naked Wiley at the bottom of the stairs seemed quite natural as far as he was concerned. He casually walked across the kitchen, picked up an apple and took a bite out of it, his rear end as smooth and white as a cue ball on a pool table. He chewed slowly. "I believe Pyune has asked you to leave, Paula, and I think that's what you should do."

~~~

They laughed long into the night. Every time Pyune turned over, she giggled. "Wiley Hanson, you done unleashed World War III. That girl will never get over the sight of you coming down those stairs naked as the day you was born."

Wiley grunted. "Suppose you're right. What was I to do — let her beat up on you like that?"

"Oh, I would have reined her in eventually. But, the way you did it was quite . . . unique. She ran out of there like that New York coat of hers was on fire."

"Wonder what she wanted with me?"

"Not a darn thing. Just didn't want you here with me."

They heard sleet hit the window and it rattle from the wind. Pyune slipped her arms around Wiley and snuggled in for the night.

"You know what?" he asked.

"What?"

"I was just thinkin'. I'm recovered well enough from my flight over the mountain to . . . ."

"To what?"

His kissed her neck and found her smooth breast. "To do this."

~~~ ~~~

Chapter 83

Paula had been to Wanda Osborne's house only once in the 20 years she had known her. She hosted a tea for her Sunday school class some years back — a dinky affair on the back patio of her home. Gnats were everywhere, and the guests couldn't wait to go indoors. Everyone had to pick the tiny critters from their little pimento cheese sandwiches as well as scoop them out of their tea.

Wanda was an attractive woman, her curly gray hair close to her head. Petite, she had the pale skin that English women prized. Her eyes, a hydrangea blue, sat in a pretty round face that seemed to hold a perpetual smile. Paula didn't like her.

Paula thought about calling Wanda and letting her know she'd be stopping by. *No, I'll just drop in.* She pulled onto Wanda's driveway and parked her Lincoln as close to the front porch as possible. The walkway had been cleared of snow and she followed it around a short curve to the entrance, noticing a small holly tree had been decorated with tinsel. It was now limp, weighted down with snow. She rang the doorbell, and while she waited she inspected the wreath that hung on the door. It looked familiar. Then she realized she'd sold it at one of her garage sales. A pitiful looking wreath, its ornaments faded, one cracked and broken. Just pitiful.

The door opened. Wanda, in sweatshirt and jeans, reached out. "Paula, how nice to see you. Please come in." Always gracious, Wanda stepped aside and Paula entered a small living room off the foyer.

"So sorry to drop in on you like this." She turned and looked at Wanda. "I was thinking we could have a little chat." There it was again. That little chat she seemed to be having with everyone these days. First William Johnson, then Wiley, then Doyce, then Pyune, then Sam, then Anne. And, now it was Wanda's turn.

Paula sat in a chair across from Wanda's pale peach couch. The redhead loved girl chats, and this was definitely going to be one of those. About men, of course. That's what women usually talked about. This chat, however, would be more interesting than usual, since it involved a pastor of The Church of Ivy Log. She tried to think of a scripture to open the conversation with, but an appropriate one would not come to mind, so she looked around for a bible. Didn't see one, so she looked back at Wanda, gave her best fake smile, got right to the point.

"I was wondering if you would like to have your letters back."

"Letters?" Wanda's blue eyes widened.

"Yes, the ones you wrote to Pastor Cobb."

Wanda, her hands clasped together, stared at Paula as if the redhead was the last woman in the world she would want to know who had written the letters; messages that anyone who read them would most assuredly say expressed physical desires.

"I believe I do want them back," she said after some time, her words soft.

Paula nodded, her eyes taking in the simple woman in jeans and tying to imagine the depth of the relationship between her and Aldelpheus Cobb.

"They're in the car. I'll get them for you in a moment. She got up and walked across soft carpet to sit by Wanda on the peach couch. In only these few seconds, she became the head of the hiring committee, her voice so authoritative that the diminutive woman seemed to shrink into the couch. "But, first, you're aware we're having a final committee meeting tomorrow regarding William Johnson's tenure as pastor of our church?"

Wanda nodded.

"I'm expecting that you'll vote for his dismissal."

Wanda inched forward, as if approaching a rattlesnake.

"I . . . I'm not sure how I'm going to vote. I like William Johnson. I think he'd make a fine pastor."

Paula swatted the air with her hand. "Oh, my. I like him, too, just not in our fine church." She reached over and patted Wanda's arm. "Remember, dear, we have our traditions to consider. I know we're progressive, but not *that* progressive."

Paula waited. It would take just a few words around town to the *right* people to expose Aldelpheus Cobb and Wanda Osborne's . . . little relationship — perhaps their excursions on church time with church funds. Who knows what all went on between them?

Paula gathered her coat around her. "You think about it awhile. I'll keep these letters a little longer, until you make up your mind. The meeting begins at 10 a.m." She headed toward the door but spun around. "Oh, one more thing. In my new position as interim pastor, I have every intention of placing you at the head of several very important committees."

She opened the door and heard Wanda walk up behind her. "Paula, Pastor Cobb and I had a wonderful few years together, and I don't regret one moment of our time with each other." She stepped closer. "And if you feel the letters are important to you, then by all means keep them."

Paula stared at the small woman and imagined her and Pastor Cobb in each other's arms.

"And another thing," said Wanda, her tiny frame lifting, "I'm not interested in serving on a single church committee you're involved with in any way."

~~~

Wanda stood at the window and watched the blue Lincoln pull out of her driveway. Paula's snooping had finally led her to who "O" was — to the woman who wrote sweet words to Aldelpheus Cobb. But there was nothing illicit in the loving words they had written to each other. They had simply been two people who'd found each other in the purest form of love, a wonderful friendship that was wholly platonic, and almost 20 years after Anne Schuyler had told Wanda about the relationship she'd had with Pastor Cobb — which had been anything but purely spiritual.

~~~ ~~~

Chapter 84

Late on Wednesday night, Sam Cobb found himself into a bottle of Old Forester soon after finishing off a pint of Maker's Mark that had been a birthday present some months earlier. To say he was a troubled man was an understatement — he was at the lowest point in his life.

Alone by the fire while William Johnson worked in his study on the Christmas sermon, Sam watched the fire. He saw angels dancing in the flames, then changing to elegant amber swans, their long bodies swaying with the heat. He reached over and tossed a couple of pieces of uncooked popcorn into the fire and watched Delilah run from the room when the kernals exploded.

Once again, he asked himself why he had abandoned Paula Jennings that long-ago summer, had left her with only the plaid shirt she sometimes slept in. His memories of her were sweet and innocent, with no malice of any kind intended when he fled that starless night. Yet, she said he had lied to her; he'd said he was coming back. He did come back — just some 30 years later. He'd studied her face after she'd told him her hurts could not be mended. Her words saddened him, but he wanted to at least try to sooth her pain. Unsteadily, he rose from his chair and slipped on his jacket. "I'm heading out for a while," he yelled to his longtime friend.

Outside, the sleet hit his face and sobered him for a moment while he pulled a wool cap over his head for the two-block walk to Paula's house.

William Johnson opened the door behind him. "You mind telling me where you're going?"

Sam held fast to the porch post. "Over to Paula's, to apologize."

"Apologize for what?"

"Never mind, for what. Jus' gotta do it." He slipped his hands in his pockets.

"Can't it wait? The weather will be better tomorrow."

"Naw. Can't wait."

"Come on, Sam. Don't be foolish."

"Leave me alone, Will."

The pastor watched his friend walk toward Main Street, singing George Straight's "Am I Blue" at the top of his lungs, "*. . . the day I lost youuuuuuuuuu.*"

~~~

Sam walked the sidewalk as though it were summertime, a lackadaisical stroll indicating neither urgency nor concern as the sleet pelted his face and the wind slapped his body. He stopped at Drake's Hardware and ogled the red wagon sitting in the window. His father wouldn't participate in the family's Christmases, giving more thought to his sermons and the care of his parishioners. Sam and his mother would always open presents together, each keeping an eye on the closed study door as his father read his bible — both repeatedly expressing hope he'd step out and join them. It never happened.

Next to the red wagon, Haskell Drake had placed a baseball glove and ball, both regulation. Sam had never tossed a ball with his dad, nor had Aldelpheus seen him play shortstop at any of his games.

Behind the ball and glove, a gold trumpet, tall and gleaming, leaned against a large red box. Some lucky boy or girl would have it for music lessons after the Christmas holidays.

Sam heard a cat meow as it scampered across Main Street and into the town square, undoubtedly planning to sleep warm and cozy in the straw in the nativity scene's manger.

He reached Dellwood and stumbled toward Paula's house. There were no lights in her windows. Even Rudolph's nose in the yard next door was dark, sleet covering the plastic face and ears.

He made it to her porch and up the steps. But he wavered and reached for the iron rail, his heart thudding in his chest. He leaned over and vomited into the snow. *That damn bourbon.* He straightened up and promptly slipped and fell into a pile of snow someone had shoveled off to the side. He laughed at this misfortune and slowly rolled over and sang the chorus of "Am I Blue" at the top of his lungs.

~~~ ~~~

Chapter 85

In the dark living room, Paula dozed in her favorite chair; it elevating her like a throne would a queen. She stirred. She was dreaming she heard music, a lovely voice singing and then someone calling her name, *"Paula. Paula."* Then, her dream went away and she continued dozing, sleep just on the fringe, when the dream returned. The lovely music began again and the sound of someone calling her name. In her dream, she laughed. She'd heard that voice before, long ago, calling her name.

"Paula," she heard again. She snapped awake and sat up. From the darkness of the front yard, she heard her name again, a long howl this time: "Paulaaaaa."

She jumped from her chair, opened the front door, saw nothing. She leaned over the rail to her right, and on the ground beside the brick wall of the porch lay Sam Cobb.

He grinned. "Hey, Paula. I brought back your pom-pom." He held up a stick with a few strands of tattered red and white paper he'd found at the parsonage and feebly waved it back and forth.

"Is that vomit in the snow?" Paula pulled at Sam's jacket. "Sit up."

"Why, I do believe it is. Not sure if it's mine or someone else's."

"You're drunk."

"Excuse me, madam. You seem to be slightly perturbed as well as misinformed. I'm not drunk."

Paula rolled Sam over. "Now get on your hands and knees and pull yourself up!"

"Don't let the pom-pom get in that awful vomit. Can't imagine someone doing such a foul thing in your front yard. Shall we call the authorities?"

"The snow's turning to sleet and it's darn cold. Now stand up!" Paula put her hands under his arms and helped him to a standing position.

"Pardon me, madam. As much as I would like to, I don't think we should be dancing in weather like this."

"Shut up and walk up the steps."

Dutifully, Sam allowed Paula to guide him up the steps, a slow process that involved their combined strength. "Oh, no," said Sam. "I can't be going inside your house." He giggled and did a little shuffle with his misaligned legs and almost fell again. "You might want to have your way with me."

"Stop it." Paula pushed him inside and slammed the door.

She turned on the lights and led him to the couch. "Sit down and don't move."

"Oh, no. I won't move a minimus muscle . . ." He held up his finger. "Make that a miniscule muscle."

Paula left the room and came back with a blanket. "Remove your jacket."

"Oh, my. I knew this would happen. Please be gentle." Sam fell backward onto the couch.

"Sam, sit up so I can take off your jacket." Paula grabbed the front of his jacket and pulled. Sam was dead weight, his eyes closed. She watched him for a moment and then placed the blanket over him and turned out the lights.

~~~

She sat in the dark and listened to Sam's breathing. Occasionally he mumbled and even laughed. But, mostly, he slept. At 4 a.m. he sat straight up. "Where the heck am I?"

Paula turned on the lamp. Sam, rumpled, his dark hair matted against his forehead, squinted and turned away. "Oh, my. How did I get here?"

"It wasn't easy," said Paula. "Do you realize you could have frozen to death if I hadn't found you?"

Sam looked stricken. "Where did you find me?"

"In a pile of snow by the front porch."

"I . . . I really can't remember."

"Of course, you can't. You were drunk."

Sam placed his head in his hands. "I'm so sorry if I caused you a problem."

"Not a problem. The problem would have been if I found you stiff in the snow when I went out for my paper in the morning."

"That bad, huh?"

"Bad. I didn't know you drank."

"I don't." He looked away. "Been a little tough. Guess I've handled it all wrong."

She nodded. "Life can be hard sometimes. I've got some hot tea for you. Want cream in it or sugar?"

"No. Just plain. Want me to come into the kitchen?"

"Can you walk?"

"Might better bring it in here."

Paula brought a mug of tea and placed it beside him. "Need something in your tummy? Crackers?"

"Oh, no. I think this tea will do it."

"You do know you vomited in the snow?"

Sam closed his eyes. "Please tell me I didn't."

"You did."

Paula reached down on the floor beside the couch. "You brought me this." She held up the ragged pom-pom.

He winced. "It's coming back to me."

"What's coming back to you?"

"My grand intentions."

"What were your grand intentions?"

He sipped his tea and leaned back. "To make things right between us."

Paula shook her head. "Like I told you, Sam, all those hurts can't be mended. There's no use trying. Besides, bringing back an old pom-pom to me is not going to change anything."

"It was a symbolic gesture. A peace offering."

She stared at him and said nothing.

"You know what," he said, "Without your makeup, I can see your freckles and you look seventeen again. No lipstick, no eyeshadow, no mascara. I like it."

"We can't be seventeen again. Neither of us."

Her words struck him hard. Maybe that was his problem — he'd remained trapped inside the 17-year-old kid who went out into the world before he was ready. *We can't be seventeen again.*

Sam sat down his mug and eased off the couch. He reached out his hand to her.

She looked at him and then his hand. When she put her hand in his, he pulled her from her chair and put his arms around her. He smelled the shampoo in her hair, felt the softness of her skin through her gown. He spoke gently into her ear. "It's time you soften that hard, hard heart of yours, Paula. It doesn't become you."

She pulled away. "A hard heart? You think I have a hard heart?"

"I know this. I remember your sweetness; those tender moments we had." Sam hesitated and watched her face. "That sweetness is still there. I just know it is."

"How do you know?" she asked, her cynicism obvious.

Sam pulled her gently to the couch and sat down. When he looked at her, his were eyes alert and a smile played at the corners of his mouth. "I don't believe something so beautiful can be lost forever. All I'm asking is for you to remember what I remember."

He watched as Paula's green eyes turned to the shadowed corner where the dark Christmas tree stood, its lights and ornaments hanging dim and still. She stared a long time without moving. Sam saw a slight nod and a reckoning move across her face, a face that was bare and exposed of more than just makeup. When she looked back at him, almost indiscernibly, a soft glimmer came from her eyes, as though she had been blind and could now see.

~~~ ~~~

Chapter 86

Sam Cobb, cold and shivering, eased through the front door of the parsonage, the crusted snow on his boots scattering with every step onto the entry floor. He took off his boots and left them by the door. The light from the Star of Bethlehem cast a soft glow in the quiet room as his gaze fell on the cold fireplace and a sleeping Delilah on the arm of the fireside chair.

"Hey, Delilah, wait up for me?" he asked as he rubbed her head and ran his hand down her back. "How 'bout a fire? Would you like that?"

He removed the fireplace screen and lay the wood exactly as he had learned in the boy scouts. He struck a match to a small piece of kindling, and the flames grew and consumed more slivers of wood before penetrating the bark of a log.

Just as he sat his tired body into the fireside chair, his friend came down the dark hall. "I thought I smelled that fat pine burning. Good fire."

He sat in the chair across from Sam, who laughed at his bright-red and black-flannel pajamas and asked, "You think I could talk you into making some coffee?"

"I'll make it for us in a minute. Until I do, I'll wait here while you warm up and decide what you're going to tell me about your visit with Paula."

Sam looked up in surprise. "How did you know I went to see Paula?"

The pastor shook his head. "Do you have no memory of

leaving here late last night? Told me something about making an apology to her. The last I saw of you, you were headed for Main Street and singing some awful country song about being blue." He squinted. "You don't remember that?"

Sam closed his eyes. Exactly what did he remember? Oh, yes, now he recalled what had happened. "If you were a good friend, you would have tackled me, tied me up and thrown me in the church cellar — that is if you have one."

William Johnson laughed. "Are you kidding? Nothing could have kept you from going to see that redhead." He leaned forward and spoke softly, the tar in the pine popping and the flames warming the room. "Everything okay?"

Sam leaned back and closed his eyes. "Will, I'm in big trouble."

~~~ ~~~

Chapter 87

Sam left the warm fire and crawled into bed, forgetting about wanting coffee. He slept a couple of hours, a restless sleep in which he dreamed of pom poms and the Nottely Lake dock and the thin redheaded girl who jumped naked into the water and called to him: *Come on in, Sam, the water's fine.*

He got up and showered quickly, dressing in slacks, a white dress shirt, and a V-neck sweater of Christmas red and green. He found the pastor in his study, drinking coffee.

"Hey, Will. Anything you want to discuss regarding our meeting? It's supposed to start in twenty minutes."

The pastor motioned to him. "Have a seat."

The two men took deep breaths and Sam said, "It's simple to me. The committee has to have a unanimous vote. Even if five of them vote for you to stay, only one has to vote otherwise and it's a standoff and nobody wins." A spark shot from the fire and briefly got his attention. "If that happens, I'll step in and mediate all the whys and wherefores. With a little luck, maybe we can end up in a unanimous vote on the second go-round." He sighed. "But who knows how it's going to go."

William Johnson swiveled his chair around to the side and propped his feet on the corner of the desk. He shrugged his shoulders and threw up his hands.

"What?" Sam asked.

"I don't understand what all this hullabaloo is about? It doesn't have to be this complicated."

Sam got up and paced the small office. It wasn't his fight,

but he was there to help his friend. "I just don't want to see you bullied, especially because . . . well . . . you know exactly what I'm saying."

The pastor's features took on a grave tone. "They don't really need a formal meeting just to tell me I have to leave?"

Sam stood in front of the desk and placed his hands on it. "Can you imagine the good you can do in this small town? Why, Will, you're the best man of God I've ever known. You live your life as every Christian should, and your message changes people's lives."

The pastor nodded his head slowly. "Shall we pray about it?"

Sam plopped down into his chair. "Heck, no, I want another glass of bourbon."

The two men laughed like crazed hyenas as they left the parsonage and walked the stone path to the church. Delilah sat in the window next to the lighted Star of Bethlehem and watched her master slowly disappear around the corner of the church. She meowed once, loud and long, her tail switching back and forth. There was not one morsel of food in her dish, the first time William Johnson had ever forgotten to feed her.

The church office was cramped. Paula, carrying the green box with Pastor Cobb's letters, paused in front of Wanda. "I won't be needing these," she said and placed them on Wanda's lap.

She sat behind Aldelpheus Cobb's desk, dressed like any female executive would present herself for a board meeting, wearing a black wool suit, a red scarf with white stripes tied at her neck. She looked pale, but every hair was in place. She folded her hands next to a file folder.

To her right, Doyce Conley, Harley Bradley and Calvin Anderson huddled in small chairs like they were in kindergarten. On a small couch by a bookcase, Wanda and Dale sat stoically, their dreary expressions making it clear they didn't want to be there.

When William and Sam entered the room precisely at 10 a.m., both of them noticed Paula looked at her watch.

"Good morning, everyone," said Pastor Johnson as he nodded to the committee. He took a seat to Paula's left.

Sam hesitated a moment and looked around the room for an extra chair. There wasn't one.

"Hold on, I'll take care of it," Doyce said, leaving and returning with a straight-back chair. "There you go."

"Appreciate it," Sam said, settling in and looking into Paula's dark-green eyes. "Shall we begin?

Paula took command. "Wanda, as church secretary, please record the minutes. I will assume I'm chairing this meeting as head of the committee?" She looked directly at Sam.

A question to position herself as the person in charge, running the show and calling the shots? Of course it was. "Yes, Paula, you are. I assume you are familiar with the correct protocol."

"Ah . . . protocol?" Her hesitation was evident to everyone. "May I state that this church is governed by our own bylaws and . . . protocol is what we deem as — "

"What you deem as appropriate?" Sam interrupted.

"By all means," she said in an authoritative lilt. "It's called an independent church." A cold and condescending demeanor spread across her as she squared her shoulders. It was her opportunity to educate those in the room, who in her opinion did not measure up to her exalted relationship with God and the teachings of the Holy Bible. She continued, "Some think an independent church is a strange phenomenon. Let me assure anyone who might be of this opinion that The Church of Ivy Log has a glorious heritage, free from outside control or membership of any kind in organizations that might dictate to us our . . . our protocol, as you say." She placed her hand on top of a nearby bible.

Sam, clearly a master of debate, responded, "There is no question The Church of Ivy Log is an independent church. I think the question is whether or not the church wants a pastor who is black."

The two statues on the couch did not move. The three men in the small chairs clung to them as though they were parachutes. William Johnson remained silent. Sam merely gave Paula a cocked-eyed look.

"Is that why we're here?" he asked Paula, whose face was now drawn as well as pallid.

She straightened a few papers on the desk. "The purpose of

this meeting is for the committee to vote on whether or not to hire Mr. William H. Johnson as pastor of The Church of Ivy Log."

Sam raised a forefinger. "Let's clarify that. I do believe The Church of Ivy Log did, indeed, hire William Johnson. The committee approved his hiring after accepting his resume and interviewing him. It was only after his arrival in Ivy Log and his subsequent meeting with you that the church reneged." Sam looked around the room. "Are we in agreement on that?"

Each committee member nodded except for Paula. "His hiring was strictly probationary," Paula said, her voice strong.

Sam tightened his jaw. "Probationary based on what and for how long? Are we back to those liberties that a self-governed church has — at its whim?"

Paula had held Sam's eyes as he talked. "There is no whim here. The committee is a democratic process. We'll vote as a whole, and the results will govern our decision." She looked away and then to each member of the committee. "Shall we get on with the vote?"

Sam sensed a softness in her last remark. Not much, but it was there nonetheless. He held up his hand.

"One moment, please. Do any of the committee members have anything to say?" He looked at the pastor. "William, do you have anything you'd like to say?"

The committee members were mute as Pastor Johnson pushed himself up from his chair and clasped his hands together behind his back. His face was aglow in the overhead lights, and his eyes glistened as he took in the room and those seated before him. His preacher's voice was humble, without blame or anger.

"I'm here because of what St. Paul said in Thessalonians," he began. "He said to cheer the fainthearted, support the weak and be patient with all. Paul also said to see that no one returns evil for evil; rather, always seek what is good for each other and for all.

"I'm here at your church in Ivy Log because I believe God wants me here . . . to cheer the fainthearted, support the weak and be patient with all. I'm here because of love. It's love that binds me to you and your lives. And where does that love come from? It comes from Christ, our Lord. Regardless of the outcome of this meeting, I ask that you love one another, support one another and find joy in worship."

The pastor sat and Sam reached out and placed his hand on his shoulder. "Thank you, pastor. Anyone else?"

No one else spoke up, so Paula handed the committee members a tiny square of paper. Everybody had brought something to write with.

She said, "Let's get on with it — y'all know what to do. Vote yes for Mr. Johnson to stay; vote no for him to go." She sat back down and marked her paper, folded it carefully and leaned back in her chair, her movements deliberate, decisive and with the cold appearance of a judge who had just sentenced a man to death.

One by one the committee members marked the ballot. Doyce's heavy chin hung down into his neck, his large fingers caressing the paper as though it was as fragile as the egg of a hummingbird. He began writing out the letters, his hand shaking, his tongue clasped between his lips in concentration. When finished, he folded the swatch of paper as small as he could possibly make it and placed it in the middle of the desk.

Next to him, Harley shifted in his seat and stared at the swatch of paper, turning it one way and then the other. In his free hand he held what he considered his lucky pen. He had voted for the President of The United States in the last ten elections — and his candidate had won each time. He depended on the pen to work one more time. He finally completed his vote and folded the paper only once and placed it in front of Paula.

Calvin held a pencil with his long fingers and licked the lead several times before he wrote dramatically across the paper. With a flourish, he folded it and placed it on the desk.

On the small couch, Dale held a book across her knees and spread the tiny piece of paper on top. She leaned over and pressed the point of her felt-tipped pen and scribbled her vote. She folded it and handed it to Sam, who passed it to William Johnson, who gave it to Paula.

Wanda looked at Paula for a long, searching moment. So long that Paula looked away and then fiddled with the ribbon in her bible. Wanda took her piece of paper and quickly wrote on it. She stood and walked to the desk and placed it on top of the other votes.

Six votes. One by one, Paula opened the folded pieces of paper and recorded the vote. Yes. Yes. Yes. Yes. Yes. Making a note of the sixth vote, she looked up.

"Wanda, let the minutes show an official vote was taken on December 23, and a unanimous vote of yes was counted. Looks like William H. Johnson will be staying for a while as the pastor of The Church of Ivy Log."

~~~ ~~~

Chapter 88

At The Boardinghouse, the news spread quickly. Doyce sat at a table with Harley and Calvin and recounted the entire meeting word for word. The now official pastor of the Church of Ivy Log, along with Sam, gathered at Paula's table with Wiley, all three eating the day's special, fried catfish and hushpuppies.

Wiley said, "Yep, preacher, the most important thing that's happened here is that you'll be able to eat Pyune's cookin' seven days a week. Now, that's an answered prayer if you ask me."

"I can't disagree with you about that," Pastor Johnson said. "The only problem I have at this moment is that my woodpile is getting quite low and we've got another three months of cold weather. Got any ideas?"

Wiley wobbled his head back and forth. "I know, I know. But you do remember my airborne descent down the mountain, don't you? And my subsequent rehabilitation?"

Pyune called across the dining room. "Who's ready for dessert?"

"Not me, Pyune," Sam said, slipping on his jacket. "I ate too many catfish already. Plus, I've got an errand to run."

~~~

Sam walked briskly down Main to Dellwood and on to Paula's house, icicles now hanging from its eves. He looked for the pile of snow where he had plummeted from the porch the night before. He found the flat spot where he'd fallen, and it appeared some snow had been thrown over his despicable vomit.

He rang the doorbell several times and waited. When there was no answer, he hurried past the town square and to the parsonage and found Will sitting by the fire, reading. Delilah jumped from his lap and ran toward him. "Ah, hello, Delilah. I love you too." He picked her up and thought about all the cat hairs she'd leave on his sweater.

"You're back rather quickly," said the pastor. "Paula not home?"

"How'd you know that's where I went?"

"Because I know you too well."

"That you do." Sam took off his jacket and sat. "Can you tell me what the heck happened?"

The pastor closed his book. "I assume you mean at the meeting?"

Sam nodded.

"I truly don't know. It definitely wasn't what I expected. Paula's vote for me to stay was quite a surprise. Any idea why?"

"Not one."

"I have a few ideas."

"Okay. Why do you think she changed her mind?"

"You."

"Me?"

"Of course."

"How do you know that?"

"She left here a minute ago. You just missed her."

"Okay. So?"

"She came by to see me — not you — I might add. She told me, while I was not her choice for the pastor of The Church of Ivy Log, you had softened her heart, as she put it."

Sam's eyes got misty. "Well, I'll be darned. Who would a thunk it?"

"That leads me to the next question."

"And what would that be?"

"Exactly how did you soften that redhead's heart?"

Sam laughed. "I don't believe I'll be answering that question, Will. And the reason is, I haven't got a clue."

Sam had lied.

In the early morning hours, he had held her, and in the midst of it, there had been desire. Long ago, their desire had been locked in a secret place — and the key thrown away. It had remained untouched, still and quiet, until time had now revealed the secret place, slowly, like the opening of a rose, one petal at a time.

When he'd touched her, he'd touched the girl she was, not the woman she had become. He had felt her give, turn into something pliable, discovering what she had lost, as if in a dream that had taken her to a place she had always wanted to be.

"Paula," he had whispered. "It's not too late."

And she had smiled at him for the first time since he'd come back to Ivy Log.

~~~ ~~~

Chapter 89

On Christmas Eve, clouds moved east and left a heavenly blue sky, the air crisp in the Appalachian cold. Ivy Log seemed like a page from a storybook as the rays from a bright sun caught the star on top of the town-square Christmas tree and lingered there, a shimmering, magical sight to behold. Pristine snow lay on the tips of the tree's branches and across the rooftops nearby, icicles clinging from eaves like giant tears of joy.

Wiley, dressed in the same suit he wore when he'd been awarded his doctorate at Georgia Tech, sat in his new red truck on the ridge above Ivy Log and looked down at "his" town. He believed there was no community more lovely on this Earth. He had left the music of the hounds and his tracks on the upper ridges when he had come down from the mountains that first time as a young man, dressed in clothes his mama had made. He found himself enchanted with the other side of the mountain, the town side — a place that pulled him to its breast and told him he could breathe there too.

When he was a child, he wanted to be a mountain, wanted to feel the groaning of the earth and breathe from its valleys and caves. Now, as a grown man, the heart of the mountain was with him wherever he chose to go.

As he looked at the misty smoke floating from the chimney at The Boardinghouse, he was glad his suit did not hold the smell of wood smoke but rather the rare scent of aftershave he sometimes wore on very special occasions. He laughed to himself and knew Pyune would carefully inspect him before Frank and Adela's wedding. He had trimmed his beard shorter than it had been in a long time. He wished he could comb his hair like he did when he was a little boy, parted on the side and slicked back with Vitalis; but, since he had no hair, this would be impossible.

~~~

At The Boardinghouse, he parked his truck by the woodpile and watched the kitchen's cats scatter. He picked up a few pieces of wood and carried them inside. He heard Pyune upstairs as he pulled his Roy Rogers cup from the shelf and poured himself coffee. *Morning, Roy.*

"Morning, Pyune," he yelled.

"Hey, Wiley," she called. "Be down in a minute."

He sipped coffee and heard Pyune's footsteps on the stairs. She rushed to him, hovering over him as she inspected every inch. She removed lint from his slacks, smoothed his eyebrows, pulled a mutant hair from an eyebrow and sniffed his aftershave. "What in the world have you splashed yourself with?"

He hadn't smelled anything bad, so he made up a story. "Deer urine. Keeps the wolves away."

"Wiley Hanson, you go into the bathroom and wash it off. It'll do more than keep the wolves away. Ain't nobody gonna get near you with that awful smell."

They both jumped when a loud knock pounded the back door and Ivy Log's postmaster yelled through the door. "Miss Pyune! Miss Pyune!"

Ivy Log's postman for 30 years, Karl Kaupa, rushed in. "Got a certified letter for you, Miss Pyune," he panted. "You got to sign for it." He held out a pen, his gloved hand shaking like a fit of apoplexy done hit him.

He kept on, "Yes, siree. When that letter came in and I saw it was certified, I rushed right over." He looked around the kitchen. "What's that smell?" He looked at Wiley and wrinkled his nose. "You done been in a fight with a bear, Wiley?" He backed away a few feet.

Wiley sheepishly looked at his shoes. "I believe I done stepped in somethin' awful."

Karl scratched his jaw. "Hope you ain't going to the wedding without washing that off."

Wiley chuckled. "Course not." He looked over at Pyune, who was sitting on a stool at her main worktable.

She slowly opened the envelope and unfolded the letter, her lips moving as she read. Abruptly, she placed her head in her hands.

"What's the matter?" Wiley asked.

She shook her head once and said, "Nothing, nothing at all."

"Well, what's the letter say, woman?"

Her face suddenly brightened as if someone had turned on a floodlight. "I won," she said softly, looking at Wiley and blinking back tears. "I won," she said again, a little louder this time.

Wiley hollered his hog-callin' yell and shuffled his feet in a hoe-down dance. "Whoooooweeeeeeee!"

He pulled Pyune from the stool and danced around the kitchen. Together, they bumped into Karl, knocked over a chair and finally ended up laughing in the middle of the kitchen, holding on to each other, the letter squeezed tightly in Pyune's fingers.

"Whew! Now, that was a celebration!" Wiley swept his arm wide. "Why, we're gonna tell this whole town that our very own Pyune Murphy's lemon pudding cake has become famous!" He stomped his foot on the floor. "Heck, we're gonna tell the whole world before it's over." He skipped across the kitchen, his bruises forgotten. "A parade. We're gonna have a parade right down Main Street and Pyune is gonna be sitting on top of Doyce's new John Deere tractor, with a crown on her head. We'll make up a giant sign, 'The Queen of Lemon Pudding Cakes!' and hang it right out front."

Wiley collapsed on a stool, breathing hard. Across the kitchen, Karl backed toward the door, the sack of mail on his back bumping into the wall. "We ain't never had nobody this famous 'round here. Hot diggity!" He rushed out the door, bumping into Vallie Thomas and almost knocking her down.

"What's all the hullabaloo about? I heard hollering clear down to Drake's Hardware." She stepped inside the warm kitchen. "Thought I'd better make sure nobody done got killed."

Pyune and Wiley stared at Vallie, their mouths open. Finally, Pyune stepped closer, her eyes glued to Vallie. "Vallie, that's Paula's New York-bought coat you got on."

Vallie grinned and pushed up the fur collar. "Yep, sure is. Shocked the heck outta me when Paula knocked on my door at 7 o'clock this morning and placed that coat in my arms." Vallie shook her head. "I couldn't believe it. I bet it cost a hundred dollars — maybe even two. Fur collar and all."

"Did she say anything to you?" asked Wiley, a wondrous look on his face.

Vallie thought a moment, her eyes wandering the kitchen. "Sure did. She said, 'Merry Christmas, Vallie.'" She wrinkled her brow. "That's the first time that woman ever wished me a Merry Christmas, and I knowed her since the day she learned to talk."

~~~

The Church of Ivy Log, minus its steeple — still sitting on the pastor's car — readied for Frank and Adela's wedding at 2 p.m., the ladies of the church swarming in the sanctuary as well as Fellowship Hall, the latter where the wedding cake sat in grand display on the center of a small table in the middle of the room.

At 1:30, the church filled with the citizens of Ivy Log, dressed in their Sunday best and bringing gifts wrapped in white with large silver bows. Doyce and Harley looked like an ad from a Sears catalog of yore; the only thing missing being a top hat for each.

Pyune flitted around Fellowship Hall, arranging food for the reception, her flock of church ladies bowing to her commands. The long red skirt she wore hugged her slim hips and fell to the top of her satin slippers.

Promptly at 2 p.m., the bride and groom walked down the aisle together. At the front of the church, Wiley, slicked up and beaming, held the ring that Henry Patton had shown him. Daly, Adela's daughter, who had arrived the day before from Chicago, stood next to Adela. Her daughter, Adela's granddaughter, Charlotte, waited nearby.

A quiet William Johnson held his bible as Frank and Adela walked up the aisle, the pastor thinking about how many weddings he had performed. Regardless of the number, he could not remember a more beautiful bride or a more handsome groom. They were Ivy Log's Hollywood couple — only death would ever part them.

The Church of Ivy Log's new pastor surveyed the congregation. Thinking this odd, he spotted Paula's red hair way in the back of the church. He saw Sam in the third pew from the front, on the groom's side of the church. He caught his eye and winked.

To his left, Wiley Hanson's face cracked wide with a grin straight from a Halloween pumpkin. The preacher sniffed the air and thought he smelled an earthy odor . . . of . . . of . . . .

The music ended and the pastor of the Church of Ivy Log opened his bible. "Dearly Beloved, we are gathered here today . . . ."

~~~ ~~~

Chapter 90

By midnight on Christmas Eve, the town that Wiley Hanson believed to be the most beautiful place on earth melted into a serene lullaby. The thousands of stars that had been hidden for so long behind thick snow clouds finally found their way to the skies above the Three Wise Men and the Baby Jesus in Ivy Log's town square, as well as Wiley's beloved Appalachian mountains.

The Boardinghouse windows were dark, the top of the chimney refusing to release even the smallest puff of smoke. Pyune and Wiley slept under her grandmother's quilt, a wood-pile cat sleeping with them. Pyune's feet were warm at last.

William Johnson and Sam Cobb walked the path to the parsonage, the pastor singing "O Holy Night"; and, indeed, it was.

Frank and Adela, now known as Mr. And Mrs. Carberry, slept peacefully in their honeymoon bed at Nottely Lake, a bit of wedding-cake frosting in Adela's hair.

In the southeast, Brasstown Bald sat regal, silhouetted against the sky, the same peak Sam had thought perfect for his talk with God.

~~~

A rim of gold crept over the Bald, spreading across Ivy Log and proclaiming it Christmas day, the birthday of the Savior, calling to worship those who centered their lives around the church and the teachings of Christ.

Pastor Johnson arrived at the church early in preparation

for his Christmas sermon. He prayed in the sanctuary where the early light streamed through the stained glass and settled on the varnished pews.

At 11 o'clock, Ivy Log's citizens came, the pews overflowing. Wiley and Pyune sat together with Sam on the front pew. Behind them, Frank and Adela were next to Doyce and Harley, whose Sears suits were still as crisp as when they took them out of the box.

The preacher took a moment to bask in the immense warmth of the congregation. It was his church, his town, his people. He would do what the Apostle Paul had said in Corinthians. It doesn't matter who you are, who you think you are, or who others think you are; if you act toward others with love, your life will be meaningful. He was home.

At the pulpit, he opened his bible and looked across the faces that were to become his flock. For some reason, he again let his eyes search for Paula's red hair, but this time he found none, not even in the back of the church.

He glanced down at his notes, and with a voice filled with passion began his first sermon in The Church of Ivy Log. His timbre was powerful and his words captivated the upturned faces that yearned to hear the words of God, as he said, "Can you imagine the incredible excitement when three wise men saw the Star of Bethlehem in the midnight sky . . . when they heard the news of the birth of a baby?"

He paused and raised his hand. "Just think, in our modern-day world, with all its wars, its turmoil, its hunger, its disease —if, on a cold night, we looked toward the heavens and saw an extraordinary light — a light so bright we stared in wonder."

William Johnson moved from the pulpit to the edge of the stage. "Why, every one of us would rush to CNN news hoping to learn what this phenomenon was, our hearts beating, our breathing rapid." His excitement flowed out into the congregation. He laughed out loud and swept his arm through the air.

"Then, the broadcaster would shout to the cameras and into the microphone. 'A baby boy has been born, and his name is Emmanuel.'"

He lowered his voice to a whisper. "I don't know about you, but every year, on December 25, I close my eyes and imagine it happening all over again . . . the birth of Jesus and the joy I feel knowing He is among us — among us not only on Christmas day, but all year long, every moment of our lives."

He paused and looked slowly at the faces before him. He put out his hand. "Here we are together . . . together in a holy place on the birthday of Christ. I want you to close your eyes with me for just a moment, imagine that bright star in the sky, that manger . . . that baby. Do you smell the frankincense and myrrh? Do you hear the cattle lowing? The angels singing?"

The doors of the church opened and a tall, thin woman walked in. She was familiar yet somehow different. She came down the long aisle, looking for a place to sit.

From the third pew, the same place he'd sat for Frank and Adela's wedding, Sam stood and held out his hand. It was the girl who had slept in his plaid shirt, the one who refused to mend their hurts. There was no turquoise eyeshadow. Her countless freckles ran across her powderless cheeks like warm pink confetti. Her black beauty mark had been left on her dressing table.

There was no hesitancy in her step as Paula walked over to Sam. He reached out and put his arm around her, his eyes grazing the face with the freckles and whispered to her, "Who says we can't be seventeen again?"

Paula smiled and lifted a small white bible from her purse and placed it in his hands.

The End

COMING SOON

Eversweet

IVY LOG'S
MOST MEMORABLE LOVE STORY

Sue Chamblin Frederick

She is known as a sweet Southern belle, a woman whose eyelashes are longer than her fingers, her lips as red as a Georgia sunset. Yet, behind the feminine facade of a Scarlett-like ingénue lies an absolute and utterly calculating mind – a mind that harbors hints of genius – a genius she uses to write books that will leave you spellbound.

A warning! She's dangerous – when she writes spy thrillers she's only six degrees from a life filled with unimaginable adventures – journeys that will plunge her readers into a world of breath-taking intrigue. Put a Walther PPK pistol in her hand and she will kill you. Her German is so precise she'd fool Hitler. Her amorous prowess? If you have a secret, she will discover it – one way or the other.

When she writes romance, her readers swoon and beg for mercy as they read her seductive stories about luscious characters. Be sure to have a glass of wine nearby as you snuggle up to her books about *love*.

The author was born in north Florida in the little town of Live Oak, where the nearby Suwannee River flows the color of warm caramel, in a three-room, tin-roofed house named "poor." Her Irish mother's and English father's voices can be heard even today as they sweep across the hot tobacco fields of Suwannee County, "Susie, child, you must stop telling all those wild stories."

She lives with her Yankee husband in the piney woods of north Florida, where she is compelled to write about far away places and people whose hearts require a voice. Her two daughters live their lives hiding from their mother, whose rampant imagination keeps their lives in constant turmoil with stories of apple-rotten characters and plots that cause the devil to smile.

Note From The Author: Now, after reading *The Boardinghouse,* I know you have some burning questions:

Will Sam and Paula get together in the forthcoming Ivy Log sequel "Eversweet"?

Will Wiley and Pyune ever marry?

But, beyond that, I'm thinking your most burning question is: ***Will the author share the fabulous lemon pudding cake recipe?***

It wasn't easy to get the renowned recipe from Pyune, but here it is. Pyune said, *"make sure your beaters and bowl are completely free of grease"* when you beat the egg whites. And, *"absolutely no egg yolk can mix in with the whites when you separate the eggs."*

PYUNE MURPHY'S
LEMON PUDDING CAKE FROM
THE IVY LOG SERIES

3 large lemons
½ cup all-purpose flour
3/8 teaspoon salt
1 cup plus 2 tablespoons sugar
3 large eggs (room temperature), separated (Ask Paula how to separate the eggs.)
1 1/3 cups whole milk
l ½ tablespoons lemon zest
½ cup plus 2 tablespoons fresh lemon juice

Zest lemon to make 1 ½ Tbs. Squeeze lemons to make ½ cup plus 2 Tbs. lemon juice.

Whisk together flour, salt and ¾ **cup** plus **2** tablespoons sugar in large bowl.

Whisk together egg yolks in a small bowl. Add milk, lemon zest and lemon juice and whisk together. Add to flour mixture, mixing until just combined.

Beat egg whites in a large bowl with electric mixer until soft peaks form. Beat in ¼ cup of sugar, a small amount at a time and continue to beat until peaks are stiff and glossy. Whisk ¼ cup of egg whites into batter. Fold in remaining egg whites gently, but thoroughly.

Pour into buttered 1 ½ quart shallow baking dish. Place baking dish into a shallow pan. Pour boiling water into the pan until ¾ inch from the top of the baking dish with the cake batter.

*350 degrees. About 45 minutes. Serves 6. *Dust with confectioner's sugar when served.*

Pyune serves her famous lemon pudding cake on The Boarding House's fine china — Old French Saxon, the Morning Glory pattern.

Made in the USA
San Bernardino, CA
25 October 2018